A SHIFTER VENGEANCE NOVEL

1

I0689758

NEVER

SILAS REAMES

Ebook ISBN-13: 978-1-961057-00-5
Paperback ISBN-13: 978-1-961057-01-2

Cover design by: Deranged Doctor Design

Table of Contents

Chapter 1

All Good Things Get Screwed Up Eventually

I slam the glass down on the bartop with *slightly* more force than necessary as I watch the news story flashing across the screen. The light of the television glints off the bottles of liquor.

Elios leans over the edge of the bar, lowering his voice as he speaks to me.

"Someone you know? One of us?" The elderly-appearing man has grey, wispy hair that is receding from the center out, forming a ring around his head. For a human, he would look pretty good for his purported age, which is seventy. For what he actually is, he looks like hell.

I shake my head, the corner of my lip raised into a sneer as I take in what's on the screen.

"Not sure yet, but it's going to ruin my week, I can tell you that much."

As if on cue my phone starts vibrating, light illuminating the lunar photo in the background. My attempt at a sense of humor. I don't need to unlock it to read the message that's displayed:

Open Contract
Sacramento: Carnival Grounds
Magical Involvement Suspected
FCFP- DOA w/ Proof

For those who don't spend their time keeping the supernatural beings of the world in check, the ad indicates "first claimed first paid," and "dead or alive." Sometimes they're not picky on the condition of a culprit as long as I can prove I've brought in the right individual ... or at least their body parts.

I'm tempted to ignore it, even with the case being squarely in my backyard. Although if I do that I'll have all manner of shifters, witches, and other magicals trawling around. I'm not sure I like that idea. Then again, I have things to do. Which is exactly why I'm sitting at a bar. Avoidance. I have a certain deadline coming up, an anniversary if you will, and I've been putting it off. Only for a couple hundred years or so, you understand. Now I've got just under a year left to accomplish something of great importance.

A second message pops up under the first.

Choice of pay: 2 million or artifact/casting of equivalent value from Magikai inventory

Elios leans over the screen and lets out a whistle. I swipe the phone back. Nosy old codger, but he's right to be surprised. Lots of magicals have amassed wealth, but for the Magikai to be offering from their personal stash is a rare gesture. They want this case solved badly, and I'm near certain the payment could help me meet that deadline I mentioned. I grab my jacket.

"Off to work then, huh? I suppose that means I should close out your tab?" Elios raises a brow and starts to move toward the till. The register is a metallic antique, complete with circular press-down buttons. Whenever people make fun of him for it, he insists that the small bell that sounds as it's opened helps an angel gain wings somewhere. Some people find that humorous and some take it seriously, because they believe in the celestial things. Not me. I, for one, have never seen an angel. But I have seen plenty of things that many of those same individuals would consider a fairytale, or a nightmare.

"One more, Elios," I say instead. After the payday they've just put out, every enforcer and freelance bounty hunter within a day's journey is going to be clawing at one another for this job. My day is about to go from bad to worse. I don't relish dealing with it before another drink. Not that I'm an alcoholic, or maybe I am, although it's near impossible for me to get drunk. Elevated metabolism and all that. Elios places the beverage in front of me, his watery, faded green eyes lingering on it before he releases the glass.

After I down the drink, so quickly that I'm upset with myself for eliminating my excuse to remain at the bar, I slap down some cash on the counter and give Elios a brief salute before I head out. As the door swings wide, I'm struck between the contrast of the darkened bar atmosphere and the unwelcome, cheery sunshine outdoors. It's cool, as if the weather has finally figured out it's fall. A bit late, if you ask me. The temperature stayed uncomfortably hot in a stubborn heatwave all the way through the first week of October. It was relentless. It's early November now, and at least I've got an excuse to transition to fall fashion. Today's look? Elegant biker chic. Fitted black leather jacket and combat boots, stone blue shirt underneath, and jeans that made even me do a double-take in the mirror on my way out. The current generation can say what they want about skinny jeans, but my ass looks fantastic. The look does not, however, come complete with a motorcycle. I walked to the bar. Responsible drinking, am I right? As I start to move east I'm hit by an onslaught to my senses.

I don't welcome the noise. Sacramento has been growing more and more crowded with each passing year, much like the rest of the world. While I'm generally happy with all the amenities this location affords me, sometimes I long to go back to the years where our kind inhabited forests and kept to the edge of small villages. Simpler times and all that.

I stare straight ahead as I plow through the crowd, single-minded in my journey to the crime scene from the news. The air is filled with the combined smells of all manner of foods from nearby restaurants, the trash that no environmental initiative has managed to keep off the roads, and the stench of both human and animal feces. It's times like this I don't appreciate my superior sense of smell. I pass several unhoused individuals huddled under the awning of a building with a 'For Lease' sign in the front window. My hard edges soften a bit at the harsh irony. Then I pass a pile of dog poop and a woman dragging her leashed husky away without so much as reaching for the bags attached to its collar. I roll my eyes.

Eventually my path leads me past the more crowded areas and through some side alleys. Here I'm subjected to the lovely smell of garbage from industrial-sized bins. The hair on my arms stands on end as I feel, before I can even smell, two men come up behind me.

I turn before they can say anything, throwing a dazzling smile their way. For a moment their eyes widen, and the shorter one takes a hesitant step back. The taller one recovers quickly, returning my smile and revealing grimy and unbrushed teeth.

"Oh, look at this one, Rob, a regular fairytale princess."

My jaw clenches at the comment. It's true: with my icy silver hair, stark blue eyes, and sharp cheekbones I have the bearings of a much outdated version of some royals, but it's not a comparison I welcome. It's a dated comment that flies in the face of the diverse nature of beauty. Not that I wouldn't take that compliment, if it were really meant to be one. I know how to use what I've got, but I don't like being objectified.

"I don't know, Dan, doesn't exactly have an hourglass figure, does she? Still, her lower half's all right."

I've always been athletically built. Not curvy, not skinny, and not that it matters to me. And those who complain once don't get the chance to do it again.

"Don't listen to Rob, princess. You're very pretty. What do you say, honey, we're both feeling a bit lonely today. Care to fix that for us?" They're a stereotypical henchman duo. One larger, one scrawny. Both repulsive, for their actions more than any of their physical features, which are unremarkable. Brown hair, brown eyes, and sallow skin for both. That's not what draws my attention, though; it's the feeling that runs over me. It breezes against those raised hairs on my arms, like a soft puff of air covering my skin. And I can just *feel* the ill intent leaching off them. It's a gift, although not always a welcome one. In this case, though, I could have determined these two were bad news without it.

I can be eloquent when I need to be, falling into the princess routine, but this isn't one of those times.

"Eat shit." I throw the words at them.

Dan, the heftier one, scowls. Rob just laughs.

"A regular ice queen, isn't she? No matter, we can help you behave."

This time I *do* temper myself. I've had hold of myself for so many years that it's second nature. I center myself mentally, a deep breath in and a deep breath out. Can't go changing features in front of the puny humans. Then again, these two clearly need to be taught a lesson, if I'm reading them right, and I *always* do.

Sure enough, both pull knives out of their pockets, flicking them open.

"Now, don't go running away. It won't do you any good, and we're not the type to appreciate a chase. If you make us run after you, we won't leave you as pretty as we found you," he threatens.

Oh Rob, you don't need to worry about that.

I allow myself the slightest shift as they get close, and I see their eyes widen just before I lash out. I know they've seen it, that flash, that otherness in my gaze. Humans never know quite what to call it, and they're not supposed to. I armbar the scrawnier one, and he sails into the nearest brick wall, slumping down unconscious. Oops. He's breathing, though, so at least I've got that going for me. The other one turns to run. I hate when they do that, because it awakens my predatory nature, but I'm well-practiced at ignoring it. Instead of tackling him and ripping out his throat, I shove him from behind.

He goes sprawling, and with a swift kick I've got the knife away from him. I grab his neck and shove him into the wall.

"We didn't mean anything by it!" Dan's clawing at my hand with dirty, stubby nails. I'm certain he expects a similar treatment to his friend. Instead of knocking him out, I pull one of my burner phones from my pocket. I always keep a couple handy. I dial 9-1-1 and shove the phone toward him.

"You're going to call, and you're going to report yourself for whichever recent rapes and muggings you've committed. Now."

He shakes his head up and down as he takes the phone. Once the call is made, I keep him in a hold until I hear sirens. Only then do I let him drop, wheezing and hacking on the ground.

"Bitch." He spits at me. I'm not fazed by it. I've heard it so many times, and almost always from lesser men.

"Stay and let them take you in. I'll know if you don't," I promise.

I hide myself down the alley and watch them get cuffed and taken away. Is it a perfect system? No. But I'll mention this to the other enforcers. The two men I've just stopped aren't magicals of any kind, but we do some public service jobs for the humans every now and again. I'm happy to add these guys to the list, just because of their commentary about my looks. I flip my hair over my shoulder, giving the scene the middle finger as I walk away. They can't see it, but it sure feels good.

Some might think that being accosted by two ne'er-do-wells on the streets of Sac would leave one in a foul mood. Quite the contrary for me. I almost always welcome an excuse to let out some justified anger. Every once in a while, that whole concept of 'no matter how many you stop, there will always be more' gets me down. Not today, though. I'm in that kind of mood where I've got plenty of excess annoyance that I'm more than happy to vent on someone. I turn as the sirens fade and make my way toward my real target.

Chapter 2

Carnage Carnival

I wrinkle my nose as I take in the scene in front of me—from a distance, of course. I'm on the northeast side of the city, out near the fairgrounds. A fall carnival complete with mobile and foldable rides has been set up. Some are still swirling with motion and lights, as though shutting them off wasn't anyone's top priority. Not that it should be. I'd wager the dozen bodies being zipped into bags and loaded into medical transport have that particular honor.

Per the news anchor I watched from the bar, one of the beverage vendors arrived to find a good portion of the carnival staff dead during setup today. It was the newscasters' mention of animals loose in the city that had drawn my attention and ire. Sometimes lost shifters—and anyone committing this crime has to be lost—are so predictable. Whoever did this hasn't even tried to cover up what they've done. Pure laziness is what it is. We live less than a day's drive from how many forested hikes? And yet here someone is, wreaking havoc in the middle of a populated area, where no one stands a real chance of writing it off as a bear attack or some such nonsense. Then again, if these individuals weren't so careless, I wouldn't have a job. If that's how I want to refer to the life of an enforcer.

I've been doing this for a long time. A miserably, wonderfully, how-has-it-been-this-many-generations long time. Any magical pack, coven, or entity that has issues too big for their own group to solve can reach out to the Magikai, and they'll send us. We also take care of general madness and mayhem, like what I see before me, where we have no idea who's responsible. The type of job doesn't matter to me, so long as someone pays up. I pace at the edge of the crime scene as I wait for the humans to finish. Maybe I don't even want this job. It's possible I could find the male I'm after without whatever payment I could get from the Magikai. Then again, if I haven't been successful for this long, what are my chances of doing it alone in less than a year? I'm running out of time.

The Magikai recruited me to be an official enforcer a couple hundred years back, when I caused a bit of a scene myself. Rather than having me terminated, the organization that governs all magicals recruited me instead. I'm sure it irks them that I insist on being more of a freelancer than someone on the permanent payroll, but we came to a compromise. They get the benefit of my services and particularly rare abilities, and I get something to do. After all, I need the entertainment more than I need the money. When I started, I'd also hoped the travel this job affords might lead me to clues about the magical I'm hunting. Even when that didn't turn out to be the case, I stayed. I have to admit my passion for doling out justice. Sometimes violently.

If I were human they'd call me a vigilante, but with my particular skills I'm much more accurate than your general do-gooder relying on their own personal moral compass. I don't go after those I *perceive* as being in the wrong; I go after those who *are*. Evil, sadistic individuals, broken in a way that can't be fixed. I've been classed as a hired gun, a mercenary, a murderer, and now an enforcer, but the most important thing I am is an intuitive. A rare genetic variant that allows some of my species to read the intent and emotions of others.

I crouch down, scenting the air for any clues. It takes a moment, but eventually, through the blood and popcorn, it hits me square in the nose.

Impossible.

What I've just scented is something I haven't come into contact with for decades. I have to be certain. I let my muzzle grow out and check again, and the smell remains unchanged. How unexpected! I'm so shell-shocked that I completely fail to hear the trio behind me until someone slaps me on the shoulder. I jump, turning with a growl.

"Never! Should have known you'd be here first." I look up to see a familiar face. Todd, a bear shifter and fellow enforcer. Some people have all the luck. Simple name, even if it doesn't fit him. Easy animal to explain in a variety of locations if woods are anywhere nearby, and fairly indestructible. He's got deep brown skin and amber eyes that, if you'd seen him shift, are an excellent imitation of the coloration of his fur and muzzle.

Standing next to him are two others. The first is a slender man with dirty blond hair sticking up at all angles and freckled skin, who goes by Lynx. Really hitting it right on the nose there, as a feline shifter with a name like that. Not that I judge. The two of them partner up on jobs all the time.

The second individual is unfamiliar. I take her measure quickly. Height is average. Her build leans toward curvy; eyes are the same green as sea glass and heavily lined. Looks to be in her teens, although who can really tell with most of us. I'm constantly guessed to be in my twenties, and that's a laughable understatement. Her hair is thick, wavy, bouncy, and a shade of wine-red that's got to be dyed regardless of what species she is. The dark hair sits in contrast to her porcelain-pale skin. I try to sniff at her in a less than obvious manner. She's doused herself in some godawful perfume, the wretch. So either she's not one of us and trying to disguise her humanity from those who would take advantage, or she's a magical outcast, or possibly even some sort of endangered species. The first, some shifters would throttle for fun. The last two mean she might have a bounty on her. I plan to find out which, sooner rather than later.

I extend a hand past the men toward her, and after a moment's hesitation she extends me her own to shake.

"Never. Charmed." I plaster a winning smile on my face, but the girl just raises an eyebrow. Her head tilts in confusion, which I feel just as well as I see, before she responds.

"Agatha, or Aggie, whichever you prefer. And you're ..." And I see where we've gone wrong.

"Never."

Her mouth opens into a surprised little 'o' as realization hits.

"Did your parents really give you that name?" she asks, tone innocent even as she delivers the offensive question.

The men both suck in a breath. They've seen me break jaws for this kind of comment before. But right now I choose to be in a charitable mood. Especially since I've scented something at this carnival that I desperately want to track, and I need these three out of my way. I have no time to squabble over first-claimed status in this case. Pissing them off is likely to lead to a competition or sabotage, and that will just slow me down.

"No." I let the one word answer dangle. The girl shuts her mouth. "And *this* girl with the grandma name is really going to make fun of mine?" I question. She stays quiet, which means she's got some brains.

Or so I think, until she leans in close, her eyes flickering off and on like a light that needs replacing.

"A shifter? Are you a wolf, then?" she asks, full of curiosity.

I round on Todd and Lynx.

"Hell's bells, you two! A witch? You could have warned me." The very human-like magicals don't have the best relationship with my kind specifically. And they're unnerving; eyes flashing on and off whenever they're up to something. I cuff each of the men across the ears, although they're both well capable of enduring far worse hits. They're also both smart enough to flinch. Not that I'm full of myself or anything, but I'm considered a *very* intimidating entity in certain circles, and for good reason.

"Never's not a wolf," Lynx volunteers, pointing at me from his place by Agatha, "she's a Were. See the mark there on her inner arm?"

More generous than I'd almost ever deign to be, I twist my right arm out of my jacket so she can see the looks-like-a-tattoo-but-isn't that runs along my inner arm from just below my elbow to just above. Abstract art to anyone not in our circles, but telling to those shifters who bother to study our history. This girl clearly hasn't.

"Like a werewolf? So ... I was right then, wolf shifter."

Lynx sucks in a breath and Todd shoots me a wide-eyed glance as he waits to see what I'll do. I reach out a hand that is starting to grow claws and wrap it around her arm, yanking her back into the trees and away from the fairgrounds. I do not put on performances for people, but this is just ridiculous. Someone has seriously let down this girl's education. That ends today. And the sooner she gets her silly questions answered, the sooner we get back to important business.

"Lynx, watch the perimeter," I throw over my shoulder. Shifty he may be, but he's also an excellent lookout. He'll spy any human a mile away, and that's not an exaggeration.

"You're good!" he shouts back.

The girl is shaking a bit now, but she's not blubbering, thank goodness. I hate waterworks. I let go of her arm with enough force that she stumbles forward a bit.

I don't waste any more time; I just go ahead and transform right in front of her face. I can see, as the color leaches from it, her eyes going wide in shock and fear. I can feel both even through her floral perfume. Luckily for me, my abilities aren't affected by smell. I change back. Some shifters take quite a while to transform when they first get going. And it can be extremely painful. For me, only the latter is true, because the human me is really more of the facade. Were is my true form.

"*Were*, pronounced like *werewolf*, not 'we *were* going somewhere,'" I clarify, "and decidedly *not* a wolf."

Not that I don't hold a bit of a soft spot for them, if I can admit to favoritism. I'm even willing to forgive the fact that somehow they've ended up with 'werewolf' as a formal title, even though the name actually refers to my species. It's true they're nearly the closest thing to what I am. Close, but not quite. Whereas the majority of shifters are a sort of dual-nature entity, living with their animal form as almost a second soul, Weres are an exception.

Our form is not fully animal; not recognizable as something specific to humans. It's much more similar to what people see in horror films, although I also like to think we're much more attractive. Bipedal, legs bent back instead of the forward-facing knees, tails, ears, a muzzle, fangs of course, hypermuscular ... the whole nine yards. Beauty and perfection. That's what I think of us. Even though the rest of the world seems to disagree. Not that I give two shits about their opinions.

Most importantly, though, at least for my health and longevity, we are quite long-lived and hard to kill. We're beat out in that area by dragons, but who isn't? Coincidentally, they're also a being whose mythical form is truly what they are. Not the human facade they wear.

"But aren't you all going extinct?" Little Aggie actually slaps a hand over her mouth, as if that's going to shove the careless words back in.

That's news.

"Real and very much still alive, thank you very much." I turn back to the boys. "Is that really what the witches are telling their youth these days? That we're basically all dead? I'm not even appreciated in my own time!" I throw my hands up, pacing. It's an outrage, is what it is. I'm torn. On the one hand, keeping a reasonably low profile benefits me. Outside of the other enforcers, at least. The

Magikai keep a record of us all, if anyone cares to go looking. Still, for one in the magical community to be so misinformed!

I round on the girl again.

"I assure you, missy, we are not disappearing any time soon." Never mind that I haven't seen another one of my kind in the last fifty-four years or so, but who's counting, really? Until today, that is. A small pang of emotion hits me at this thought, and I actually rub at my chest. Emotional mess, that's what I'm acting like. I need to rein it in. I make an effort to turn their attention back toward the carnival of murder behind us, just as another ping sounds. The males and I pull out our phones. They've no doubt received the same message.

Sacramento
Rogue magicals holding valued kidnap victim
Unknown species – obtain alive
Pay increase to 4 million or equivalent from Magikai stores

I nearly drop my phone. That's a heck of a payday. And it should be. Trying to take on an unknown number of magicals who have slaughtered a dozen human or possibly non-human victims is tough enough. To do it while having to decide which of them is actually a victim that needs to remain alive ... nigh impossible. At least alone. I feel an idea coming on.

"Listen, we all know that the odds of a single shifter, or any magical, taking down a dozen foes without someone getting away to spout some half-believed story about supernaturals to the police is as likely as this witch teaching me about the foundations of magic. So, I propose teamwork. Or rather, separate work that we will compile again at a later date, since I've no desire to be around others on a continuous basis." I clap my hands together, pleased with myself.

The two males give each other a look before nodding in tandem. Agatha stands behind them, tight-lipped. I take this for agreement.

"Excellent! I will scent and follow any leads. Lynx, if you'll follow up with the police and find out what they know. Hacking, spying, however you'd like to play it. Todd, evidence collection along with the witch? She can scry for clues or bewitch the investigators or whatever her key quality is." All witches have one: a key. It's part of what makes them useful. Sounds callous, I'm sure, but as a general rule they can be a nasty bunch. I'd like to say it's part of the reason they get depicted in the media the way they are; then again, look at how my kind is portrayed. A Halloween villain. And we're basically perfection.

No, I think they're terrible because of rotten luck. Spells, potions, fortune telling. It all costs something, and it's much easier to go the sacrifice-the-kiddies route as a witch than it is to walk the straight and narrow. Not that we abide by the same rules and obligations as our human neighbors, but you've got to have *some* boundaries.

The magical world operates on a few very basic principles enforced by the Magikai. One, no harming the innocents. Now, that is a fairly broad rule. For instance, what to many appears to be an innocent hiker is a guilty trespasser to a bear shifter whose territory has been encroached upon. We tend to let each kind draw their own lines there. Children are off the table, though. Second rule: we settle our differences through preapproved means. Again, a stray kill between arch enemies is going to get overlooked, but there are ways of settling full pack or species disputes. Because, thirdly: no exposing ourselves to the humans at large.

Why? I'd love to say, just because we like them. The average human mind, no matter how much they purport to adore magic, is not equipped to handle our reality. Trust me when I say I've seen people attempt it enough times, and it almost always ends badly. There are some notable exceptions of individuals entrenched in our world, but those are few and far between. Could we take them all out and rule in the open? Undoubtedly. Why don't we? We're not grade-A assholes for one, at least not most of us. And then humans would be our responsibility. No one wants that. At least no one with half a brain. Aside from the destroy-all-humans crew, the rest of us realize we'd then have to form some sort of human-magical co-governments. We'll let them handle their own disputes, with the occasional behind-the-scenes assistance, thank you very much. The last thing we need is to take on their drama. That leaves us free to exercise our natures in the background. A much better arrangement.

"Meet you at Elios's later this evening to share findings?" Lynx asks. The bar does have an actual name, The Lusty Lute, but the aged barkeep is the fixture everyone knows.

"I'll confirm that we're taking this as a shared job to the Magikai. That way, no one else can claim the contract," Todd offers.

The trio head toward the scene of the crime, a large patch of dirt between a blood-spattered carousel and equally messy Ferris wheel. The cops have dispersed by this point, and if the witch is worth anything she'll be able to do at least a mild shielding spell on them while they rummage around.

I turn my nose back to scenting what caught my attention before. After all this time, I've found another Were. Now to determine if this one is the victim or the murderer.

Chapter 3
New Leads & Old Enemies

It becomes clear by the time I hit the airport miles away that my search isn't going to be a simple one. Hell. Normally I don't mind a good chase, but this isn't a time where I like leaving things unanswered.

I curse myself for getting distracted by my temptation to find the other Were, if there even is one. Maybe someone's found a way to trick even my nose and abilities. After all, despite what I told the witchling, there aren't very many of us left. Comparatively fewer in the western hemisphere, and even fewer than that roaming large cities in the USA.

What I should have done is get a closer look at the bodies or go with Lynx to gather reports. That would tell me whether the wounds are even consistent with one of my kind. Sometimes I'm an idiot. I ran all the way here, strictly because my target did. Or at least that's what my nose led me to believe. I debate grabbing a cab back into town but decide against it. I can at least double back and see if there are any other scents I missed in my rush.

I'm cutting through one of the parks on the north end of Sac when the scent of Were grows stronger again. This time, though, it's different. Distinctly male, and also familiar. Surely I'm imagining things. I've been searching for so long and have gone years without so much as a single clue.

I feel my body react in simultaneous and contradictory ways. Physically? I'm drawn to the smell, and I feel my knees going all melty. Emotionally and mentally? I'm in shock. Torn between fury and fear as I fight back a flurry of flashbacks.

While I stand frozen in place, deciding what to do, I feel a pair of arms wrap around me. Even after all this time, their weight and warmth is familiar. I need to get myself under control, and fast. I settle on my most frequently used strategy: he's an enemy until proven otherwise.

"Hello, Never." The Were behind me nuzzles at my neck, taking in my scent. I shove him off, fuming.

"*You're* the Were I've been scenting this whole time? Damn it, Damien, why didn't you just show yourself? Could've saved me a lot of time."

"Or maybe you're the Were *I've* been tracking. Have you thought of that?"

He smiles, canines pointed. The male never did like to keep his form fully human for long. Which is a damn shame, because it is pretty to look at. Muscled, statue-perfect form, eyes that humans have to lean in close to discern whether they're blue or grey. Grey is the answer, if anyone was wondering. His hair was longer last time I saw him, although that's been a good century or so, not that I keep track. Now, it's longer on top and shorter on the sides. A combination of grey and brown, although the stubble on his face is still deep brown. No one would mistake him for old, even though he is. "Silver fox," most people would say, which is really laughable to me, given what a rarity that would actually be.

He moves in close again, muscled chest visible through a tight shirt. He reaches both hands up, looking like he's going to grab my arms, but he must catch my expression. Damien pauses as I curl my lip at him, letting my own canines lengthen to points.

"Try it, and you'll be going home without your hands," I warn.

Does it sound harsh? Good. I mean for it to. Now, I like to consider myself a fair Were, but trust me when I say he's got it coming. *Damien* ... the origin of the name means to tame or to subdue. It's nothing I've ever been interested in, and he must have decided it wasn't a possibility when we were together, because he abandoned me two hundred years ago. After I was dumb enough to let myself fall for him. Even that wouldn't have left me feeling salty this long, except he happened to leave me alone in the woods with all manner of enemies closing in on us at the time. He got away. I didn't. At least not for a number of years. I shake my head, hair whipping my face as I banish the memories. Moon knows, when you're as old as me you've got enough of them that you'd rather forget.

"Would you mind telling me just what you think you're doing, tracking me in my own city?" I seethe.

He just grins, damnable man. His teeth are points of pearly white perfection.

"As luck would have it, I'm *not* here for you. Although I have to say it's a most welcome excuse to run into you. I'm here for the girl; the other Were."

Aha, so my nose was right. Another female. Thank goodness, because these walking and talking male appendages are the last thing I need more of. I tell myself I'm just curious because she's probably one of the suspects the Magikai has me tracking.

"Find yourself another girlfriend to use and lose, then?" I mean for the comment to sting, but he doesn't take the bait.

"Would it bother you if that were the case?" he asks, but doesn't wait for an answer. "No, she's just a target. Barely a mature Were, from what I've heard."

It's more information than I've been given. And the Magikai is powerful, so how is it he's got details I don't have?

"Just who are you collecting her for?"

He grins again, grabbing my hand and planting a kiss on it before I can pull it away.

"You were always at your most attractive when you were scheming. That information is private. But I might be willing to trade for it. I need to know what's happened to my elusive prey."

"And you think I might have some idea where she is or how to find her?" I saunter closer to him, placing a hand on his chest. I hear it when he sucks in a short breath, and I know I've got him. Two can play at this game.

"As you said, it is your city." His voice is tight. Good. That means he's actually having to work for control, which means his brain isn't the organ in charge. It seems that even though he was more than happy to dump me like forgotten garbage, he's still got some reaction to my charms.

I slowly climb my fingers up his chest, letting claws begin to grow. I rake them slowly across his neck, making sure my voice is sultry as I look up at him.

"I might have some information," I croon. "But is that really all you want? After all, Damien, it's been *so* long. I've missed you." I lean in on the last words, and I can feel the tension of our mouths less than an inch apart. His lips part, and his limbs go slack as he leans towards me. Which is when I knee him right in the crotch.

For the record, it's just as effective with Weres and other shifters as it is with human men. Free self-defense tip there.

He buckles at the knees but doesn't go down. Strong male.

"Damn it, Never!" A true snarl is on his face now, extended muzzle and all. He slashes out at me with a furred and clawed hand, but I dance backward. Dare I say I'm enjoying myself?

I waggle a chastising finger at him.

"Now, now, Damien. Let's not be angry for no reason. I'd say after what you did to me you have it coming." I let the playful facade drop for a moment, and I *hope* he can see the betrayal in my eyes. If he has any soul left, he'll feel at least a little guilty about it.

"Never, I —"

"Save it! You didn't come here to apologize. You came for the girl, right? Well, it may interest you to know I don't have her. I might have some leads, however, not that I'm in the mood to share with the likes of you. And since you're clearly here on a hunt, you'll have to catch me fair and square, just like any other prey." Before he can react, I put on some muscle and roundhouse him in the jaw. It'll piss him off, of course, but he'll be fine.

I turn and run. Not my most badass moment, but you have to know when to fight. And this is a battle I want to have on my own terms.

"She's got intuition, Never!" he screams at my back.

It's a testament to my professionalism, really, that I continue to sprint away, jumping on a trashcan and catapulting myself into a tree. Parkour may be growing in popularity with humans, but we magical folk have honed that talent for centuries. His words echo in my head as I move. Were are already so limited, and even among those of us left I'm the only one with my abilities that I've ever come across. My parents were both thrilled and terrified when they realized my gift, because even at that time I was the only intuitive they'd heard of.

Once I'm past the park and several rooftops over, I know I've lost Damien. After all, he was right about it being *my* city. His presence does present another problem, though. Not the fact that he's likely to be able to track down where I live, or even that he's in competition to find the girl. I don't know who he's working for, but even that isn't an insurmountable issue.

No, it's inconvenient timing, since now I have two missions, and I'll need to decide in what order to approach them. He's the deadline that's been looming over me recently.

You see, I made a vow all those years ago when Damien abandoned me, and I'm a Were who keeps her promises. In this case, I'm a Were who has to. He may have been my friend, and my lover, but none of that matters now.

I'm going to kill him.

Chapter 4

Concocting Plans Over Cocktails

Todd and Aggie beat me to the bar. He's got a comically large tankard in front of him. I can tell by the scent it's an amber ale. She's got hot chocolate, complete with marshmallows. Either she is a giant goody two-shoes, or she's actually young instead of just appearing that way. Maybe both.

I swing by the bar, leaning over to wave at Elios as he rings someone up. Two shifters next to me go wide-eyed as my cleavage presses into the counter. It's not as much to work with as some folks have, but it gets the job done. One shifter whistles and the other snickers. Pigs. Not literally; one is a wolf and the other smells a bit like a reptile.

"Eyes up here, boys." The words are friendly enough, but when they look up, they're face to face with an angry Were in full shift. They scramble back.

"Sorry, ma'am, drink's on us," the wolf stammers, putting cash on the bar. *Ma'am?* What am I, a thousand years old? That's almost worse than the ogling.

Elios arrives and lets out a sigh as they move themselves away from the bar and toward a pool table.

"Trying to scare off all my customers, Never?"

I smirk, leaning over to scratch under Elios's chin.

"Then I'll have you all to myself." I wink. He just rolls his eyes. One thing I appreciate about the barkeep; he's immune to me. My flirtations, my temper, and my jokes. It would be preferable if he appreciated that last one, but I'll take two out of three. It's nice to be around someone who is not impressed, intimidated, or looking to profit from you in some way. With the exception of drink prices, of course. I slide the cash over to him.

"Corpse Reviver, please."

He grumbles but moves towards the till. The thing about Elios's establishment is, it's really more of a dive bar than a classy cocktail joint. And he prefers it that way. He would much rather sling draft beers, cheap wines, and straight liquor than anything else. He humors me, though. And to be fair, he makes an amazing cocktail.

Once I have my drink in hand, I saunter back to the table. I take a sip from my glass and let out a sigh. Delicious, as always.

"Now then, I'll start. I came up with absolutely nil. What about you two?" I stare over my glass at Todd. I'm not quite ready to share about Damien.

"Not much better. The cops cleared out almost anything useful. I did find this." He places a cooler on the table. "Underneath the carousel. No telling if it was already there, but it's got blood on it, so it's possible one of them dropped it."

I open it, preparing to see a body part or something that needs to be kept on ice. It's a cigar. A gigantic cigar. Partially smoked. And it reeks. The smell of bodies must have covered it from the humans' senses. I slam the lid shut again and wave a hand under my nose to disperse the scent.

"You could have warned me!" I level a glare at Todd through watery eyes. He just grins. The jerk. "It's not much of a clue. Did you see anything else?"

"We weren't able to. More of the humans came back and we had to leave. Todd heard their cars before they'd even gotten to the street with the carnival," Aggie offers. Of course he did. He's a bear. Since we are apparently having no luck on the 'explore the carnival grounds' front, I change topics.

"Just how old are you, witchling?"

"Eighteen. Why?" She's genuinely curious. I can feel it. Bless her, handing out her real age so readily. Often it's an innocuous enough piece of information, but she doesn't know me well enough to share these things. Naive.

"Country coven?" I ask.

She nods, smiling with wide eyes.

"How did you know? Your intuition? Todd told me how you can figure out things. Like mind reading? Or psychic abilities?"

I'm torn between laughter and annoyance. I decide it amuses me.

"An urban witch would likely have already known about Weres, and a lot of other rare creatures. That, and you're way too optimistic to be from here. Also, no. Intuition does not let me read minds. Although it does let me know if you lie, so keep up the honesty."

She nods earnestly.

"I will."

I'm about to ask what her key is, because she just might tell me without it costing an arm and a leg. Witches hold that information close unless they're profiting off it. The thing that comes out of her mouth next distracts me.

"You can trust me. I'm from a light-magic-only coven." Pure and total honesty to that statement, as far as I can feel.

"No shit!" I slap a hand on the table. Agatha wrinkles her nose as I cuss. Sue me. I've been alive too long to censor myself. And it's a really, really, rare thing to find a whole coven practicing light magic only. Hard enough to find a lone witch doing it. I lean forward, eager to pepper her with more interrogation.

Before I can decide on my next question, Lynx walks in. He pulls a file out of a messenger bag he's toting. He slides into the booth, making a face as he settles on a piece of cracked vinyl. Renovations have never been much of a priority for Elios.

"Managed to get some illicit copies made by a shifter intern I know," he explains as he sets the file on the table. Todd opens it and pulls a packet of papers off the top, revealing a set of photographs. I snatch the first one.

I was the one who sent Lynx to the cops before, but mainly to see what they did and didn't know. It's not often they have any information on a scene that we've missed. In this case, though ....

"Seems one of the detectives thought to take photos of the crowds that showed up after all the bloodshed. Guilty parties may revisit the scene of the crime and all that," he rattles off as my grip on the photo I'm holding grows tighter.

"You've really got to hand it to humans; just when you think they've gone as close to the edge as they can without going over, they build up an obsession for true crime. Do you know there's actually one girl in these photos with a camera that the files say they tracked down this morning? She was vlogging the whole thing. Had a bunch of followers online just watching as she livestreamed mutilated bodies while they tried to get bags on everyone." He continues. Any other time, I'd be happy to banter with him about the depravity of humans vs. that of any magical being. The obsession with the morbid.

Now isn't one of those times.

I clench my hand and my claws rip out, unbidden, shredding holes in the photograph.

"Damien," I seethe.

Lynx raises a brow over one vibrant hazel eye. Although they're really more green-gold than greenish-brown.

"Someone you're familiar with? A potential suspect?"

I shake my head and change the subject.

"Go home, Lynx. Surely Fiona's missing you by now, assuming she's still able to put up with your particular brand of charm."

He just grins. Most official enforcers are as single as myself, but Lynx is an exception. Unlike some of us who travel extensively for contracts, he and Todd stick to the west coast. They take odd jobs as they come to the area. Lynx has a strict perimeter he tries not to leave, because he has a mate.

"Fiona has excellent taste. All right, then, but we'll check back in with you tomorrow."

I barely register his words as he slinks out of the booth, all silent and sinuous feline.

"At the carnival. We should go over the scene again. I scented another Were. We need to track them down," I state.

I'm not prepared to open up about Damien, but I should let them in on this particular detail. Lynx stops and turns.

"You *what*?" he demands. Luckily for me, Were scents *are* similar enough to wolf shifters that they clearly overlooked her presence at the scene. Damien's in this photo, though. He was hunting her, just like he said, and closer than I thought. I want to get to her first.

"Either she's involved or she's innocent, but she was there, and we need to track her down. Honestly, I'm leaning toward thinking she's the kidnapping victim."

I don't say anything about her supposed intuition. That's something I want to confirm for myself. They agree readily enough without that detail. It's the best lead we have. A young female Were, possibly with my abilities, stuck in a violent scenario. I'd be lying if I said I wasn't drawn to our similarities. It's always a possibility I'll have to catch or kill her, if she's on the wrong side of things. For once, I'm hoping against a violent outcome.

After the bar door shuts behind the others, I go back to staring at the photo.

A good number of magicals have fated mates—some weird ability to just *know* they're supposed to be with someone. I can't knock it, because it's eerily similar to my intuition, which ironically seems to malfunction only in the face of those feelings. Quite a few other species can go through mating ceremonies that bond them much deeper than a human marriage ever could. Almost all of them are willing to die for each other, and some literally cannot live without their other half.

Not Weres, though. There are some similarities. We tend to be hyperprotective of our loved ones, and once mated do tend to remain monogamous. That being said, we operate strictly on the basis of choice, not fate or design, when it comes to picking that mate. And boy, did I nearly choose wrong.

The next morning, I'm up early and headed back to the fairgrounds. There are a few leaves scattered around, their orange and gold hues in stark contrast to the dirty grey sidewalks. Let no one say I think myself above basic bitchery, because I am sipping on a fall-themed oat-milk latte from one of the local roasters. Brown sugar, not pumpkin. That particular squash belongs at the entrance to a corn maze, not in beverages.

I start my work at the entrance of the carnival, scenting methodically toward the rides where the bodies were found. There's a dizzying number of smells. There always are, in a city as populated as Sacramento, but I've learned to block it out most of the time. When I'm on a job, though, and sifting through all the options, it can be overwhelming. The whole scene has been cordoned off with stereotypical yellow tape, which I duck under.

Luckily for me, and them, there are no cops in the area. Hopefully they got everything they wanted yesterday. The ticket booth has been tagged with graffiti, but the scent of the artist is human and fades out not far after, so they didn't stick around. When the others arrive, I'm sorting through a pallet of beverages that the vendor abandoned yesterday after stumbling onto the bodies.

Lynx and Todd move toward the walk-through attractions: haunted house and corn maze. Aggie stays near the entrance to work us up some kind of protection.

Which reminds me: going back to that whole topic of keys, every witch has a skill they excel at far beyond anything else. Not to say any decent witch isn't well-rounded, because they are. But as mentioned before, spells, potions, conjurings—it all costs something. Except for when it doesn't. A witch's key, as it's so aptly called, unlocks an ability without the typical cost. That's also how they tend to make their living, if they have a good or especially powerful one.

Witches are often wily, unscrupulous beings, but I try not to hold that against them. It's the luck of the draw. If I had to sacrifice a pile of toads every time I needed my claws to come out, I can't say I wouldn't make the same call. The pro to being one is the camaraderie of a coven, sometimes a very cool and unique skill, and, I personally would like to add, a fantastic wardrobe. Since most of them house up together, they've almost always got an endless supply of outfit swaps, and beautifying charms are surely someone's forte in the house. Aggie's sporting some turquoise overall corduroy dress that ought to look ridiculous, but doesn't.

Fashion isn't everything, though. Witches do get the shaft on quite a few other things. Save an anti-aging potion, they tend to live much shorter lives than your average magical. Hundred and fifty years, tops. Nothing to scoff at if you're human, but frustrating when your pals are two hundred–plus and not aging a day. And they *do* age, if they're not draining power to prevent it. Also, when it comes to sheer physical abilities, all tricks and potions aside, they don't have nearly as much to speak of. Any shifter could wipe a witch off the map easily if it comes down to physical strength alone. All in all, not the best deal in the magical world. Even the vamps are better off, if they'd get off their lazy behinds.

This makes it even more impressive, or boneheaded, depending on who you ask, that Agatha's from one of the rare light-magic covens. I'm fifty-fifty myself. They have to work so much harder for everything and utilize much more complicated spells. A waste, really, when you're on limited time and resources. Still, she seems to be getting along with some shielding spell just fine, so I go back to sleuthing.

I move toward the actual murder rides: the Ferris wheel and carousel. I'm a few yards back when multiple shifter scents hit my nose in a deluge, and they don't match the profiles Lynx's intern put together in the file. I know, because I stayed up late digging through it. Damn.

Yesterday, I got so caught up in scenting the Were that I didn't check for other leads. Stupid, stupid, stupid. Not that Todd and the witch caught on, either, but I know better than to farm out an important job like this.

"Hey, musketeers, get over here!" I yell at the three of them. I point at the leaf-strewn spot that I've been scenting. "Tell me what you can discern from this area."

"Aw, hell." Todd catches on first. "We didn't make it this far before the cops came back yesterday. Looks like there definitely *were* shifters involved in this. And is that vampire I smell?"

He's right. A motley crew of magicals. At least seven, against the dozen or so carnival workers that were hauled off in body bags. And amid all that ... the Were. Now that I'm here, the trickery is obvious. The Were's scent is very strong leaving the fairgrounds, in the middle of all the others' scents, and in the opposite direction of where I went yesterday. A false trail.

"They must have anticipated enforcers arriving and taken something of hers to throw us off the trail. Another sign that she's the victim here," Todd suggests, his opinion aligning with my own.

"So where are they, really?" Lynx asks as he scans the area. We're able to follow the actual trail to a side street several blocks away. Then nothing. They must have pushed her into a car. We fan out, trying to find any clue of where they've gone, but no further scent hits my nose. I pull at my hair.

"Damned kidnappers making things difficult," I complain. When we catch up to this group I am going to be less than polite. Partly because I want to find that Were, and partly because I am on a deadline and they're costing me time. Something glints in the sun down the street.

"Thank the moon!" I shout as I run over to it. A license plate reader. Terrible for people concerned about privacy; very useful for finding car registrations. I turn back to Lynx.

"Can your intern friend look into information on the cars parked on this street yesterday?"

"Sure, for a price," he offers. I wave a hand. I assume Lynx already paid him for yesterday's services. I'll happily foot the bill for this piece of information if it leads us to our culprits.

Three hours later, Lynx walks to the parking garage where the rest of us are waiting. Thankfully the neighborhood we were in is one of those nobody parks on the curb places. Which means there were only two cars there all day, and they're both registered in the same town.

"Boys and girls, we're headed to Susanville," I announce.

Chapter 5
Cabins and Kerosene

Around this part of California, they like to give everyone what I call the "in just a few hours" speech. If you live in Sacramento, you can get to all sorts of fun places—redwoods, the bay, Tahoe, numerous forests and waterfalls and hikes and restaurants and amenities—in "just a few hours." It appears that speech also applies to getting me from our murder scene to our next clue.

This particular road trip takes us through the beautiful scenery around Lake Tahoe and into Nevada and the casino lights of Reno. Depending on traffic and construction, this way is actually faster than staying in-state. For about the seventeenth time, Todd adjusts himself, bent over in the backseat.

"I still don't understand why we couldn't take my truck. It's much more equipped to handle the forest roads, and it's more spacious," he complains. As a bear, Todd is an absolute unit. As a man? Big enough to be immediately noticeable, but not so large that he can't fit inside a regular vehicle. He's just jealous Lynx is sitting in the front. The feline shifter in question has already been slapped on the shins twice for trying to put his feet up on my dash.

"Sorry, friend, but you know I get carsick in the back," Lynx says, turning toward his fellow enforcer. It's a half-truth. He gets carsick sometimes. It's enough of a risk that I'd rather have him in the front. A little over two hours into the drive, I've had enough of the bickering between the two shifters. They may be unlikely cross-species best friends, and business partners to boot, but they fight like an old married couple. I make a sharp turn into a casino parking lot as we enter Reno.

"Okay, everyone, pile out. Quick bite to eat, then back in the vehicle." It's a sleek orange sports car I chose strictly for color and not at all for practicality. What can I say? Magicals like shiny things. Or expensive things. At least some of us.

"Do we have time for a bit of gambling?" Lynx asks, eyes going bright. Given that we put our lives on the line all the time for work, it's no surprise that he's fond of games of chance.

"Eat and lose money at the same time. That way we can multitask and get on the road."

Four cheeseburgers, several slot machines, and less than an hour later we're back at the car. I for one have made back the money I paid to the police intern, which has put me in a chipper mood. Even Todd doesn't complain as he squeezes himself into the backseat.

My happy emotions falter as we turn down the street indicated by the car registration Lynx got us. Both vehicles were listed under the address of a cabin a few miles out of town and up in the woods. I pull us off the road near a neighboring drive to avoid suspicion as we take in the scene. At the end of the street uphill are several cop cars, lights flashing. There's also a firetruck and an ambulance, and a body bag is already being loaded. Behind the vehicles is the cabin, and a good half of it has either been burned down or blown up.

I have no desire to wait for another hours-long law enforcement comb-over of the area before we're able to go look through the scraps. This time, we need a different plan. Something big. Something frightening. Something that will grab their immediate attention and firepower while we do a quick look around.

"Oh, Todd?" I turn to him as I sing-song his name.

"I hate when you get that gleam in your eye, Never. This is precisely why Lynx and I don't partner with you very often. It always involves some harebrained and half-thought-out scheme."

I'm near certain he's thinking of the last time we worked together. Which may have involved Lynx burning his whiskers off. But we did catch our targets.

"Yes, I do, and as I recall, my plans always get us paid," I counter. "Now, I think it's more than feasible that blood of this amount might draw in a wild animal or two. Perhaps a bear comes looking for dinner?"

He just growls at me, which is always more humorous when magicals are in their human form.

"I really don't want to get shot today. I hate when that happens. It burns," he grumps.

"As much as losing out on a payout from the Magikai will burn? Along with our reputation as enforcers if we can't gain some traction on this job very soon?" After all, he officially accepted the contract for us. Which means every other enforcer will know we botched things if it comes back up as available. And it will, if it's determined we're taking too long.

He doesn't respond directly but walks off, grumbling to himself about "half-assed ideas." About a minute later, an impossibly large bear resembling a grizzly goes barreling toward the smoldering, half-ruined remains of the cabin from the trees. He lets out some low huffing noises as he turns and veers away just before reaching the cops' perimeter. It has the desired impact.

"Jesus Smeeth! Did you see that?" I can hear the local sheriff shouting to one of the others.

"Well, what the hell do we do about it? Have you ever seen one that big, and this close to town?" another man chimes in.

"Must be the corpses drawing him in. Let's get this wrapped up, gentlemen."

Everyone quickens their pace as they bring out another couple of body bags. It's no good. We need to examine those individuals. And as much as it turns my stomach, if the Were is among the dead, I still want to confirm it.

Todd lets out a growl as he makes another pass at the cabin. He stops near the end of the driveway, which runs downwards toward where the cops parked. He draws himself up on his hind legs, and I have to hand it to him, bear-boy is impressive. What did I say before? Absolute. Unit. He's at least the height of a polar bear when he's drawn up like this, and from their vantage point downhill he's got to look even larger.

A shot rings out, but Todd's already running back into the woods, and I don't smell any new blood.

"Don't shoot it, Perkins, dammit. We'll just end up pissin' it off. Call animal control and get them up here to handle this mess," the sheriff instructs.

"But sir, what do we do with the rest of the bodies and the crime scene in the meantime?"

"We leave it. Get in your vehicles and move further downhill. Something that big could topple our squad cars right over, and I'm not having anyone crushed in a rollover. We'll just have to resume once animal control has the situation handled."

They hastily pack themselves into their cars and drive off. They'll still be able to see the front of the cabin from where they've stopped downhill, but that's also the intact part of the house. We should stay blocked from view if we're careful. I signal to Lynx, and we start moving around the back half of the cabin. Todd keeps up his routine of making passes at the house, at one point ripping some casing off a window.

I pick my way through the charred remains of what seems to have been a bedroom. I catch the faintest scent of Were under the desolation. I move to the entrance of the room, and there are still two bodies left that the cops didn't get around to. The first is charred beyond recognition or scenting, even for our noses. The second must have been thrown by the blast. He's burnt on one side, but the left part of his body has unblistered areas. And, very telling, he's missing a head.

This "meth lab explosion," as I overheard one of the cops guess, has magical written all over it. I notice the charred-beyond-recognition body does have some visible, deep slashes on it, as if they were attacked by a very large animal.

"Unless they were mauled by a bear with a penchant for arson, it would appear our carnival killers have struck again," I suggest, side-eying Todd to see whether he'll take the bait as he saunters up behind me.

"Smokey would be so disappointed," he opines dramatically, shaking his head as he laughs at his own joke. Not all bears have a sense of humor, but Todd's an exception. I feel a smile tugging at my lips. Getting too chummy with anyone is dangerous, but I'll enjoy the faux-camaraderie for the length of this contract.

Aggie pokes her head out from behind the bear shifter, nose wrinkled up at the smell of burning flesh.

"Gross. But if these guys are the ones who took the other Were, who's the person or group killing them?"

"Precisely what we're here to discover, little witch!" I throw a finger up in the air, full-on detective mode activated as I deduce clues from the scene. Are we dealing with two groups, or a fight between the original kidnappers? I turn back to my headless buffet of clues. Underneath the soot, something on his lapel glints. I reach down and rip it off. It's a bejeweled pin. Real gems; very expensive, given the clarity. A set of diamond dice with inlaid rubies, and surrounding them a bejeweled mouth with ruby lips and diamond fangs. One is biting into a dice, a pear-shaped drop of gemstone blood underneath. It's a vampire coven sigil, and I've got a good guess which one.

"Vegas," Lynx states behind me, leaning over my shoulder.

"Yep. Seems we were on track with our casino stop earlier. We may need to pay the Vegas coven's lord a visit. See if he's aware he's got vampires out here murdering and kidnapping other magicals."

It wouldn't be unheard of, but it would go against Lord Costas's nature. I make it a point to be aware of potentially powerful or well-funded factions anywhere near my home. Lord Costas has headed up the Vegas faction for over half a century. He's more into profit and comfort than anything else. Makes his money off casinos and other entertainment-related venues, not hiring out his coven members as mercenaries. Contrary to popular belief among humans, vampires are generally not active killers. They're hedonistic and lazy. One thing humans got right is how attractive most vampires are. Not that our burnt body has retained any of what I'm sure must have been gorgeous features.

"I vote we go see the vamps," I put in.

Todd groans, human again. Lynx hands him a pair of shorts. They must have been keeping spares in the backpacks they'd tossed into my trunk earlier. Occupational hazard for most shifters. Always be ready for nudity.

"Just great. Several more hours crammed into your backseat. We'd better find someone alive to deal with when we get there." Todd pouts as he pulls on the shorts.

I concur. I'm sick of chasing bodies. My abilities are only useful when I can communicate with someone living. I go into furred form and give a last sniff as animal control officers make their way up the hill. I haven't detected a strong scent of the Were, so it's possible whoever blew up our villains took her, or that one of them was able to get her away from the scene. She's not among the dead, though. We move back behind the house and into the abutting woods before the humans descend. I'm determined to at least get a final look around the perimeter before we leave.

The heavy smoke and smell of death is choking whatever other smells may be out here, and I'm about to call it a day when I hear it, from deeper in the woods.

A howl.

The Were is here.

Chapter 6
The Key

"Northeast!" Todd yells, zeroing in on the source of the sound. I don't wait to see what the others are planning. I go barreling into the forest, fur standing on end.

"Never!" I hear Lynx yelling behind me, but I don't stop. I raise my snout, sniffing the air. Now that I'm away from the scorched cabin remains, I can smell her easily. I hear rustling and skid to a stop as I hit a clearing.

There's a girl, roughly Aggie's age in appearance, hands held behind her back by a large male. Another male is crouched in front of her, trying to stuff a gag into her mouth as she struggles. She's got to be the Were.

"Hold her sti—"

I cut the crouching male off with a snarl, launching myself at him. He ... runs? Not very magical of him. The male behind her shoves the girl at me and starts to shift.

"Who?" she starts.

"No time! Can you fight?" I demand. She just shakes her head, windswept auburn hair sticking to the sweat on her face. Just great.

"Get to the trees, then, that way!" I point her back toward the others and turn to face her larger captor, who is now fully shifted. A bear. Hopefully Todd will be here soon. This guy's not quite as large as my fellow enforcer, but he's awfully close. He's got brown fur and a massive snout, which I get a close-up view of as he pulls his lips back and roars.

His breath is foul. I wipe bear saliva off the side of my face.

"Are you done?" I taunt. Then I jump, using the offending snout as a foothold. I tuck and roll as I sail over his back, swiping my claws down each side of his spine. He lets out another roar, twisting toward me. He's bigger, but I'm quicker. I manage to slash his face before a paw catches me in the stomach, sending me flying backwards. That smarts.

Some people, namely the few humans I've met who have been introduced to our world, are initially under the mistaken impression that being magical means being invincible. Wrong. The bigger and badder and tougher you are, the longer you get to stay in a fight and get pummeled. The more pain you get to endure. It breaks some people.

I love it.

I charge back toward the bear, but a giant furry blur collides with him first. Todd is here. The two bears shake the ground as they trade blows. I turn my attention to the trees where the smaller male went. It takes only a few seconds to spot him. He's running back toward us, with three others in tow: a female and two males. The girl shifts quickly as she runs, a talent not everyone has bothered to perfect. A white tiger. One thing I do enjoy about feline shifters—the sheer variety. I focus on her as she sprints past the others. I hold my ground as she gets closer, gaining momentum. When she's several yards away, I lean forward and let out a howl, flexing my claws. She's about to barrel into me when I twist to the side and kick, taking her front legs out. She goes tumbling. She's quicker than the bear and is already righting herself when I dive on top of her, pummeling her face and neck with my claws. As she starts to twist away, I dig in, not breaking my hold as she attempts to fling me off.

Eventually she twists enough to loosen my grip, but I slide my claws down her shoulder as she gets free. It throws her off balance just enough for me to force her over on her side, and I dig my claws under her ribs. She yowls, pulling away, and then runs off, limping toward the trees. Where the heck is Lynx? Or even Aggie, for that matter? The tiger was overconfident and almost too easy to handle, but now I've got the other three closing in while Todd faces the bear and ... What. The. Hell.

"Never," Damien calls, holding up a palm as he emerges from the trees behind the others, "let's all calm down for a moment. Calvin! Stop!" he yells to the fighting bears.

I risk a side glance over toward them, and the grey one breaks away. Both are bleeding from several gashes and panting. No clear winner.

"*Calvin*? Really? What idiot named him? He's not bald." I can't help it; my fascination with names transcends even the most serious of moments. "What about the wolf shifter you've brought along? *Bunny*, perhaps? And you've even taught him to heel; what a good trick for a pet." In front of Damien is a nondescript grey wolf. There's also a vampire, and the male who had tried to gag the Were girl. I can't quite place what he is; some sort of shifter. A varied crew indeed.

Calvin huffs as he lumbers back toward Damien, his offense clear even if I couldn't read it. As it stands, it's rolling off them all heavily. Particularly from the wolf. Calling a shifter a *pet*? It's rude. Worse than almost any other insult. But I'm in a foul mood, so he'll have to deal.

"Never." Damien frowns at me. Is he disappointed with my brash demeanor? Impossible to say, which only makes me angrier.

"Fancy seeing you here, Damien. You did tell me we were both looking for the same girl. Did you beat me to it, or did you follow me here?"

"Don't respond! She'll just read us," the unidentified shifter to his left instructs. Silly shifter, they don't need to speak for me to tell if they lie.

"I'm already reading you. I can tell I've annoyed you." That's because of the tic in Damien's jaw and the way his eyes tensed when the other man spoke. My intuition never worked right with him after

... well, it doesn't matter now. My ears prick up as I hear steps behind me. Todd stays in bear form to my left. Aggie moves in by my right. Silly witch. I would have told her to wait in the car.

"Where's Lynx?" I whisper.

"Taking the girl back to where we had lunch. I, uh, had to put her to sleep. Sorry, she was getting a bit hysterical. Lynx said you'd figure out our transportation and we could meet him later."

At least somebody's head is in the right place. Get the girl as far from here as possible until I can figure out this mess. Having her unconscious isn't a bad plan, either. We really don't have any idea how she'll respond to our 'rescue' attempt.

"She removed the intuitive?" the vampire laments across the field. Damned magical hearing. "We have no choice then, Damien. He'll want a —"

"Say, sweetheart, care to clear something up for me? Those boys down at the house, yours? Or was there another guest at this party?" I yell toward the bickering group.

"Never," Damien growls a warning, but I keep right on going and bat my eyes at the vamp.

"I wasn't talking to *you*, you overgrown wolf." It stings me to insult my own kind, but he deserves it. "I was talking to the vamp."

"We came as backup. There was a disagreement on what to do with the girl. Things escalated," the vampire volunteers. All the truth. "And you'll end up in a similar situation if you don't provide us with that intuitive immediately."

I catch the flash of a pin on the vampire's clothing.

"Was that dead vamp part of your coven? Killing one of your kinsmen? Now, that's cold. What will your lord have to say about that, I wonder?" I examine my claws as I speak, as if I've got all the time in the world to debate vampire politics.

"She's stalling!" the shifter I still can't quite place accuses. "This is ludicrous. Regardless of what you've said, Damien, I'm certain

he'd rather have this intuitive than no intuitive. Let's just take her."
Damien's body tenses, and I can see the fur break out along his arms,
but he doesn't disagree.

So, they want an intuitive. And they were going after the easier
target?

"Well, if it's me you want, boys, I'm right here." For the record,
I'm inclusive. I would have said *boys and girls*, but the tiger's still
hiding herself in the trees. Hopefully too injured to fight.

"Come and get me." I lean forward as I blow a kiss, or the closest
imitation I can get through a wolfish snout. They can choke on it.

The vamp moves first. He's clearly more used to threats than
fighting. Todd's able to body-slam him to the ground easily as I
relieve him of his head.

The wolf at Damien's side snarls, and the other shifter's eyes go
yellow. Another feline, perhaps? I'm about to find out, because he
starts to move. I put myself in a defensive stance, preparing for him to
shift as he reaches toward the vest he wears, flipping it open. I register
a glint of metal as he draws several weapons out of a hidden place and
throws them at me.

Damn and double damn. I dodge, but two of the blades make
contact. One slices into my shoulder and leaves a graze. The other
lodges into my forearm, and I grit my teeth to hold back a yowl as
I pull it out. Blades sting. And unless I'm very mistaken, these are
tipped with something. Poison, perhaps? Aw, hell.

I start to get dizzy, dropping to a knee but managing to keep
the shifter in my sights. He stays in human form and doesn't throw
anything else. He just watches. If he wants to bring me back to
whoever his boss is, it seems he's doing only enough damage to
subdue me.

I feel small arms wrap around me.

"Never! Oh no, oh no, oh no!" Aggie's voice is trembling. She grabs my forearm, and I hiss at the sensation of pain it sends up my arm.

"Watch it!" I snarl. I'm not the nicest when I'm in pain. Then again, is anybody?

"Sorry," she mumbles without loosening her grip. Then I feel it, or rather I don't feel it. The dizziness ebbs. Is her key healing? I mutter a thanks as I start to pull myself back up again. I see the shifter move and throw, but I'm ready this time. I fling Aggie out of the way and roll. Three small throwing knives embed themselves in the dirt.

He tries twice more, and when those shots don't connect, his face pales. I can read it in his face and his emotions: he's scared now.

I grin. Or at least what passes as a grin when you have a muzzle.

"Seems you're empty. My turn."

I sprint toward him, and as I do he reaches for one final blade strapped to his calf. This one is much larger. The wolf shifter breaks away from Todd, headed toward me as well. Damien's finally looking like an actual Were, and he's right on the heels of the wolf as it sprints toward me.

Three against one? Fine by me. I'm in no mood for niceties. Then I see the edge of the blade. It's glowing. Whatever was on the others, it'll be nothing compared to this. It's packing some serious power, and I sense regret rolling off the shifter. The realization hits me before the blade does. Regret that their deal is about to go bad, because this blade is going to damage me. I keep running. It's my only option. As the four of us are about to collide, I hear Aggie's scream in the background.

"No!"

I'm thrown to my knees as a strong wind buffets the air. The shifter drops his blade, losing balance as well. When I look up, the wolf shifter is back in his human form. Stark naked and straining like he's trying to shift back. Damien's back to his human self as well.

I turn and look back at the little witch, who's wide-eyed and horrified.

"Oh shit, she's a stripper," I say to myself. Now, typically I'd be the first to acknowledge the potential humor in our naive little country witch having a key that makes her sound like a worldly provocateur, but this isn't the time.

Strippers, well, strip. Strength, power, abilities. It's an immensely powerful key, but I can see why she's not setting up shop somewhere to farm it out. Because *no one* likes a stripper. Not in the magical sense. Villains and the Magikai alike will use them, but they're basically everyone's nightmare. No magical relishes the idea of their identity—and that's really what our abilities are to us—being stripped away. There are legends of witches who could remove them permanently, but I've never seen it. I scent the air. Damien still smells like a Were, the wolf still smells like what he is, and the third man still smells as frustratingly impossible to place as before.

The men are all huffing, out of breath and exhausted, with only a human level of energy to pull from. Across the clearing, Calvin is still in bear form but unconscious. Seems Todd bested him after all. I stand up and dust myself off.

"Well, boys, it's sure been fun, but if you'll excuse us."

Let no one say I am unsportsmanlike. I think Aggie's done quite enough to these men at present. Or rather, I refuse to have a final showdown with Damien when he's in this state. When we meet, it will be one-on-one. Winner takes all. And I'll expect him to come at me with everything he's got.

I stride back toward the witchling.

"You won't get away! We'll hunt you down. You and the girl." The unidentified shifter is stumbling toward us, brandishing the blade. He veers and moves toward Aggie.

"And you!" He lunges at her, and she squeaks, scuffling back.

I reach over with a clawed hand and swipe the blade away.

"That's quite enough of that. Keep your words to yourself, shifter, or they'll be your last." Do I sound ominous? Perhaps not, but I am holding a bewitched blade of some sort, a fact that has him quite upset.

"You power-stealing little bitch!" He throws the insult after her, pointing an accusatory finger at Aggie. She cringes, looking even smaller than normal.

I've officially had enough. I swipe the blade through the air, severing a finger. He screams. I'm more than happy to wait and see what the effects of the blade are, but we don't get the chance. Todd bowls into him, and while I'll spare the details, there's no need to watch for poison's effects on a corpse.

Damien and the wolf smartly keep their traps shut as our bear escorts us back down to the cabin. We skirt around the edges and walk until we come to a small grocery store in town. I borrow us a vehicle. It's a truck, much to Todd's delight. I'll report it anonymously when we drop it off in Reno and meet back up with Lynx.

For the moment, I want to put some distance between myself and Damien.

Chapter 7
Clearing Things Up

This is probably a good time to quickly mention a couple of very important things.

Item A: Damien. It really ought to be clear by now. But just in case someone is wondering about the whole 'holding a grudge for two hundred years' thing. If you're looking for someone who doesn't believe in an eye for an eye, or a limb for a limb, I'm not the heroine for you. You may as well put the story down and walk away. Truth be told, I'm not much of a heroine at all. Unless accidentally freeing a village of people while traveling down a path of bloody revenge counts. In that case, throw me a celebration. Oh wait, someone already did. But more on that later, or before, as the timeline goes. "An eye for an eye leaves the whole world blind" may have worked for Gandhi, but not for me. If I'm fighting someone and they take an eye, I aim to level the playing field. That's how you stay alive.

That reminds me.

"Here ... wrap this in something. There may be some napkins in the glove compartment. Maybe even a bag of some sort," I instruct Todd, shoving the severed shifter finger at him.

"Are you kidding me, Never? You brought a *finger* along on this drive? The hell for?" Clearly, Todd is less than impressed with my brilliant idea.

"It serves a purpose, I promise. That finger is our plan B." I can still feel the disdain rolling off him. Not for the severed limb; after all, his hands, or muzzle, aren't clean either. But he doesn't go around collecting souvenirs. Still, he accepts the appendage, wrapping it in a coffee store napkin from my glove compartment.

"We'll stop at a gas station and grab a cooler and ice," I announce.

"Um, Never," Lynx interjects from the back, where he's squashed against a window with an unconscious Were between himself and Aggie, "now might be a good time to discuss Plan A, actually."

"Fine."

But first. Second? Item B? How were we listing? Whatever. Item one: Damien. Item two: the girl. Intuition. As much as I like to credit myself for my enforcer feats, in my thank-you speech I'd certainly need to mention my sometimes troublesome but always useful ability.

Weres are rare
But rarer still
Are those who
Possess such skill
Intuition, see inside
All the secrets which they hide
Much adored and much revered
For the wicked also feared
Used for good or used for ill
Watch to not become the kill

Not that I've gone in for such things as predictions and prophecies. Maybe in the older times. Either way, though, I have to admit this particular prophet and fourth-century Were philosopher hit the nail right on the head.

Intuitives have a much more honed version of exactly what the name suggests. Luckily, because I'd hate to be burdened by most shifters' inane thoughts, I don't read minds. Or the future, thank goodness. I can't even imagine how many folks would be breaking down my door for that particular curse. Nope. I get *feelings*, which is really just such a tame word for what I can do. The difference between my feelings and those of most other people is that I'm right. Not just some of the time, but all of the time. Well, nearly almost always.

Clearly, when it comes to the men in my life, or at least one, I have made a serious error in judgment in the past. My massive misstep with Damien is what convinced me that love has to interfere with intuition somehow. Which is part of why, while I'm more than happy to buddy up, drink, carouse, and hook up with other shifters when the mood strikes me, I do not let myself make the mistake of genuinely caring for them. Not to that extent.

It also means I need to be very careful in how I approach the girl. If she really is an intuitive, she'll see straight through any lies, which means I need a very good reason why she should trust me. Perhaps she's much less skeptical than I, and 'because I just saved you' will suffice for the present.

Oh yeah, present. Plan A. Back to my conversation with the others.

"Plan A is twofold. We need to get the Were back to a safe place, namely my house. Then, once we've all had a nice rest and showered any lingering blood or dirt off ourselves, we'll be headed to Vegas. Where I will be meeting with a certain vampire lord whom two of our deceased combatants were working for."

"Uh-huh. Okay, *so* many comments," Lynx begins. "Why your place? No offense, Never, you're a formidable opponent, but why not some sort of safe house? They could figure out how to track you. You're not exactly inconspicuous."

I'd like to say, "because she's like me, and will be most comfortable with her own kind." I don't, though. That's me projecting. I don't even know if it's true. Instead, I settle on ...

"I may not be inconspicuous, but I'm private. You'll find that while my property was purchased quite legally, there are no standing records." I've had them all bespelled. Paperwork can save and end lives, kids—remember that.

"She could stay with me. Bears are more than capable of looking after her," Todd grunts from the passenger seat. I can tell he's reluctant. He doesn't tend to involve his kind. Bear shifters don't exactly live in a traditional pack. Not the same way as wolves, anyway. They keep to a certain general area, but they maintain more solitary lives, with less oversight. They do have a ruler, and the northern California crew is run by Todd's brother, Rex. Literally born with a name fit for a king. Not that either twin would appreciate the name-related humor. Todd is a loose cannon, a comedian, compared with his brother. Still, bears help bears.

"I'd actually prefer she not stay with us, if it's all the same to everyone else," Lynx says. I don't have to ask why. As the one mated individual in the car, whose spouse has a baby on the way, I doubt he wants to bring trouble any closer to his door than it already is.

"What about you, witch? You've been quiet back there. Not going to insist on having her shack up with whatever nearby coven you're living with? Where exactly are you from, anyway?"

Aggie's staring out the window. It has started to drizzle. I hate that. Northern Californians suck at driving in the rain. She's just watching the droplets roll down the glass, a lingering sadness of homesickness wafting off her.

"Canada. I'm from Canada. And I don't have a coven here. I'm staying on my own."

Well, we will be getting into that later. My curiosity is piqued. A light-magic stripping witch with no coven?

"No good, then. She stays with me. Todd, thank you anyway, but after that nasty piece of work we just encountered in the woods, I doubt she's feeling particularly amicable towards bears. Even if she was, I'd like to have her somewhere with a perimeter that's very easy to identify. It would be too much to ask of the bears to guard every square inch of every mile of their territory." It's the one way I can think of to insinuate they wouldn't be capable. Without starting a fight.

"Stubborn Were," he accuses. But he doesn't argue it again.

"How long do we have until the girl wakes up?" I throw the question over my shoulder at the witchling. I am less than impressed when she shrugs.

"I can't say for sure. Consciousness spells aren't my key. I'd say I could keep her under at least until we get to your house, though, if that's what you need."

The girl is proving quite versatile. And she's reeking of discomfort, uncertainty. I take a guess as to why.

"It's not a bad thing, by the way, that you're a stripper. Witches don't get to pick their keys. Even if they did, there's nothing wrong with your ability. Don't apologize for being strong."

She doesn't respond. But a small smile plays on her lips.

"Powerful women do not say *sorry* for kicking ass," I continue, "and witchling, you kicked quite a bit of shifter ass out there today."

Several hours of awkwardly silent car ride later, and after a stop to put the finger on ice, we're back in Sac. Now that we're here, I need to figure out a few things before moving the intuitive into my home. Then we'll need to reach out to the Magikai. One problem at a time. Lynx waits in the car with the unconscious girl while I walk with the witchling.

We make our way up to my place. I scent the air, but that and my intuition confirm for me that no one has followed us. All the better for me. I'm still a bit worried Damien will seek me out, more because it would be an added complication than out of fear. Either way, he can enjoy getting past the security system. I'll see him coming before he crosses the property line.

Over the years, I've relocated my life several times over, but I have to say I'm pretty fond of this place. It's smack-dab downtown. Close enough to easily walk to all the best dining spots, but a few blocks away, so you can pretend you're in a more secluded area.

The gorgeous stone and white stucco exterior, set against a wood door and black trim and roof, give it a Tudor vibe. But the shape and layout is all Victorian. It's got a wonderful bay window out front, and concrete steps leading up from the sidewalk. The inside has been totally modernized to my taste. Lots of bright natural light, wood flooring, clean surfaces. I've adapted to and appreciated many technological advancements that humans have come up with over the decades, but honestly I could go without electricity. I'm not scared of the dark, and sunlight is a much better way to brighten a room. But I digress.

"We're going to need more than my regular home protection," I admit to the witchling, "a heavy layer keep-out-or-get-blown-to-smithereens type spell. Any chance you've got one of those lying around?"

Agatha shakes her head, as I knew she would. Stripping for a key quality *and* a proclivity for the magic I need would be a near-impossible good bit of luck.

"Although," she says, tapping a finger on her chin, "I can get us one."

That's got my attention. The witches capable of doing what I have in mind are few and far between. And also wildly expensive. Not that a new Were isn't worth the price, but I've grown a bit accustomed to my lifestyle. I'd prefer not to have to sell my spare New York loft just to pay the witch off.

"How much?" I question.

"She owes me one. It shouldn't cost too much. Actually, I think I could barter the use of your abilities for it."

That's flabbergasting. My abilities *are* intensely valuable, but only sought after by a certain audience. Global domination–hungry maniacs seeking to vet the reliability of every henchman they have available? Check. Individuals wanting a one-time-only look into their own or others' emotions? Most people tend to mistakenly head toward fortune-telling psychic spots for that.

"Who's the witch?" I'm well-versed in our options around here, and I feel like I'd know if someone with such skills were close by.

Aggie blows out a breath.

"Promise you won't make fun of her name," she demands, crossing her arms in front of her.

A new name? An odd name? Now I'm intrigued.

"Cross my heart!" I swipe my left hand in an x over my chest, while crossing the fingers of my right hand behind me.

"She's just a couple years older than me. Her coven visited ours. It was for a skills exchange a few years back. She works out of the Joshua Tree area, but she doesn't usually use her key, so it's not widely known."

Interesting; why not utilize such a bankable skill? Still ... more important things.

"The name, witch."

"Chrysanthemum." She cringes as she makes the admission, and I can feel the hesitation. In this case, though, she has nothing to fear from me.

"Flower of death? Very nice. Poisonous, too. Odd name for someone with a talent for protective measures, I'd say."

She gives me a small smile.

"Yeah, her family thought the same thing. The whole lot of them are skilled with old-fashioned potions—every single one. Mostly the poisonous kind, although antidotes for each as well."

So she's the odd bird out, then. I can relate to that. Even if I couldn't ...

"She's our best shot. Give her a call." I don't have time to be picky.

While I wait on the witch to get ahold of her friend—thank goodness for cell phones—I go through my house. I walk past the entry and into the living room, surveying the area. Given that I've got little to no shame, there's really nothing I care about another Were finding, but I do like my personal space. In the name of that,

I pack away the array of nail polishes on my coffee table, along with a pile of DVDs. I know what you're thinking. Who watches those anymore? Me, I do. Not all the time, of course, but there are a few black-and-white films I can't depend on finding via streaming services that I enjoy. After a second of thought, I also swipe a couple of photos off the wall. None are too revealing, unless you know what you're looking at, but then again, she might. I'm not familiar with this new Were.

"Never!" Aggie's voice sounds in the entry. I pad back through the hall, the soles of my feet chilled against the hardwood. A testament to my control, really, that despite my claws it's in pristine condition.

"Will she do it?" I call around the corner as I make my way to the door. I halt when a cell phone is shoved in front of me, the face of another teen girl on the screen. She's got spiral curls all around her head that are old-woman white, in stark contrast to her bronzed and youthful skin.

"I'll protect your house. If you'll help me with my boyfriend," she announces, getting straight to the point.

"Deal. Help how, exactly? Need advice? Need him dead? I'm not picky." Okay, I probably wouldn't kill him, unless he deserved it.

She shakes her head, curls bouncing.

"I need to know if he's hiding a second girlfriend in Los Angeles."

That's it? A teenage dating drama? My lucky day.

"Not that I can't help; more than happy to. That being said, couldn't someone in your family just slip him a truth serum or something?"

She rolls her eyes.

"They could. But would they? I'm not sure. They're not exactly fond of him to begin with, and who's to say they won't give him something poisonous instead? And I've got no talent for potions, so I might kill him by mistake. No, I'm only bringing my family in if my suspicions are confirmed." Her violet eyes flicker on screen, just as Aggie's did when we first met. I read people all the time. Witches pick up things about people occasionally. The lightbulb effect is a dead giveaway, though. I assume she's verifying my ability in some way.

"What species is he?" I inquire.

"He's a vampire."

I have to work *hard* to keep from rolling my eyes. Now, understand I'm all for judging each individual ... I do it all the time. That being said, in the magical world at least, there are certain stereotypes that ring generally true. And vampires being hedonistic, blood-guzzling lust-monsters? Accuracy. This will be too easy. The hardest part is going to be tracking him down, which we don't exactly have time for.

"When do you need this accomplished?"

"I mean, I'd prefer now. But if he is cheating, I'll handle him my family's way whenever he gets back, so it can wait until he's here in Joshua Tree. After all, I assume if Aggie's asking for this spell you have your hands pretty full."

I can hardly believe it, but my lips pull up in a genuine smile. Finally, a reasonable witch. Where did Aggie dig this one up? Perhaps there's hope for the next generation after all.

"Great. Done. Now then, how soon can you get up here for spellcasting?"

She shakes her head again, stray curls dropping over her eyes.

"No need. I can do it through the phone."

The joys of technology, like their detriments, truly are endless. And she's not even profiting off this skill. After this is all over, I may have to toss her some career advice for free on top of handling the wayward boyfriend. Least I can do, really.

I clap my hands together.

"Okay, let's get to it, then!"

"Aggie, can you hold me up in front of the house? Then I'll need you to walk me around the perimeter, and after that the interior of the home. Never, you'll need to grab something meaningful to you that ties you to the house. It's got to be something you truly care about, and it's got to be something connected to the home somehow. I'll need you to burn it."

There's always a catch. I'm not complaining, though. Cheapest spell and easiest bargain I've had in a long time. While Aggie begins walking the perimeter to set up initial protections, I run back in the house and into the kitchen. I tug open the bottom drawer of a series next to my pantry, revealing the item. A small stuffed animal. I'm a badass, and that's just solid truth, not showboating. Still, that shouldn't suggest I'm not sentimental at times. I get one to celebrate each new house I have, for personal reasons I won't get into at present. Could I also burn the very expensive, very limited-release bottle of Ardbeg I have in my pantry saved for a special occasion? Yes. Would that result in burning my kitchen down? Likely also yes.

When Aggie and Chrysanthemum join me inside, I'm instructed to boil water on the stove and then drop the item in. With Aggie doing the witchy work on our side of the phone, it dissolves into a pot of blue and gold water instead of burning my house down or setting off the fire alarm.

A darned shame, too, because who doesn't love a hot fireman? Not this time, though. I need to greet my houseguest.

Chapter 8

Introductions

After protective preparations are complete and I've reiterated my promise to help the young witch with her dating woes, I head out to grab Todd and Lynx. The feline is in human form, but Todd's gone back to bear and towers on his hind legs.

He carries a still-unconscious Were up the front steps. She looks soft, too soft for our kind.

They're hardly past the front steps when she shoots out of Todd's arms, her own transforming as she pops up, scratching and hitting. He takes a hard slap across the muzzle, and when he swipes his paw across his snout, it comes away bloody. He snarls. Damned shifters, so easily upset.

The girl spins in a circle, taking in the rest of us.

"Listen, I get that you're probably very upset right now," I offer.

She scoffs, drawing herself up to her full height, which quite frankly isn't much by Were standards.

"I am not. I eat beings like you for breakfast. So you'd better back off, if you know what's good for you. You have no idea what you're dealing with." Her voice shakes in spite of her tough words.

Todd still looks murderous behind her. And I'm exhausted, not that I'm likely to get any sleep tonight. The draw of comfortable pajama pants and a less cluttered house is high, and I have no time for this tomfoolery.

"Wrong. You are losing it. You're nervous, confused, have no idea how you got here, and are feeling very mistrustful of us. You're a Were, and aside from myself, perhaps the only living intuitive."

Her claws drop and her eyes widen as she locks her brown-eyed gaze on me.

"*You're* Never?"

"My reputation precedes me. Excellent!" I beam at her and hold out a hand.

She chokes back a sob, only half successfully, as a tense sound escapes her throat. Then she launches herself at me, arms wrapping around my middle as she squeezes me into an unwanted hug.

This is unexpected.

"*Gracias al cielo!* I've been looking for you for weeks! And you're the one who came after me in the woods. Did my family ask you to find me?" she cries as I pry her off.

I cast a pleading glance around at the others. I've had my fill of emotional teens for the day, and I do *not* like people invading my personal space.

Todd is laughing over his bloody and bruised nose, back in human form and stark naked in my entryway as Lynx giggles and hands him a set of clothes. I keep spares of various sizes in the coat closet. Not because I host a lot of social gatherings, but to have on hand for the occasional male visitor.

"Well, it looks like you've got everything under control here." The feline snickers at me.

"Toodle-oo!" Todd calls as he grabs Aggie's arm and hauls her out behind them.

I sigh, resigning myself to the situation. This is what I wanted, after all. What I demanded, really. I told them she had to stay at my place. Me and my big mouth.

I give the girl a few conciliatory pats on the shoulder before prying her off from where she's clung onto me again. I take a couple of steps back, assessing her as she sniffles and gets herself together. After a few snotty snorts, she dries her eyes and smiles at me. She's got deep-set brown eyes and warm, golden skin. The few words she's spoken indicate English isn't her first language. Nothing but respect from me on that front. It's not mine, either. Takes a lot more intelligence to learn multiple languages than monolingual speakers give credit for. I'll figure that piece out in a moment, though.

"It seems you know me. What's your name?"

"Nadia," the girl responds.

I tuck a finger under my chin, considering. I haven't really gotten far in my plan, past getting her here. Out of harm's way. I still need to figure out who had her and why. Also, determine what to do with her when this is done. That also means I'll eventually need to get around to contacting the Magikai, which I've been solidly avoiding all day. Aw, hell, I'm bushed and it's been a long day for her as well. Spelled sleep isn't restful sleep. I'll ease into things.

"So, your name means *hope*. You do represent hope for the species, I suppose."

She shakes her head, glossy auburn hair sliding over her shoulders.

"Not because I'm a Were. Because I can do what you can do."

Astute. She's trying to use intuition to glean the information she wants from me. I bite back a snappy comment. *No one* can do what I can, least of all this female, hardly more than a pup. But that's not a very charitable thought. Still, I barely keep it to myself, because being considerate of others' feelings isn't always a strength for me. She flinches a bit, so clearly I didn't hide it that well.

"You have intuition," I allow. She must read a more calm demeanor from my direction, because she nods and continues.

"Yes. Our pack was very excited, my parents told me. But also very wary. They've kept me close growing up. I was told the ability can be a gift, but it can also make others uncomfortable. Or it could be used for ill. That's why this is the first time I've traveled." She rattles off the information, all truthful, without an ounce of hesitation. I was banking on her trusting me, but she's putting even more stock into me being her ally than I'd hoped. Maybe she's more sheltered than I realized.

"Traveled outside of your home country of ..."

"Colombia," she volunteers, "and I've only rarely left the edges of our territory. Until last month, that is."

"And what spurred that?" I pay close attention to how she answers this question.

She just blinks.

"Well, because I was being chased."

I smack my forehead at the truthful but useless answer.

"Caffeine. We're going to need *lots* of caffeine. And we should get you somewhere comfortable. It's putting me on edge, having this whole conversation standing in my entryway."

I walk through the kitchen and over to the coffee bar. Now *this* is progress I can get behind.

"French press? Pour-over? Espresso? Latte?" I tally off the choices, but Nadia's not looking. She's spinning a slow circle in my living room, looking around.

"*This* is your house?" I'm surprised that she sounds surprised. I'm a Were. Of course the house is luxurious. Any magical being who's been alive this long and hasn't managed to stash away at least some cash isn't doing it right. Even the altruistic ones. To be fair, in many cases we're being bankrolled by a dizzying amount of generational or pack wealth.

"I'm going to go with pour-over for both of us," I announce, grabbing a bag of single-origin beans. I raise my voice over the whir of the grinder.

"What was your home like before?"

"Extravagant, palatial, but more crowded." She gives a shy smile as she turns back to me. "We lived at the edge of the jungle. Uninhabited areas, of course. You all seem to be right in the middle of humans here. Larger cities were hours away, growing up. Not to say several of the pack didn't go back and forth quite a bit. I actually saw Bogotá a time or two, but they preferred to keep me safe back at our grounds."

Ah. Group housing. I get it. Kind of. It's not that Weres have zero pack mentality; we do. It's just that there aren't many of us left. I've had to override the pack desire myself.

"Just your family?" I pass her a speckled grey ceramic mug with a terra cotta base, steam wafting off the top.

"No. There's several families," she hedges, beginning to catch on to the whole nature of the interrogation. Now that she's getting comfortable, she's becoming more aware of what she should and shouldn't share. I can tell she's being honest, but she's not giving up everything. "A variety of other shifters, too, that do business with the pack. I've only come face to face with a few, though. They didn't want me to share what I am with other magicals."

"What was that like?"

Instead of answering right away, she wanders the rooms. Her bare feet pad along the floor, shoes abandoned near the couch. I'm not overly surprised. I told her she could stay, which means I've pretty much granted her free access to my den. She'll stay out of whatever place smells like I sleep there, so the bedroom, but the rest of the house is now a perimeter she has to check out. At least, according to Were standards.

After she's wandered through the study, lined with books; the butler's pantry, containing a sizable wine fridge; a guest bathroom in the hall; and even out onto the covered porch, she makes her way back into the living room. She bypasses my room, as predicted. As she passes the stairwell leading to the second floor, she pauses and makes her way toward the seating area instead. She flops down on the couch, careful not to spill her drink as she answers.

"Our housing was colorful. A lot of other extravagant multimillion-dollar mansions outside the cities are more modernized and monotone, but we like the bright shades. A lot more space outside than this, of course. Not that I'm judging," she rushes to assure me, "I'm just not used to feeling this cramped in by humans and houses."

"Don't worry. It takes getting used to. I myself keep a cabin up past Tahoe for just such a reason. Although the more popular that spot becomes, the more likely hikers are to wander by. I'm considering another property entirely." Not that she needs to know my real estate plans.

I let her take a few sips without peppering her with questions. When the coffee is mostly gone, I lob another one at her.

"How did your family get you up here? Do you know any other Weres in the area?" *Do they know Damien?* I want to add, but don't.

She shakes her head again.

"No Weres. We're just lucky that my parents have trustworthy friends. They warned us that they'd heard of new magicals in the area looking for an intuitive." She sets the cup down on a coaster and starts wringing her hands, a most un-Were-like gesture.

"And that resulted in your joining a traveling carnival in the USA, how exactly?" I press.

"We have a kapre that lives with us, Alab. He's mated to Selena, another one of the Weres. Oh my God! What am I going to tell Selena? I got her mate killed!" Nadia's chewing her nails now, as they lengthen to claws. A medium-tinted brown fur begins to make its way up her forearms.

I skim right past commenting on a Were name based on the moon—so typical—and to the more interesting thing.

"You had a kapre living with you? A tree-dwelling, smoke and fire, gigantically tall kapre? And how does that involve the carnival?" *So that's where the huge cigar Todd found came from.* Kapres constantly have one. I should have known.

She's sniffling now. My lip draws up as I see a hint of snot dripping out her nose. I can deal with all sorts of blood and gore, but

I *detest* snot. I hand her a box of tissues, touching them as little as possible as I pass them across in a pincer grip.

"Thank you," she snivels and blows into one of the tissues. "Alab used to travel with them sometimes. At least any time their itinerary included a location with large trees he could hang out in. He left them once he met Selena. But he still had friends, and he suggested to my parents that it would be a safe option."

"How do I fit into all this? You knew who I was. While I do like to have a reputation in certain professional circles, I would not be thrilled to find myself some sort of magical celebrity. I don't need that level of publicity in my life." *Particularly now that my ability has become a hot commodity.*

"Don't worry. One of the carnival workers mentioned you. Their sister's an enforcer in Washington. We thought I could move with the carnival; disappear without a location for whoever was after me to track. I'd find you, the one other Were with my abilities. Get your insight on our gift, and what others might use it for. Maybe you would even know who was after us, because surely they'd want you, too? Then, when it was safe again, I'd go back to my family."

Well that's clearly not happening any time soon. Although even I'm not sassy enough to say it out loud. Or, not in exactly those words.

"I think you'll be staying here for the foreseeable future. At least until we figure out who's after you and what they hope to gain from your abilities. I don't suppose you have any ideas or clues from your time in that cabin?"

More sniffles.

"No. They kept me locked up in a basement. I only escaped the explosion because when the second group of people showed up and fighting broke out, several of them took me to the woods."

"And which group was which? Were they working together?" I lean forward, eager for the answer. I'm certain she can tell. Her shoulders slump and she stares down dejectedly at her half-empty coffee cup.

"No idea. I'm sorry. I'm not much use, am I?"

I don't say it, and I really try not to think about it, but I see her lips droop into a frown. Aw hell. I'm not used to someone mirroring my own talents back at me. I change the subject instead.

"So they sent you to me. Without notice. Why were you so certain I'd help?" This is an important question. Everything costs something. Surely they weren't naive enough to send the girl up here with not only no heads-up, but no payment, no bargain they were trying to make. Not even any blackmail?

All I read from her is blank confusion.

"We're the same. Weres help weres."

As if it's as simple as all that. It seems to her it is. It's more than just her belief; it's an actual unspoken code of our kind. Or it was, back in the dark ages. Seems some of us are still noble enough to stick to it.

I kick my legs as I push myself up and off the couch. I walk toward her and grab her empty cup off a side table.

"All right! That's enough chit-chat. Pajamas and off to bed!" I announce cheerily. I'm sure, because I would be able to, that she reads something is off. I give her credit for not mentioning it.

"I don't have pajamas. I don't have any, anything."

Well, crap. After a second of indecision I put my smile back in place.

"Tonight, borrowed pajamas! Tomorrow, shopping!"

Chapter 9
There's So Much To Do

In the morning I'm up before Nadia, and I make myself another drip coffee while I wait. We've got lots to accomplish, but I doubt the girl's had much sleep lately. I consider myself tough but fair ... to my allies, at least. So I'm not going to knock her out of bed if it's not necessary. I use the time to take care of an unpleasant to-do item instead.

"Hello?" The voice on the other end of the phone sounds both official and annoyed.

"I have an update to provide for an open enforcer contract," I inform the woman. She sighs, and I can envision her eyes rolling.

I've spoken to quite a few secretarial types for the Magikai over the years. I picture this one being the sort of individual who provides you form A and then is mad when you don't return her a completed form B. Luckily our conversation is short-lived, as the phone clicks and I'm transferred to someone higher ranking.

"This is Representative Unkai. You have an update, Enforcer?" The male voice that answers is low and rich. Luckily for me, he's also a representative I'm familiar with and one who doesn't grate on my nerves too badly. Unkai is a raiju. While most often drawn by humans as a wolf-like creature, that's not quite accurate. The male is more of a wolf-weasel meets sky-dwelling sea monster. Quite difficult to describe with accuracy. His head, and the rest of him, are in the clouds. Literally. No one said all magicals are as easily integrated into humanity as shifters.

I tell him we've obtained the kidnapped Were and took out several of her captors. I leave the stripping out of it, as well as Damien. I focus more on Nadia's safety and the fact that we still don't know who was after her.

"She certainly can't go back home without our being guaranteed of her safety and catching those responsible. You, more than anyone, can appreciate how her ability could be misused," Unkai states.

"Did you know what she was?" I demand. "That she was a Were, and an intuitive? Did you already know exactly who you were asking us to track down?"

A pause on the other end. A heavy one. I can feel the hesitancy before he chooses a truthful answer.

"Yes. We knew it was a Were, and an intuitive. We knew she traveled from South America, but not her exact pack origin or age. And we always treat information as rumor until it's confirmed. The thinking was that your being on the case was a bit of good luck for us. You'd be able to determine whether she was who and what we thought, before we started creating any plans around it."

A prudent choice. The Magikai monitor all sorts of magical threats. Individuals and organizations who could do us harm. If one of them had an intuitive? They'd easily be able to sniff out any Magikai spies, along with recruiting members they could be absolutely certain were committed to their cause. A foolproof vetting program. Also, a great chance for me to mention my plan.

"Yes sir, which is why I think she should remain with me until we're able to settle that matter." I hear him splutter on the phone, and feel determination. I'm certain he'll speak over me if given the opportunity, so I plow onward. "You're right; she can't go home. And if she's turned over to the Magikai before we know who's responsible, she's still in danger. This group had a lot of knowledge about her, and we all know those at Magikai headquarters are the most well-informed. There could be someone there working against the representatives." I won't accuse him or the others directly, but making them paranoid about those who work under them? That might just do the trick.

He pauses for a moment before he responds.

"Very well. But some of the other representatives won't like it. We prefer to keep a close eye on our most gifted magicals, particularly those of an age to train."

The Magikai have their own sort of unofficial academy, which they use to train up full-time enforcers and others who work for them. Whatever they do also seems to involve instilling unwavering loyalty in their authority. It's the part that I missed out on and have never been good at. I don't know Nadia well at all, but the idea of them recruiting her rubs me the wrong way.

"Understood. How much time can you give us?"

"I'd say you have maybe a few weeks at best. It would help if you could find out who's behind this. Do you at least have a lead?"

"Yes," I answer, thinking about the bejeweled vampire pin. We'll need to track down Lord Costas soon.

"I suggest you find the information quickly. And Never, I feel inclined to remind you that the Magikai tolerates you because you have historically benefitted us. The girl could, as well, but we'll want a closer relationship with her. Do not make us put you on a short leash." The words are clipped. A snarl rips from my throat before I can even consider stopping it. Representative or not, it's an insulting phrase.

"Sorry, sorry, poor choice of words. But you know what I mean. Having you with her is good because you're alike, and for the same reason a risky decision for our organization. Do not try to keep the girl from us. It would be a choice you'd regret."

I don't even get to read the intention behind the words before he hangs up. I bristle under the threat, literally, a stripe of fur growing down my spine. The enforcer gig benefits me because I get to dole out violent justice while getting paid, but I do *not* like taking orders. Both a natural Were tendency, and from personal experiences. I'm smart enough to know I can't exactly take on the Magikai directly, but they're going to be sorry if they think that means they have control over me.

A good thirty minutes after the call ends, Nadia stumbles into the living room, eyes bleary. I'm cross-legged on the couch, and I frown down at my coffee when I realize it's empty. I'm sure she could use some as well. In one smooth motion I twist off the couch and cross the room. Maybe a French press this time. I add cinnamon to the grounds as I get to work.

While I do, I answer her question from last night about how I found her. I tell her about taking a contract with the Magikai, and that the others work with me as enforcers.

"Tell me more about the Magikai."

She plops herself down cross-legged into the papasan chair in my living room and stares expectantly over her coffee mug.

I roll through a brief lesson in government, if that's what you can call the Magikai. Ages ago, different species and classes of magicals came together to reach a bit of a truce. Not between one another necessarily, but when it came to the humans. Could we wipe them out fairly easily? Yes. Did some particular magical groups vote for subjugation? Also yes. Thankfully, they got voted down. For all the brutality human lore credits us with, not that it isn't well deserved, we can be largely logical when it's necessary. And as a group we determined that it behooved us to live among the humans without revealing ourselves. I for one am relieved. I don't want to hunt them, and while I don't mind helping, I am also not interested in being a nanny to a lot of defenseless, magicless individuals.

Now, that's not to suggest all species get along with one another, or that humans aren't targeted. We've generally agreed on some guidelines, though. No leaving bodies with hard-to-explain wounds that would point to us. No cursing or turning unwilling humans into magicals; that one's mostly for the witches and vamps. Pretty straightforward stuff. Different regions have their own rules on what an "acceptable" number of missing humans is.

"So you're saying we don't care about killing humans, as long as no one can point toward a magical source?" She's making a face at me now, mouth twisted into a disgusted little line. Ah, to be that naive and idealistic. I guess living near the rim of the Amazon didn't create a lot of opportunities for human interaction. Or really many interactions at all outside her pack.

I start pouring refills, then get to work on eggs and bacon.

"No. I'm saying it's a concession that's made. If all the magical factions went to war every time a human or someone in an opposing group was taken out, we'd have decimated this planet centuries ago. Despite what people like to think, most rules have to run off compromise, not extremism."

One of my more temperate views, but I have no desire to destroy the world. Just the evil in it, for a price.

"But it's murder!"

I don't deny it. Then again, we're not the same as humans. We operate under a different set of morals.

"You're awfully high and mighty for someone who hasn't been around these mortals for long. I would have thought, living in a pack in the wilds, you might have been raised more traditionally," I observe.

I throw breakfast onto two plates and make my way back to the living room. She's chewing her lip when she takes it this time, one fang showing.

"We might have been. I was kept separate from most of that stuff. My family didn't really tell me much about humans, to be honest. The focus was always on my ability. The importance of using it the right way, and of keeping it hidden from the wrong people. I learned how to hide, not how to fight."

"They kept you sequestered like a piece of dragon treasure, and used you when it was convenient," I observe through a mouthful of bacon.

That earns me a glare, and it seems the new Were does have claws after all. They curl at the edges of her coffee cup, raking scratches into it. I frown; I like that ceramic. I grab it back before she shatters the thing and stains the fluffy cream papasan as well.

"That was rude!" she accuses, canines lengthening. Time to nip this in the bud, Were style.

I transform my face and roar.

That snaps her out of it. This is one of those times humans and Weres are different. They think yelling is rude. And it is, the way they do it. We rely on body language and certain displays to communicate things that are easier done than said. She retracts her claws and holds out a hand with a small smile.

"Sorry about the cup," she apologizes as I hand it back. "It's just, I don't like thinking of it that way. The pack cared about me. They protected me. There's people out there who would use me for my abilities; surely you understand that. Maybe it wasn't right, and I did hate being locked away at the compound. Still, they were doing what they thought was best. Can you get that at all?"

I nod, changing my face back with the movement. I do get it. Intuitives are useful to others for a variety of reasons. If you're good, you acquire one to sort out bad guys, help choose leaders, even counsel relationships. All sorts of functionality. If you're bad, you either acquire one and force them to do your bidding so you can spot betrayal, or you murder us to get us out of the way. It's part of why I've relied on building a big-bad-Were-wolf image for those I work around, keeping my profile low outside certain circles, and working with the Magikai, who could provide protection, even though I'm no fan of authority.

"Let's try another topic," I suggest. "Magicals."

First we go through what she has seen. Weres, several wolf shifters, a feline shifter or two of a jaguar nature, the kapre, and a few witches.

"So the felines here are different species?" she asks. I wonder if she's thinking of Lynx.

"Not exactly. Again, we don't classify exactly like humans. So the terms are loose adaptations. Weres and wolf shifters are different species. Whereas the human is just as much their real form as the wolf, it's not the same for us. They have a twin soul. We, on the other hand, *are* the Were, and the human is just altered features, as I'm sure you know. Felines are all from the same grouping. Different variations may gravitate towards certain climates, but it's not a given. You could have a tiger and puma pair give birth to someone like Lynx, for instance."

I'm not a magical geneticist, and I have no interest in that level of research. I know our different qualities, abilities, and weaknesses. I've studied how packs and loners think, and what drives different magicals to kill. That's my version of learning.

"What about the other groups? Ones that don't have a second form?"

"Witches and vampires. The witches are mainly running a business. Probably the most integrated with our human companions. They sell their specialties to others. Some are great at poisons, others love spells, others have combat-related gifts, or more sensual talent." I waggle an eyebrow, but her face stays blank. "Never mind. The most common thing they're hired for nowadays is magical shields. The kind that makes humans overlook us and what we're doing. Every pack worth its salt keeps a witch or two on the payroll for just such a thing. Nowadays they have it done on a monthly basis. Almost like lawn maintenance."

Necessary in this day and age, and even I made use of such things in the past. Chrys's spell is a whole new level, though.

"And the vamps?"

I shrug.

"For all the media attention they get in human lore, there's really not too much to say about them. Other than the rogues that I hunt down, they're generally content to keep to themselves. They're typically not any more violent than other magicals, and in truth often less so. They, like many of us, have amassed obscene amounts of wealth over the years. The difference is they're fairly content to sit in their castles and spend it on a secluded, extravagant existence."

I really can't hold it against them. It's just not my style. I need to be moving; to have a purpose and action. Still, I have no problem with the blood suckers. Whenever they *do* have a rogue or a group trying to bring back mass slaughter, they're some of the most cooperative with the Magikai. Their leadership does *not* want bad press. It's why I'm hoping the Vegas coven will prove helpful. Whereas shifters, even when well-intentioned, are driven by a need to protect their own, vampires protect their best interests. And their best interests include feeding and spending in peace. Simple as that.

Once coffee and breakfast are cleared away, I get Nadia set up with a short sundress of mine, which is an ankle-length dress on her, and we head to the boutiques. While I detest shopping when it's a necessity, I enjoy it quite a bit when I'm in the mood for it. I end up with several new outfits. Nadia, who I'm bankrolling for the time being, starts off shy. She walks around the first boutique and runs her fingers over a few shirts without trying anything on. After a couple of hours, though, she's in the swing of things. Soon enough, she's loaded down with bags and wearing a new outfit. She's even smiling, and it's genuine.

I almost hate to ruin it.

"All right, time to go meet the others and get the ball rolling on this plan."

Chapter 10
Teenage Takeover

We meet at a wine and cheese cafe near downtown. I grab a glass of red and a charcuterie. Todd looks almost ridiculous sipping from a delicate champagne flute. He's just so large, and the stemware is so fragile. He sets the glass down and licks his lips.

Lynx, being the closest to parental in the group, thought ahead and got the two teens hot chocolate and pastries. They're chatting away together as our bear shifter gets down to business.

"If we're going to officially be on this together, how exactly do you recommend we split the pay?" Todd asks, bringing up a question I'm shocked we haven't addressed before now.

"Four ways, of course. Equal," I declare. His mouth hangs open at my response. Look, typically, I'd love to barter a fifty-fifty deal. They're working as a trio and I'm planning to do a lot of the heavy lifting with the vamps. The fact remains, I'm still on a deadline. And honestly, helping Nadia is going to be payment enough. I poked fun at her naivety, but I really do like the idea of helping another young Were. It would be like helping myself, or at least giving her the assistance I never got.

"What about me?" the Were in question pipes up, raising her hand like she's in a schoolhouse.

I laugh.

"You? *You* are the target, not an enforcer. You get to live. You don't get paid." Harsh, right? Maybe so, but the honest truth. Without our bodyguarding, this girl is going to be taken and used for who knows what. This service isn't free, and my kindness stretches only so far.

"The payment's up to four million, or equivalent magical item or casting. You know the Magikai; we can split it, but we have to choose one form of payment. Are we going for money or magic?" Lynx brings up the most important question.

"Magic," I answer instantly. The boys aren't as concerned with finances. Todd's pack is well off enough, and their lifestyle doesn't require a lot. Lynx and his mate, given she's expecting, might be able to use it, but he's not typically picky about payment types. Aggie protests.

"I could use the cash," she admits. "I'm beginning to like it here, but this place is expensive. And my apartment isn't exactly in the safest area. It's starting to make me uncomfortable."

My ears prick, itching to go furred with curiosity.

"Do tell."

She fidgets, twisting her arms, crossing her legs, staring at her feet. The whole nine yards. I can feel her reluctance, but underneath that is the memory of fear. It burns my nostrils, or maybe that's just my imagination. Intuition is more a mental than physical sense.

"Well, there's these guys in an apartment down the hall. They like to throw loud parties, drink and do drugs. Not that I'm trying to judge." She holds her palms up. "But if they catch me in the hall or coming into the building they yell things and get really grabby. One tried to follow me into my apartment last weekend."

I feel my muscles tensing. I narrow my eyes.

"Hex them?" I suggest.

She shakes her head again, wine-red hair bouncing. She's curled it today. One benefit of witches: you can alter your looks a lot. Shifters default back to their original features when they transition, unless they're paying for serious spells.

"I'm not the best at combat magic. I can keep them out of my apartment, but having continued confrontations is tricky. Maybe if I used dark magic, but I don't. They've started getting more aggressive. Saying if I don't start loosening up, being more fun, they'll have to *show* me how to have fun. I really need to be able to buy my own place." Her eyes have gone all watery. *Aw, hell.*

"Can you strip them?"

She sniffles before answering.

"No. I don't strip strength, I strip magic. It's why I was able to help you with the poisoned blade. I'm not a healer, but I pulled the magic out of the wound."

Great. So she's a sitting duck for these human jerks, and I have a fresh reminder that I owe her one. I cannot *believe* what I am about to suggest.

"Stay with us."

She hiccups, a tear already streaming down her face.

"What?"

"You heard me. Stay at my place, at least until the case ends. I still vote for taking the payment in magic, but we'll figure something out. Maybe by the time we solve this whole mystery your party boys will have found another building." Or they'll have found themselves forcibly removed by me. Either way.

"Oh, Never, thank you!" She runs forward, wrapping her arms around my middle. I pry her off.

"Stop that!" I hiss. My house is turning into a teenage girls' slumber party. I don't think I like it. And I'm not doing it to be nice. I'm doing it to get this case solved. That's it. And I'll keep repeating those reasons to myself until they feel true.

"Okay, well, if that's settled for now, what are we doing next?" Todd asks, steering the conversation back to our contract.

"Visiting the vamps, and I'm suggesting I go in to meet Lord Costas alone," I say, leaning over the table to whisper to the others.

We end up deciding to make our way to Vegas the next day. We. I'll go into the vamps' dwelling alone, but Lynx will monitor the perimeter. I tried to argue against the girls going at all. With the spell Chrys has over my house, they'd be safer there. No dice.

"Nope. We *hope* the protection will hold, but if they break through, the girls would be sitting ducks," Lynx argues.

"Not exactly. I could strip them," Aggie suggests, but I can feel that she's hesitant.

I sigh, forcing my eyes into a *dramatic* roll.

"He's right. We're supposed to be watching Nadia, and the Magikai are going to skin us if she somehow gets stolen back. Either choice is a risk, but at least this way she'll be attached at the hip to one of us the whole time. But I still go in alone. If they are working with whoever took Nadia, that means they're after an intuitive. And they're about to get one."

Once we're back at my place, I find myself restless. I work out, but it doesn't help. Normally I'd head out to The Lusty Lute and bother Elios, but I don't want to leave the girls. I know I'm in for a long few days, or weeks, depending on how things go, but I won't be able to sleep.

I head down to my kitchen instead, opening the pantry to find a snack enticing enough to take my mind off of exes, vamps, and Weres. Then I see the popcorn.

"We're doing a movie night!" I yell. In under a minute I hear two sets of feet running through the hall.

"Sweet!" Aggie announces, already in pajamas and throwing herself onto the couch like she's lived here forever.

"What's the plan?" Nadia inquires, grabbing the two of them blankets from a basket in the living room. Weres don't get all that cold in fur, but I like the soft feel. I prep the snacks and am prepared to pull up some options on one of a dozen streaming services; then I remember my DVDs.

"Ladies, prepare to experience *true* entertainment," I announce, falling back onto the couch cushions.

Aggie giggles, scooping up a handful of popcorn, a stray kernel falling onto the blanket over her legs. She looks over at me.

"Oops!"

"I may be fierce, but if you think I haven't had my fair share of crumbs in here, you're wrong. Just try to keep it to a minimum."

Nadia is quiet, sipping coke out of a can with a bendy straw. She smiles when Aggie passes her one of the flavored buckets of kettle corn I had on hand and murmurs a thanks.

"What are we watching?" she asks.

"*His Girl Friday*, which you will appreciate because the leading lady is tough, sassy, and holding her own in a male-dominated field." Or maybe they won't. We can't all have good taste in film.

As it turns out, the girls love old cinema. Which leads to a bit of a movie marathon. After also watching *On The Town* and *Citizen Kane* to give them a well-rounded look at comedy, musical, and dramatic cinema, I am beat.

I leave the empty popcorn bowls for future me before dragging myself to bed.

I've had maybe four hours of what I will generously refer to as sleep when Todd's pounding on the door. And it's got to be the bear, because it's strong enough to echo through the house.

"I'm awake, dammit!" I yell, none too generously, as I roll out of the sheets.

I'm right; it's the bear shifter. I open the door and my annoyance gives way as Todd averts his eyes. I look down to see that I am in a pair of boyshort undies and nothing else. Shifters are unclothed all the time, but as I've paid an excessive amount for a particular spell that prevents my shifting back without clothing, it's not something he's ever seen.

"Drag me out of bed this early, and you get what you get," I state, in response to his unspoken embarrassment.

"Early? You're the one that wanted to get to the vamps before the sun sets! Benefits of the light and all that. Now, get those girls up and let's get moving!" His tone is harsh, but I feel the softened edges when he speaks about the girls. He likes them just as much as I'm beginning to.

"Yeah, move your ass!" Lynx yells from the car before winking at me. I'm not fooled. He's so devoted to Fiona they need a new word for that level of commitment, but he likes to tease.

I head back inside and yell for the girls, but they're already in the hall. Nadia's pulling on a jacket while Aggie finishes combing out her hair. I let out a sigh.

"Guess it's just me, then."

We've been in the car all of five minutes before I yell at Lynx, leaning over to pull on the steering wheel.

"Stop! We need to grab coffee!" I instruct. I am *not* doing this without caffeine.

"Dammit, Never!" he gripes before doing as I instruct. "You all have a problem!" he accuses as the girls cheer my decision from the backseat.

"If you prefer, we could stop by The Lusty Lute and wake up Elios as well," I offer, knowing the old goat lives above the bar, "but I don't think the owner would appreciate it."

He grumbles but parks so we can all grab drinks. I get a brown sugar latte for myself and Todd, who I know has a secret affection for them. I cannot talk the girls out of ordering pumpkin-flavored monstrosities. I even grab a cortado for Lynx, who despite all his arguments guzzles it down quick enough.

Hours later, we see our destination. We don't actually have to drive into Vegas proper, although Todd plans to wait down there with the girls.

"But no gambling!" he instructs, although I can already feel their determination to ignore him.

Lynx will be in the canyons surrounding the vampires' sprawling estate. And I will be meeting with Lord Costas. Lynx arranged it with a single phone call. A formal message from an enforcer telling you that some of your vampire buddies are running rampant against the Magikai's orders lands one an invitation easily enough.

I don't change myself for any man, or monster, but I don't mind a bit of dress-up. Vampires are among those magicals who appreciate sparkly things, and so I put on something a bit more formal for the occasion.

The obvious choice would be a turquoise or sapphire outfit, to complement my blue eyes. I don't go that route, though. I'm wearing what can only be described as a dress with its own leggings. A combat ballgown, if you will? It's deep green on the top, with slashes of green and steely grey as it moves down. I've got heeled boots and several rings. The jewelry could be useful for cracking jaws as well as adornment.

Lynx drops me off at the gate. An ornate, taller than Todd as a bear, metallic eyesore that encases the perimeter of the palatial estate. Many magicals respect power and intimidation more than compassion, which is part of why I choose to lean into an icier persona.

I stare down at the vampire greeting me.

"I do hope I'm not expected to walk all that way." I wave an arm toward the mansion entrance not even a quarter-mile uphill, if I judge the distance right.

He sweeps into a bow.

"Of course not, madame." He's staying safely under the awning of a toll booth–like structure at the gate. Vampires do not burst into flame when they hit sunlight, but it is uncomfortable for them to varying degrees. Depending on whether or not they've paid for some witch-provided sunscreen.

Truthfully, it would be quicker to run up to the entrance, but I wait for the limo that arrives a minute later. The vamp at the gate didn't feel evil or violent, merely inconvenienced. Still, I'm on guard as I'm dropped off at the house.

Chapter 11
Negotiation & Vexation

Castle really might be the more accurate term for the structure I'm entering. It doesn't have the age or legacy of a real one, but it certainly has the style. Large turrets, stone facade. None of those modern lines or floor-to-ceiling windows for the vamps. For what I would think are obvious reasons, they value a thick curtain and a shuttered window much more than natural light. By now, Todd and the girls will have reached the Strip and are hopefully keeping a low profile as they blend in with the many casino patrons.

Vampire lords can be very touchy creatures. I don't want this one to feel ganged up on. A vamp butler of some sort—I admit to being rusty on the hierarchy—sees me through a yawning entrance. A curved, dual staircase climbs to the balcony of a second floor. The faintest glimmer of a chandelier glints in the fading light as I step through double doors, then disappears as they shut behind me.

I'm led through the cavernous entrance and into a room that somehow manages an even higher vaulted ceiling. If I had to take a guess, this might have hosted balls back in the day, were it a true castle. But it's now been turned into a throne room. Plush red carpet laid over a secondary gold fabric layer runs from the double doors through the center of the room between a set of columns, and straight up to a dais that surely the vamp lord had built in. The throne is the height of at least three grown men and is inlaid with gold accents, alongside black and crimson jewels. Gaudy, I would call it. Very on-brand for a vampire lord, though.

I'm feeling in my element today. Acting alone, going toe to toe with other magicals. The teens are all right, and I've got no personal grudges against Todd and Lynx. Still, I'm used to a certain solitary lifestyle. This is much more me.

I stride forward with my entourage, or a set of two vampire guards, depending on your point of view. The butler trails us as well. On each side of the rows of columns are different groupings of vamps huddled together. They wear a bizarre mix of modern fashions and outdated looks. I'm seeing fitted jeans and crop tops next to intricate ball gowns that must boast lots of tulle underneath. One thing that's constant is the over-accessorizing and use of high-end materials. They're all decked out in glistening rings, necklaces, or tiaras. Some are drinking from crystal, while others are holding solid gold goblets. A few are pretending to be engaged in their conversations, but I can feel the curiosity coming off them in waves. Also a stray hint of hesitation, fear, and animosity, depending on where I focus my attention. I decide to put on a bit of a show. I need to establish myself as a serious player right up front, before they make up their own minds.

As I move forward, I transition to Were mode without so much as a hitch in my stride. A few gasps ring out around me as the dress rips and falls in shreds to the floor. I don't turn to look, but I can see from my periphery that they're all staring now. It's no small trick to be able to make an instantaneous change like mine without so much as a grimace. It'll let them know that I am not to be messed with, since I can clearly handle pain. Then again, it's also possible that they're more horrified by the wasted clothes.

At the end of the aisle sits Costas, lounging on his throne. He's the only vamp who manages to look outwardly bored at my entrance. He's seated sideways, legs kicked over one arm of the throne as his back rests against the other. He's almost too stereotypical for words. Black hair that's slicked with some sort of gel but manages to fall over his forehead in a devil-may-care style. Red eyes, gaunt but handsome appearance. Snowfall-pale skin. I'd guess he was turned and his aging permanently halted somewhere in his early forties, but he clearly was well on his way to silver fox status as a human. Not a wrinkle in sight.

We come to a stop several feet from the throne, and for an uncomfortable minute or two nobody speaks. I can feel his awareness of me, and even if I couldn't, vampire senses would make it impossible for him to miss me. Still, he remains silent, a gold-topped cane in one hand as he waves it around like a maestro, conducting music only he can hear. Maybe he's trying to portray the image of being a bit unbalanced, but I know better. His name means *stable*, and he is that. Odd, perhaps, but not unhinged.

I'm happy to wait him out, but the butler clears his throat. As he does, the vampire lord freezes, slowly turning to face us. He's glaring, canines bared. I hear my guards shuffle backwards a few steps. I stay put, furred hackles rising. Costas's features relax into a smile. He kicks his legs forward and stands, slamming the foot of the cane on the floor as he does so. It echoes.

"Ah, Never. My honored guest. I must say I was so happy to receive your invitation. Although I had hoped to see more of your retinue?" So far, he's telling the truth. He raises an eyebrow and leans forward as he glances around me, as though the others will appear.

"While I'm certain they would have appreciated your hospitality, they were otherwise engaged."

I'm quite sure he doesn't need to be intuitive to read into that half-truth. Vamps aren't known in the magical community for being nearly as evil as some species, but that doesn't mean I'm taking chances. Where one rogue came from, there could be more. Best to keep Nadia and myself separate.

He waves a hand in a dismissive gesture.

"A shame, but your auspicious company is more than enough. Now, do have a seat and we can discuss our business over refreshments."

"It's more comfortable for me to stand in this form, actually, but I will take that drink," I counter. It's a small rebellion, and an easy way to test his temper.

"Very well." Costas inclines his head. I get a faint hint of annoyance, but that's all.

Another butler scuttles forward, holding a silver-gilt serving tray. Several glasses of various materials are on it, each with a different beverage. I don't smell anything suspicious, and the servant isn't giving off any deceitful vibes. I pluck a flute of champagne off the tray and sip. Drinking daintily from fragile objects is not an easy accomplishment with a muzzle, nor is handling a champagne flute with claws. I manage both.

Costas smiles, and I see just a hint of red glinting off one fang.

"Marvelous."

I give him a summarized version of what transpired with the carnival, and the dead vampire rogue from the cabin bearing his coven's seal, as well as the one whose head we ripped off. I omit who was responsible.

"Andre always was a bit more of an adventurous type. Turned during the Spanish American War when he served as a mercenary," he says as I mention the second vampire we faced off against in the woods.

"Interesting." And it is. With *warrior* for a name, though, it's not surprising. "But I'm less concerned with his beginning and more concerned with how he came to his end. How is it that a vampire under your control ended up in a rogue magical group, on the payroll as a mercenary, without his lord's consent?"

He steeples his hands, resting his chin on them.

"Now that *is* the question, isn't it. I can assure you, I'll be investigating the outcome of this whole affair. And looking into the organization responsible." All honest answers, from what I can feel.

"And are you aware of the organization responsible?" I push, my tone demanding. I stare with black eyes, unblinking. He sweeps his hands out and shrugs.

"The Jeweled Claw, I would presume."

I nearly drop my drink. I do snap the stem of the champagne flute, and only just manage to keep a paw over it to cover my brief slip in temperament. I work to keep my tone calm.

"I haven't heard that group's name in quite a long time, I must say. Many are under the impression that they're no longer around." Including me, until this moment. "May I ask what leads you to that conclusion?"

"The Jeweled Claw always had a talent for scrimping its ranks from a variety of magicals, particularly those with a propensity for violence. Nasty group; lots of animalistic shifters, not that I'd include our present company in the same category as the house pets, I assure you."

A distasteful comment, but one he sees as truthful.

"So it's the varied members of the group and their methods that make you suspect the Claw is back?" I press, trying to glean more information. He knows more than he's letting on. There's something hazy at the edge of his honesty. Something effortful.

"I was approached by an individual claiming to represent them. Seeking members and funds. I told him I don't raise armies; I run casinos. He's long gone but must have taken those two vamps with him. I do my best to keep track of my coven, but they all get some measure of freedom in traveling. I'm afraid I'll disappoint you in much more than that. I can't give you a headquarters or the name of a leader for the Claw."

I bite back a snarl when the words ring true. A wasted trip, then. Disappointment eats at me, and I can't quite manage a civil 'thanks for your time.'

"Well, if that's all the information you have for me, I'll be on my way," I quip, preparing to turn and storm out of the throne room. The Magikai are not going to appreciate a dead end. And they're *certainly* not going to want to hear about the potential return of an organization that was once the greatest threat to all magicals. I don't relish being the one to tell them, and I won't be doing it until I have proof.

The need to find evidence is at the forefront of my mind as I distractedly move to leave. Something cold and metallic snaps around my neck, a lock clicking into place. *What in hell's moon?* There's a chain connected to it, gold and heavy. I feel along the edges of the collar as I try to pry it off, and there are raised edges that I assume have to be some sort of magical incantation set into the metal.

"What is the meaning of this!" My voice rises as I pull at the infernal thing.

He just smiles.

Frantically, I think back through our conversation. Costas reeked of covetousness when I arrived, but then again, I have that effect on power-hungry beings fairly often. Most of them aren't dumb enough to cross me, and they lack the opportunity. This vamp is going to pay. But how did he trick me?

Then it hits me. It's not a deceit. He's totally at ease with this plan, and vampires have dampened emotions anyway. Makes them much trickier to read than your average magical, and unfortunately I've been distracted. He never denied working with the Jeweled Claw, just that he didn't raise them an army. He never said outright that he lost track of his two vamps, just that they had freedom to move around. And he is very happy to see me, because he's down one intuitive and I've delivered myself up on a silver platter. *Stupid, stupid, stupid.*

The king's voice echoes across the hall.

"Our deal with the Claw was for the younger Were. There's nothing to say we can't acquire you as well, though. Have you any idea how much you'll fetch on the right market?" Costas's loyalties aren't with us, and I doubt they're truly with the Jeweled Claw. They're with greed.

I force myself to stand still. I'm still a Were, furred and fanged, so the choker clearly doesn't impact my form. But I can feel the drain in strength. What did this lovely accessory cost him? Whatever it was, he obviously thinks he can make back that price and more. It's also not the first one I've come in contact with, and I shove away the onslaught of panic as I focus back on the vamp.

"Then again, I could keep you for myself. A vampire lord has plenty of enemies. Particularly amongst our own kind. You could be a valuable tool in my arsenal. Imagine the relief I would feel if I could know for certain which of my coven are truly loyal to me." He sweeps a gaze around the room at the crowd of red-eyed vamps surrounding us.

I try very hard not to hyperventilate. It's not going well. This scene is too reminiscent of one from two hundred years ago that I'd really rather forget. I remind myself that magicals respect strength. Not blubbering. I force on a false face of bravado. Given my usual level of confidence, I'm hoping it comes off.

"You hardly need me for that, Costas. It'd be a waste of my talents and time, but if you're so concerned, I'm happy to give you pro bono consultation right here and now. That whole group to your right is useless. They're a bunch of blood-guzzling gluttons who would just as soon gut you as glorify you, but they're too lazy to put proper effort into either." I sweep an arm out over the vamps in question. Some of them go wide-eyed, and a few hiss at me. Tasteful. I point to another cluster of his followers.

"The vamps over there seem a bit shady to me, but I'm betting it's because of the embezzling of blood and funds they've been doing, rather than an outright attempt at a coup." I gesture to a small group huddled near the throne. One of them drops their jeweled goblet, crimson spreading across the floor. It's a guess, but I'm thinking a good one. They've been staying as far across the room from me as possible, which means they've likely got something to hide. They're not fighters, though; that much is obvious. Add to that the obscene levels of bedazzlement on their adornments, even by vamp standards, and I think I'm close enough to correct.

Costas narrows his eyes in their direction, and a few of them are smart enough to cower. He speaks through his teeth, his voice clipped as he continues to stare at the group I've indicated.

"A most impressive display of talent."

I clap my hands together.

"Always happy to help out a magical ruler." Utter bullshit. He can rot, for all I care. "Now then, if that's all you'll be needing, I do have a rather busy schedule to get back to." I'm unsurprised when I take two steps, only to be pulled backwards by the chain.

"No, I don't think so. Why give up something so valuable? And really, Never, free advice? What is it the humans say, why buy the cow?" I ignore his awful understanding of human idioms. I lower my muzzle, glaring and letting saliva drip down my fangs as I growl.

"Are you absolutely certain you want to do this, Costas? I am a vindictive Were. I can promise this will not go well for you." I wish he were intuitive in this moment; then he'd be able to feel every ounce of hatred that I hope is portrayed through my black gaze.

He shivers, but smiles, and the smallest bit of pleasure oozes off him.

"Delightful. I do love magicals with some fight in them. They should've called you Vicious, my dear." I actually like the sound of that. "Lock her up." That, I do not appreciate. He waves his hand and three vamps pull on my chain, hauling me back down the carpeting and out of the ballroom. They'd never be able to manage it on a normal day, but I can tell this thing has weakened me physically, and it seems to be building the longer it's on. It's all I can do to stay upright as they pull me along.

"Damn you, Costas! When I get out of this, I swear —" The door slams shut behind me before I can finish the threat.

Chapter 12

Plans Are Made To Be Broken

I rake claws down the stone wall of my cell, and they barely even leave a mark. Pitiful. However this collar works, it's stymieing my abilities a ridiculous amount. A very powerful witch made this, if I have my guess. Or warlock, perhaps; I'm not prejudiced, they're just less frequently found. Either way, they're dead when I find out who they are. I am an expert at holding a grudge.

It figures that a vampire lord in love with the old world would go so far as to build a medieval dungeon into the basement level of a Vegas mansion.

Growling, I shake the thick chain links that connect my collar to an iron ring on the wall. This place is dank, dark, and claustrophobically cramped. That being said, things could always be worse. I'm just struggling to identify how that could be in this exact scenario.

This is no time to panic Never. Just history is repeating itself.

I like to convey the tough-gal persona, but I'm not obtuse. My current predicament is less than ideal. I'll have to rely on the others figuring out I'm in trouble, but if the girls show up, Costas will have a chance at Nadia. I stay in Were form, not wanting to be any more vulnerable than I already am. I smack my head softly against the stones a few times.

"Stupid, stupid, stupid," I repeat my earlier mental mantra aloud.

"Um, no arguments from me, but could you stop slamming your cranium and come to the door?" Lynx's voice sounds from the other side of a wooden door with a barred peephole.

I have *never* been so relieved to hear that feline shifter.

"Lynx? Thank the moon!" I'm not especially religious, but the occasion calls for it. I move toward the entrance, as close as the chain will allow.

"All right, Never, we're going to get you out of here. I'm picking the lock and Aggie's working on whatever 'keep out' enchantment they've got on the door."

I hear an urgent-sounding whisper before he speaks again.

"Oh, yeah. Aggie says you should stand back for this part."

"If I need to stand back, then why did you ask me to come over to the door?" I snap, anxiety getting the better of me. He just chuckles.

"Ah, now there's the demanding and surly Never we all know and tolerate."

I take several steps back, until I'm up against the chilled stone wall, my tail sweeping against a cobweb. Mere seconds later, the door blows off its hinges, rock tumbling down around me with a bang and a cascade.

As the dust settles, I see Aggie and Lynx, illuminated in the dim torchlight of the hall, eyes wide. Aggie's mouth is rounded in that ridiculous surprised expression she makes every time something doesn't go according to plan.

"Oops!" she squeaks.

"So much for quiet. May I presume we will now need to make a much speedier exit?" I question.

"I'd say so." Lynx nods, then shifts. He'll be much more helpful against the vamps in feline form. Aggie makes her way over to me, stumbling over the rock. She pulls a vial from her pocket, which she holds above the gold chain. A few glowing orange drops land on the metal, and with a hiss the links begin to melt away, gilded flecks dripping onto the dirt floor.

"Witch, I am running up quite a tab with you." I don't like debts, but I'm happier with this than the alternative. She's sweating, breath labored.

"Don't mention it, and don't thank me just yet. I can handle the chain, but not the collar. Whatever they've done to it isn't responding to my stripping. It's like somehow they've separated your strength from the magic that lets you shift. You're stuck with the thing until we can get somewhere else. It'll take a while to figure out." Not ideal, but better than I anticipated. I'd prefer my strength, of course, but I can make do without it.

The minute the last droplet of the chain link Aggie is working with falls, I spring for the door, tugging her along. Or rather, I grab her and she runs with me, because even witchling weight is more than I can currently handle at this moment.

The three of us make it as far as the stairwell to the main floor when a few vampires come stomping down to check on the noise. Lynx savages the first one, fangs right to the face, a true artistic move. Aggie squeals but manages to shoot something sparking out of her hands at the second. He claws at his face and topples down the stairs, breathing but unconscious. The third lunges for me. With an attack unlikely to be successful, I do the next best thing and sidestep. With the help of Aggie's leg sticking out, he goes tumbling down the stairs as well. Not as graceful as your typical vampires, but we got them by surprise. I doubt they expected that I'd actually manage to break out. I don't think the main floor will be as simple.

We're greeted with darkness and eerie silence as we hit the foyer. Nighttime must have fallen. There's not even a playful hint of sunshine at the edge of the thick curtains that line the limited number of windows. Then, in the corner, a small flame the size of a matchstick head illuminates. It's lowered onto a candle, and a ring of fire spreads around the room. Some sort of linked candelabra system. Costas stands at the door, his glittering and bejeweled entourage lining the walls. He lifts a hand and snaps his fingers.

As he does, the crowd of vamps converges on us.

"Don't hurt the intuitive! We need her!" he calls out. "Leave the witch living as well. She might have a key that's worth something. Kill the cat."

They go after Aggie and Lynx first, and I can feel from those rushing past me that I don't even register to them as a threat. Aggie screams as she shoots sparks at them, losing intensity with each blow. Lynx is slashing and clawing, but he'll never take down a dozen vamps, with more joining in. Our situation is desperate, and I do the only thing I can think of.

"Royal Challenge!" I scream with as much volume as I can muster. My throat is hoarse from sucking in the dust of the dungeon, but it has the intended effect.

Costas snaps his fingers again and the other vampires go still, receding to the walls. Lynx collapses against a frantic Aggie, several wounds visible on his hide. He's keeping his feline form, so he's not terminal.

I stride up to Costas, drawing my shoulders back as I stand up to my full height. As I suspected, I'm taller than him. I take full advantage and curve my neck so I'm staring down my muzzle at him.

He just looks up and smirks.

"My dear Never, I think you must be mistaken when it comes to our customs. Royal Challenges are for *vampire* lords. We challenge each other to expand our territory, or topple leadership in our own coven. It only applies, however, to our royalty and nobility. Which you are clearly not."

I shake my head.

"I don't think so. Check your history books if you must, but you'll find that *you're* the one who is mistaken. Your laws clearly state that 'any royal may challenge the current vampire lord for control of his or her coven. Disputes are settled combat style, to the death, winner takes all.' *Any. Royal.* The challenger doesn't have to be a vampire."

His jaw goes slack, red eyes blinking at me rapidly for a few moments. Then he laughs, wiping at his eyes as if he's flicking away a tear. Not that vampires can cry.

"I have to give you full marks for entertainment value. Are you seriously trying to tell me that you, an enforcer and magical mercenary, are of royal stock? The absurdity, Never, honestly."

I grit my fangs. He finds it comical, and I find it an unnecessary fact of the past that is just as well forgotten as the rest of my former life before I went all murderous vigilante. Still, the truth is the truth, and it's the only way I can think to get us all out of here. At the very least, it gives us the chance.

"I *am* royal. Not all of us lord our lineage over others like the vampires. I think you'll find if you look back that Weres used to operate differently when there were more of us. We had pack alphas who were ultimately under one regional king of the wolves. My father was our region's king, which makes me the very sophisticated, always beloved, fairytale fucking princess of the Weres of Denmark, Norway, and the Schleswig-Holstein region of Germany, thank you very much."

He gapes, fangs hanging in his open mouth as his jaw works up and down like a fish.

"Impossible. A bluff. Weres don't even have royalty."

"Correction, bloodsucker, they don't have royalty *now*. Oddly enough, as human technology increased and connections became easier, territories became smaller. That's the way of the world, though. There's much less need for an ultimate authority to handle disputes when you can just video chat another alpha if you need input. However, regional royalty among our kind was common until the 1800s, and it was never formally dissolved. It just went out of style. Therefore, I am still very much royal, and very much meet the requirements for your little challenge. Now then, procure me a weapon." I turn my snout up at him, my tone haughty.

He snaps his jaw shut, brows drawing down in a fierce glare. I've upset the vamp. I happen to know Costas wasn't turned until the 1770s, and as vamps tend to be at their most out of control and bloodthirsty for the first few decades, I doubt he paid much if any attention to the ways of Weres during that time.

He turns and waves towards someone in the crowd. A male vampire wearing a formal suit complete with long tailcoat comes scurrying forward. I can feel his worry. He whispers his message to Costas, but it's useless. The sound in these cavernous rooms echoes.

"She's correct, sire. Technically. Our law doesn't outright exclude royals from other factions. It's just never come up before. She has a right to fight. And per the magically binding nature of the document in question, if you deny her you may risk curse-related repercussions." Costas snarls, backhanding the male. I guess him to be the vamp historian. Most magicals with large packs, covens, or groups keep some sort of equivalent to track our ways. I breathe a sigh of relief. I'd been hoping the contract was magically binding, but that had been a gamble on my part. Costas doesn't seem like the type of being to follow rules any other way. Lucky me. As the historian scuttles away, Costas straightens his shirt and turns back to me, offering a smile that I'd read as false even without intuition.

"It would seem you have yourself a duel, *Princess* Never, although I stand by my earlier pronunciation. You are a *vicious*, spiteful thing. Troublesome. I'll be sad to lose the profit I could have gained from your abilities." He shakes his head as he waves an arm, and a few more vamps go scurrying off.

I can feel that he's convinced he's going to win. I'm not certain he won't. After a few moments, the others return, proffering a variety of weapons held up on silver trays or in their arms.

"Ladies first," Costas offers and sends a woman toward me. She's in a sparkly plum evening gown, and it stretches against curves as she dips into a curtsy in front of me. Impractical clothing for a fight; then again, she's not the one who has to best the vampire lord.

I make a big show of glancing back and forth at the offerings, though I'm already building a mental strategy that doesn't require them. After a minute, I pluck a pair of sai off a silver platter. Typically I'd rely on my own appendages, but using a weapon is part of the ceremony.

After I've grabbed them, the vampire servant retreats, and new trays are brought forth for Costas. They're all holding serious firepower. He picks a street sweeper off one of the trays.

"Ah, now here's a nice choice. Then again, I'd hate to shoot holes into my castle," he muses, setting the gun back down. Showboater. He has to give me a weapon, but nowhere does it say mine has to be as good as his.

"This will do nicely, I think." He holds up a revolver, of all things, and then grabs a bullet off the tray. He holds it up so that it glints in the candlelight. "Silver bullets. Just for you, dear." He blows me a kiss and then begins loading all six.

Cocky man, no pun intended, to think it'll only take six shots. Silver bullets are a myth. And bullets aren't going to kill me anyway, although they'll sure as hell hurt. I assume he's going to try to subdue me before deciding how to get rid of me.

He waits for the servant to back past the nearest column as I await whatever formalities start this thing.

"Begin!" he yells, pointing the gun at me.

Chapter 13
Don't Play With Guns

I hardly have a chance to register the word before he's squeezing the trigger. I tuck and roll. I'm much slower than normal but manage to dodge it as the shot goes wide, chunks of stone or marble blowing off the nearest column. I'm on my feet and running as he takes the second shot, weaving between the columns, my movements sluggish. This bullet hits the floor and a piece of marble ricochets, slicing my ankle. I hobble a couple of steps before I can get my movements back in check. I can't tell if he's just a bad shot, or he's toying with me. Probably the latter.

I'm even weaker than I'd realized. I'll have to improvise. First things first; I need him to run out of bullets. I twist behind a column as bullet number three slams into the side of it, the sound of the impact ringing in my furred ears.

"No hiding, Never. This is supposed to be a fight," he taunts as I duck my head around the column. He's smirking. His red eyes are a lighter shade than before, almost pink. He's getting hungry. If he were starved, that might give me an advantage, but I doubt that's the case. I've just whetted his appetite, which makes him even more dangerous. As if to validate my point, he licks a fang.

"I have to say, dear, I'm enjoying this. It makes one feel so alive. Even the undead." He taps the revolver against his chin. "Perhaps when this is over, I'll keep you after all. Lock you back in that dungeon and bring you out whenever I need your *services*." I don't care for the emphasis on the last word at all. Double innuendo, anyone? In his vampiric dreams. I don't sleep with the undead.

I fling one of the sai at him. It spirals through the air, and my aim is all right, but the force I normally have is gone. It doesn't have nearly enough momentum, and he knocks it aside easily with his revolver.

"Temper, temper. Maybe I don't need you alive after all." He shoots before I can duck back behind the column, and the fourth bullet slams into my collar, knocking me backwards. I feel myself go wide-eyed, the shot far too close for comfort. I'm panting now, physically exhausted from running. I growl in frustration at my predicament.

I don't get a chance to move again before the next bullet hits my arm. It burns, and I drop my remaining sai as I clamp a hand over my injury. My leg quivers and I'm tempted to drop, going lightheaded.

"Never!" I hear Aggie scream across the foyer. I don't want to think of what Costas will do to her and Lynx if I lose. He doesn't know she's a stripper yet, but he'll find out. If that happens, I'm willing to bet she'll get a collar to match my own. In spite of myself, I'm growing quite fond of the little witchling. Even if I weren't, I'm not about to let some sick vampire capture her.

I do a quick count. Just one more bullet. I can do this.

I lock my legs in place, keeping myself standing out of sheer willpower. I stare at Costas across the room.

"Waiting for me to recover?" I ask.

He grins.

"Seems only sporting to let you gain your footing before I plant this bullet between your eyes." Confidence oozes from him. He's already won, the way he sees it. This is just an entertaining way to pass the night. He lifts the gun in the air over his head and lowers it back down slowly. I'm not sure if he'll actually do it. A shot to the head is risky if he hopes to keep me alive. Without the collar, I'm pretty sure I'd survive it, but I'm not sure of the impact its magic has on my healing. I don't think he knows, either, and indecision is flashing off him in short bursts. Either way, I call his bluff.

I snarl, then charge straight toward him. I'm slower than normal, but by this point I'm accounting for that. I launch myself, but to his right. I hear the click as the last shot rings out, aimed where I was standing moments before.

If I'd tried to rip out Costas's throat, I'd have been right in its path. As it stands, I'm colliding with a vampire behind him. Vamps stick to a largely liquid diet. Blood and often alcohol. This one is holding a brimming cup of vodka, the scent burning my nose. I swipe it and fling the contents on Costas.

It drips off his face, and he runs at me. Vampires are quite fast on their feet when they're not lazing around on a throne. He pins me against a column, squeezing my throat above the collar.

"Insolent. Cheeky. Insufferable." He's slamming my head back with each word. I reach my damaged arm up, managing not to grimace. My hand grips the brass base of a candelabra and I swing. I hit him in the throat with the flames and press down with as much force as the collar allows.

He screeches, dropping me. I hold on to the candelabra with one hand, my other around the back of his neck as I use all my dwindling strength to keep them held together. I can't gain a lot of ground, but I manage to put him off-balance and we topple over. Costas falls to the floor and I'm kneeling on his chest, pushing the flames down his throat.

Here's an interesting fact about vampires and humans. Humans are largely water. Not so with vampires. They may consume blood, but their bodies aren't technically alive. The only reason they don't have sunken, dried-up zombie features is due to the nature of their species, but they're certainly not what I'd call hydrated. They have a lower burn point.

He presses a hand into the floor, pushing upward against me. My arms shake with effort, and I search the room for any other option as my grip threatens to fail me. Then I see the sai. The one I threw at him before. I lunge for it and just manage to wrap my fingers around it while keeping hold of the candelabra with my other hand. Before he can see what I've grabbed, I slam it down, blade first, into his palm. The tip goes through and embeds itself into the floor. Not as damaging a wound as I'd like, but it keeps him sufficiently pinned. My fangs may be weaker right now, but so are the more burnt and crispy areas of the vamp. I go for the throat and clamp down tight. Even this simple motion aches.

Costas stills. I wait for the red to fade, his eyes going blue. That must be the color they were previously. Before he was turned. I'm not taking chances, though. My breath comes in shallow heaves as I lean over and twist his neck, then knock another few candles on him, just in case.

Ashes to ashes, dust to dust and all that. The former lord of the vamps is now a pile of cinder next to me.

I try to push up with my arms, but I can't stand. I'm aching, and bleeding on the floor, which is making a few of the vamps lick their lips. They've abided by the challenge rules thus far, so I chance it that they'll continue. My voice creaks, but their eyes lock on me when I speak.

"Someone get this damned collar off of me."

For a moment no one moves; then one of the more provocatively dressed women steps forward, a glittering crown on her head.

"Were you his queen, then?" I ask as she pulls a long necklace with a key on the end from her negligee.

She shakes her head, glossy black curls swinging.

"He didn't have a queen. He had a harem," I scoff. Generally I abide by a 'to each their own' model. She is, however, dripping with disdain as she looks down at the pile of ash. I'm not certain everyone in his harem was there voluntarily. I hold out my uninjured arm and she places the key in my palm. I fumble around a bit, trying to find where to place it, before Aggie steps forward.

"Here, let me." In just a few seconds she's got the lock undone and the collar drops off. I can't help but breathe out a sigh of relief as my strength rushes back. It makes me go lightheaded and I nearly topple over again as I try to stand up.

The vamp historian steps in front of me. I tense, readying for a fight. Instead, he sweeps into a deep bow.

"My lady."

I blink at him, wondering as he straightens up what color his eyes were before he was turned. A useless thought in the present moment.

"What are you talking about?"

"You won the duel. By the magical bindings of our contract, you have replaced the lord. You are now the ruler of this coven." He states this as the other vamps drop into curtsies and bows all around the room.

"Oh, shit." Not the most formal words for a new ruler, but I'd been more concerned about the whole getting-out-alive piece of the contract when challenging Costas. Not ruling a vampire coven. Not to be species-ist, but they're not my favorite magical being. By far. Not even the top five. I don't think I can easily be rid of them, though, unless one of them wants to challenge me.

"First off, help Lynx," I command, buying myself time to think. Several of them run over to the injured feline shifter. I pace back and forth as I consider what to do next. I could use this to our advantage, but I'm not sure how. I need more time to reason this out.

"You." I point at the historian. "What's your name?"

"Hugh," he responds. I look at him more closely than before. He's got textured, caramel-colored hair. Like most vampires, he's handsome. Unlike most vampires, he's more bookish than devilish. He's got the slightest bit of an English accent still clinging on, but it's faded, so I'd guess he was changed and brought here some time ago.

"Intellect," I respond, referring to the meaning behind his name, "I'm going to trust that you have enough brains not to betray me.

After all, you understand the nature of that contract. I am in charge here until someone legitimately challenges me, or I get assassinated. Is that correct?" He nods several times quickly. Technically, vamps do off each other that way. A formal challenge only has to be honored once both parties agree. Hugh's dripping a healthy amount of timidity, and I'm getting no signs of deceit, so I don't think he'll double-cross us.

I turn and address the vamps around the room, raising my voice.

"I'm going to be away for a while. In the meantime, Hugh will be in charge. There will be no unsanctioned vacations from the grounds until my return. And no meeting with other magicals, with the exception of procuring your ... food. I'll be back when I figure out what to do with you." I say the last sentence quieter, but I know they can hear. If it's possible, Hugh pales even more, in spite of his bloodless state.

"And whom shall we announce as our new leader? We must contact the other covens to inform of this change. It is the law. Will the title of 'Lady Never' suffice?" he asks. I snort. I am anything but ladylike, and I have no desire for the rest of the magical community to know I've won a coven. At best they'll think it's a power-play move. At worst, it'll tip off the Jeweled Claw. I shake my head.

"No. Everyone here is forbidden from mentioning that your new ruler is a Were, or any magical not a vampire. You shall refer to me as—" I smile, lips rising over my fangs as inspiration hits. Thanks, Costas, for all your wonderful insults. "You shall refer to me as Lady Vicious."

It has a nice ring to it. Maybe I'll keep it. I'm always careful about names, but an alter ego or two wouldn't hurt. I try it on for size.

"Heed me in this. If I hear that any vampire of this coven has left the perimeter of these lands, or told *anyone* about my identity, heads will roll." My intuition is overwhelmed, as fear, trepidation, and even admiration hit me.

I'm already out of place in my fur around their jewels. Just to make a point ...

"Fetch me a crown!" I yell to no one in particular. Several options are proferred up from various vamps around the room. I select one that is thin and intricate. Silver, just for kicks, with a marquis diamond in the center. It's got both emeralds and sapphires adorning it. As I set it on my head, I let my features go human.

In spite of the ludicrous amount I paid for this particular charm, the outfit I get when shifting is fairly low key. Fitted jeans, ankle boots, crop. It's outlandishly simple compared to my crown, and the other vamps in the room.

Still, I put a swing in my step and do my best imitation of a queenly walk as I exit. The vampires bow as I pass each of them on my way out.

Chapter 14
I Need A Drink

There's no rest for the wicked, or in this case a new vampire lady and exhausted Were. The very next day, we're all back at The Lusty Lute, trying to cobble together a plan. I am not going to approach the Magikai about the Jeweled Claw without some evidence.

After some discussion with Hugh, and some very pointed questions to ensure he wasn't working around my abilities, it's clear we're in trouble. Costas played the details very close to the chest, and the only other vamps in on it seem to be deployed out with the Claw. Killing him was the worst thing I could have done if we wanted answers, but as our lives were on the line ... not sorry.

"So we've got absolute squat," Todd grumbles back as Elios drops off a pitcher of beer and my cocktail.

"That's not exactly true. Never here got a whole load of vampire groupies. Assuming they're not all currently plotting how to overthrow her and celebrate her imminent demise." Lynx snickers. I ignore him. I'm just lucky he and the others decided against Vegas proper and stayed so close to the vamp mansion. I wave down the bartender as he passes the till.

"Did you poison this drink, Elios?" I yell, leveling a steely stare at him.

He just sighs resignedly and starts to wipe the bar top with a questionably clean cloth without looking up, his tone bored.

"*No*, Never, I did not poison your beer and absinthe, you insane Were." He rolls his eyes. I ask him the question at least once a month or so. I'm mostly kidding, but it's still reassuring to feel the honesty each time he answers.

I throw the beverage back and lick my lips.

"Ah, the satisfying citrus and mint tang of a Green Devil." I wink at Nadia, who is staring wide-eyed at the remains of the drink.

"What *was* that lime-green monstrosity? It looks like sludge." She sticks her tongue out.

"Judgy, judgy. But correct. Lime and mint. Very refreshing." I smack my lips again as I pick up the empty class and stare discontentedly.

"Something is very wrong with you," Elios accuses from behind the bar. The male serves all manner of odd species, but according to him, I'm the only one who orders this particular combination.

"For so many reasons, bartender. For so many reasons." I raise my brows at him and let my eyes flash with the slightest change. They darken like the sky before the rise of the moon, or so I've been told by my admirers.

"Don't start flirting with me now, girl, it'll scare off your competition," Elios teases good-naturedly. When did he grow a sense of humor? Todd guffaws, falling backwards. Lynx just grins as the bear passes him over a twenty-dollar bill.

"I told you I'd given him something to say to throw her off her game."

I have to hand it to the house cat—I'm surprised. Not in a bad way. Elios could stand to cheer up a bit.

I, on the other hand, am not thrilled with the suggestion I have for the group. I wait until I've got a refill and take a deep drink of my Green Devil. I let out a sigh that even I have to admit is just a tad overdramatic. But I *really*, really don't like what I'm about to propose.

"We need to go see the Bone Reader."

"Creepy!" Lynx's nose scrunches up, tongue flicking out in distaste.

"He's still alive?" Todd questions.

"What is a Bone Reader?" That comes simultaneously from Aggie and Nadia.

Moon save me from other shifters and witches.

I place a hand between my eyebrows, kneading at my forehead in an attempt to assuage the headache their questioning is bound to cause.

"He's alive. What's to kill him now, if not thousands of years of existence? And yes, he is creepy, but he's also the best at what he does. Also ... a Bone Reader, or *the* Bone Reader in this case, is just that, a reader of bones."

Aggie raises a questioning eyebrow and Nadia tilts her head. More explanation, then.

"You bring him a bone, and he will use it to tell you all sorts of useful tidbits about the individual it belonged to. You'll see."

Agatha sticks her tongue out and makes a 'blech' sound as Nadia scrunches her nose.

"Okay, that's not just creepy, it's disgusting!" Agatha accuses.

Very judgmental generation, this one. She and my new protege are going to have to get over some of this sensitivity. The Bone Reader is just one of several entities in our world who are distasteful, but necessary, or at least no one's figured out how to kill them and so they're tolerated. All the better that this particular individual is helpful.

"Todd," I begin dramatically, waving an arm through the air, "the finger."

He rolls his eyes but produces the cooler I asked him to bring. He pops it open to show the severed finger from the shifter who threw those poisoned blades at me when we rescued Nadia.

"*Que hijueputa es eso!*" Nadia yells.

"It's decaying!" Aggie complains as she makes a retching noise. You'd think a witch would have a stronger stomach. It's all that light magic.

"This is going to provide us the information we need to track down, and once and for all eliminate, our murderous kidnappers!" I announce, pulling the bagged finger out and holding it up. Even Todd looks a bit green.

"Nope! No! Not in my bar. I draw the line. Do you want to get me shut down for health code violations?" Elios shuffles back over, waving a dirty dish rag toward us in what I find to be an ironic gesture.

"My dear barkeep, we both know you don't follow anyone's health codes but your own," I counter.

"Fine, then I'm banning it just because it smells! Put that stink bomb of an appendage back in the cooler from whence it came, you unhinged woman." He turns and walks back to the bar, confident his directions will be followed. I figured it would send him into fits. I don't think Elios would kick me out, but I have seen him do it to others. Old-man facade or not, surly or not, he's won over enough of the local magical community that no one really messes with him.

Without another word, Todd tucks the finger gently back into the ice and shuts the lid.

"It may not be the most convenient option, or the most tasteful, but it's the option we've got. Those men that had Nadia were connected to the Jeweled Claw, if Costas was right. This is the best way to get information on them, hopefully even a location. I've booked us tickets for tomorrow morning. Meet at my house, and be ready to leave by seven sharp. Pack warm for your human forms."

As we exit the bar, Nadia tugs on my sleeve and I feel myself tense, teeth clenched.

"Small Were-ling—"

"That's not a thing."

"If there can be a witchling, there can be a Wereling. Now, as I was saying, as a general rule, other individuals do *not* touch me without my express permission. Unless they're looking to lose a hand." I put my hands on my hips, staring her down. She doesn't flinch. She's gaining confidence.

"And yet, you're not annoyed. I can tell. I think I'm growing on you." She grins and starts walking. "About my question?"

"Yes?" I turn to her while we exit the bar, back into the breezy sunshine of another glorious blue-skied California day.

"How does Elios know so much about magical stuff? Aren't humans knowing about us like, super rare?"

I blink at her a few times before I catch her meaning, then double over laughing.

"What's so funny?" she demands, actually stomping a foot on the pavement.

I wipe a tear from my eye. If only Elios could have heard her. That would have got his gruff up.

"Elios *is* magical."

She blinks back at me, bewilderment cascading off of her.

"But he's so *old* looking!" she protests. "He's got to be, how many thousands of years old, to look like that?"

In truth I'd hoped she was going to comment on him. It is jarring to see a magical look like he does.

"He says he's seventy. I'd guess much older. But that's unimportant. He doesn't look like that because of his age. He's cursed."

"Cursed? He's your friend though, right? Are you going to undo it?"

I shake my head.

"He'll have to do that himself. It's a contract curse. Not easily breakable, and only by the individuals in the contract, if he rights what he did wrong."

Elios keeps himself to himself, but given my particular gift for wheedling information out of people, I got the story out of him once. Truthfully he may have just wanted to confide in someone, and I was available. It was a rare wet and rainy morning in Sac, misting outside and cloudy. No one here drives well in the rain, nor do people prefer to get out in it if they have no cause. That, combined with the early hour and the fact that the bar sign stated Closed had kept the rest of the place empty. On that particular Tuesday—likely another reason the place was emptier than a tomb—I'd barged in, knocking the door nearly off its hinges as I broke the lock. I still remember fondly the look of surprise and indignation on Elios's lined face.

"Dammit, Never! You're wrecking my fine establishment!" he'd seethed.

I'd just waved a dismissive hand at him.

"I'll pay for it." I then proceeded to dump a bag of coins on his desk. Old Scottish, fifteenth century. Magicals barter in all forms of currency. We need money to spend in the human world, but between magicals it makes little difference to us how things are paid for, as long as it's valuable.

"Get that filth off my bar," he growled at me through clenched teeth, eyes locked on the bag I'd dropped on the bar. That had caught my attention. The contents were worth a hundred times what it would cost to replace the measly bar door.

I knew why I was surly. I'd taken a contract because I'd thought it had a connection to Damien, due to rumors of Were involvement. It had been a decade since my last news of him, and I'd been thrilled to finally have a lead. It hadn't been him, though, just a saber-tooth shifter. Poor guy had lost his mate and gone a bit unhinged with age. It happens sometimes to the most ancient of us. Especially those species who have too few of their own kind left. That had also left me jarred. Not only had I not found my ex, and had to put down a rare shifter, but I'd been knocked in the face with my own potential future if I wasn't careful.

Suffice to say, I'd earned the drink I'd gone looking for in Elios's bar. He, on the other hand, had no reason to refuse the money.

I didn't even ask him; just followed his gaze to the bag of coins and stared at it. Waiting in silence. And eventually he let out a sigh, shoulders drooping as he ran a hand over the top of his balding head. He pulled away and stared at his empty hand.

"There used to be horns up there, you know." And then he confessed the whole thing.

My gruff barkeep had once been a bit more risky and mischievous. He'd been traveling in Europe and fallen in with a group of magicals he met while out drinking and carousing in Scotland. One, a kelpie, asked him in on a job that involved the stealing of a rather valuable object rumored to reside in an abandoned castle there. The only problem was, they weren't the only group after it.

Long story short, the contract involved not doing harm to anyone else involved or their families. A way to prevent anyone from taking the item or the money and running, or blackmailing the others, as it were. When they showed up to the castle, one of the other groups was already there, and a scuffle ensued. It was only after Elios threw one of his opponents off a battlement and onto the wave-hammered rocks that it came to light his murdered assailant was the sister to the kelpie in his contract. It didn't matter that he'd been under attack. It didn't matter that he hadn't done it intentionally. He'd broken the contract by harming his associate's sibling. And the curse had taken hold. The kelpie brother had disappeared, along with the rest of the gang and the stolen goods, and Elios had been left penniless and looking like a wizened old man instead of a carousing young satyr.

"So he's not even going to try and break the curse?" Nadia demands as I finish summarizing the woeful tale.

"That's the question, isn't it? But a question for another time. We've got work to do. Come on!"

In truth, when I'd first heard the story I'd been about to ask Elios the same thing. Then a pack of wolf shifters had walked through the door, dripping and smelling of wet dog, to grab a morning drink and take their chances with the limited food items Elios passed off as a menu. I'd let it drop, and he hadn't mentioned it since.

I had no idea what the terms of the contract were or if he even could break the curse. It had been on my mind to pursue the matter further a few times, but he'd never asked for help even knowing my line of work, so I'd left well enough alone. I feel the urge to ask if he wants my help once Nadia is safe, maybe even to offer it.

Being around all these other magicals is doing something to me. I'm not sure I like it.

Chapter 15
The Bone Reader

"Basic economy? Are you kidding?" Lynx pouts as he makes his way towards the boarding area.

"Uh, uh, uh. She who purchases the tickets picketh the seats!" I pronounce, handing out assignments.

"Extra legroom? Thanks, Never! I knew I was your favorite." Todd winks at his feline companion as he walks toward the line at the gate, hoisting a duffel over his shoulder.

"No, you're just the most obnoxious whiner," I correct. "I am *not* enduring a repeat of the complaints about the lack of space in my car."

He just shrugs.

"Either way."

I give the girls tickets, together with the feline. *I* will be flying in first class. After dealing with shifter business partners, a teenage witchling, a fledgling Were, a coven of vampires, *and* the reappearance of Damien, I feel it's deserved. Or at the very least, necessary.

I pull out a book as we take off, then within five minutes laugh at my own optimism. Instead, I grab an eye mask and put that on before kicking my feet up and grabbing a nap.

We get a rental once we land in Alaska, then drive it to what I deem a decent point to leave it. I instruct everyone to don a few extra layers of clothes if they're planning to make the walk without fur.

I'm the quickest of us by far as we make our way across a snowy landscape in search of the Bone Reader. I can hear the incessant chattering of the others' teeth behind me; it's been a bother since we left the car. Todd has chosen to travel in his bear form, which is a wise decision. He walks alongside me and is the only one I'm not currently tempted to throttle.

"H-h-how much f-further?" Agatha questions, a prolonged whining tone entering her voice. I roll my eyes even though she can't see it from behind.

"Ancient magical beings do not reside in places of convenience." For a reason. What the Bone Reader provides is a valuable service, and if you want it you're certainly willing to travel, along with paying his price. In fairness, as someone raised in a snowy environment, it bothers me less than the others. I have largely chosen to eschew the wintry landscapes of my youth, but that doesn't mean I don't have a tolerance for them, if not a fondness.

I'm walking as a Were since we're far from prying human eyes. That helps. Lynx's feline form isn't any better adjusted to the snow than his human one, and he and Aggie are stuck carrying our packs. Nadia is bundled up in coats, insistent that she's too nervous to show herself as a Were still in case we're being followed.

As the light falls and the wind starts howling, I find myself also secretly wishing the Bone Reader had chosen somewhere warmer, like Miami, for his home. At long last, I see the rounded mouth of his ice cave ahead of us. Whether he keeps the humans away through sheer location, uses his own magic, another's, or just devours any who get too close, I'm not certain. I can't even say for sure what the Bone Reader is. Truly maddening.

With my intuition I can read him better than any other magical can, according to the Bone Reader himself. A trait that thankfully he finds delightful and charming, instead of intrusive. I suspect he could snap my spine as easily as a human's if he chose. Or maybe not; maybe he's all panache and flair with no substance. Then again, my intuition tells me he's unspeakably powerful ... a chaotic neutral being on nobody's side.

I hear sighs of relief as we enter the cave, and I know that's what they are because I can feel it coming off the others, like their breaths that fog the air.

"So, where is he?" Nadia peers into the darkness beyond us. As she steps forward, I throw out an arm, blocking her path. One does not simply walk deep into the Bone Reader's home.

"We remain here. He'll come to us," I inform the group. I can sense him in the darkness, all eagerness. I suspect he'll make us wait, though. The Bone Reader likes to make an appearance.

"I suggest we sit and warm ourselves," Todd says, back in human form and pulling on trousers from the pack Lynx lugged along.

I shake off my Were form, which, as much as I keep referring to it, is really still just me. Still, simpler terms.

"You're not naked!" Nadia exclaims. The surprise spiking off of her sharply. I guess this is the first time she's seeing my party trick.

"Yes, a brilliant deduction from the young Were." My tone is sarcastic and she blushes, but someone has to keep her on her toes.

"How *do* you do that?" Aggie questions, dropping her own pack on the icy floor of the cave as her green eyes scan the darkness beyond.

"A monumentally costly spell from a witch."

This particular individual was quite talented. I didn't like the idea of tying a witch's spell so close to my own abilities at first, but it was too convenient to pass up. At no point in history have naked women wandering around been considered typical. It was the practical thing to do. I watch the darkness as I respond, but nothing moves.

A good two hours later, smoke begins to billow out from the depths of black beyond us. Typically that might obscure the view, but at the same time the interior of the ice cave lights up brilliantly. Glistening bluish walls reflect back at us. The large cavern is devoid of furnishings, save those made of snow and ice. In the center of the room stands a large goblet atop an ice pedestal. Behind it stands the Bone Reader.

"Guests," his voice booms in several tones at once, echoing in the cavern, "welcome to my home. I do hope you've brought me something of interest?"

I step forward and proffer the box containing the finger. I lean it toward Aggie first, and she removes the cloaking spell we used on the plane to disguise the smell. The Bone Reader opens the small black box with relish, hand remaining still over the contents for a moment before he lifts the appendage off the red velvet.

"Exquisite. All the way down to the last knuckle, a nice clean cut. Very well done, Never." His gaze sweeps over to me. He isn't guessing; the Bone Reader knows I'm the one who removed it.

Without a word he drops the finger into the goblet in front of him, and a hiss sounds as it's dissolved by whatever liquid is inside. After a few moments he reaches his own hand in and pulls it out undamaged, although the finger we've brought has been reduced to gleaming bone.

He holds it up, and his gaze is adoring as he twists the bone this way and that under the light. A tongue flicks out and he gives it the smallest taste, then sweeps the bone into a pocket in his attire, out of our view.

"Origin: Pacific Northwest. Below the Canadian border, so you're looking for someone US-based. Male. Olive-skinned, hickory hair with the slightest wave. Cut above the ears, in that style all the males seem to embrace these days. Blue eyes of a medium shade. Average build and height. Oh, Never, I think you'll like this. He's fairly unique. A bird shifter—picture something like a phoenix. I know how you appreciate your rarities." He winks, and the effect is unnerving.

"Do I need to worry he's going to rise and incinerate us all?"

A small shake of his head.

"Not unless you burned him alive, and I can tell you didn't. Or if you did, this bone isn't aware of what happened to its former body."

"We didn't burn him," I confirm.

"Just how often have you visited this magical being?" Nadia whispers. I shush her. One does not interrupt the Bone Reader. He must notice, because his speech stops. The sound he makes is practically a crow-like laughter as he leans toward her.

"How delightful. A new intuitive. You *must* barter your bones to me, dear. Think about your price. Don't feel hurried; I have all the time in the world. But do let me know when you determine the cost and we can settle on something."

Nadia stares, open-mouthed, at the being behind the goblet. Then she turns to me.

"Have you promised him *your* bones?" she questions. I don't respond to that either, and shush her again instead.

The Bone Reader goes back to rattling off the information about our mystery shifter. One strange thing about this ancient magical being: he gives the information first, and settles payment later. It's something I haven't told the others. He'll let us know what's due when he's done.

"Works for The Jeweled Claw, has —"

"But they haven't existed in centuries!" This time it's my own voice interrupting his many voices, but I can't help it. Until this moment I'd held out hope that Costas had been deceived. Perhaps an upstart group of magicals imitating the power of the fallen group. As far as everyone is concerned, the Jeweled Claw was eradicated years ago by the Magikai. There were rumors for a while afterwards that some of their numbers had survived, but they never surfaced and the rumors died out.

Unlike Costas, the Bone Reader's words are absolute.

"Oh no, dear, I don't think so. It's all quite clear here in the bone. He was a lieutenant of some sort. On a mission to find *her*."

He raises a finger and points past me towards Nadia. "I can't get you the full motive; probably above his pay grade. As far as he's concerned, though, his leader is in need of an intuitive for their schemes. They've got plans to obtain one and then set about toppling the power structure of the magical world. My, my, my, that should lead to an exciting event. And we've lived relatively peaceably for so long. I do think I'll enjoy the change."

As always when I visit the Bone Reader, it would be very difficult to tell whether that was true from his tone. His voice echoes and waves over itself, sounding like multiple voices at once. It's only because of my intuition that I can tell he's sincere. He's more than happy to embrace the chaos that would come with a war between the Magikai and the Claw. *Intrigued* actually might be a better word. He likes the excitement.

"Where has the group been gathering?" I ask. We'll need to inform the Magikai at once and root out the rest of the group.

"Romania." He supplies the answer readily, as I knew he would. I groan at the information. That'll be a long trip.

"Though it may interest you to know they've taken up residence in San Francisco for the time being. At least, that's where this shifter was for several months before coming into contact with you, along with several of his peers and superiors. That seems to be their western hemisphere home base."

Truthfully, I might have preferred Romania. Sacramento is fine, but San Francisco is far too hustley and bustley and noisy and crowded for me. Just too much in every way. It's also quite easy to hide there.

"He arrived in San Francisco in July and went to Sacramento the last week of October. Then was relieved of his finger by you less than a week ago. Is all that correct and helpful?"

He knows that it is. This is just part of finalizing the deal.

"Yes. The information has been helpful and correct, to the extent of my knowledge. What do we owe?"

I don't visit the Bone Reader on a frequent basis but have used his services enough over the years to know the routine. And, as much as I might like to say, "thanks for the disturbing info, how much will it cost me?" the Bone Reader requires a bit more old-school formality than that. And he's one of the few I'll provide it for. Ancientness means something in the magical world. Older species generally means stronger species.

He claps his hands. "I do enjoy this part; now, let me think." He taps a hand on his chin several times. "I believe I would like the sound of rain on a Scottish loch in fall, when the leaves have gone golden and auburn, please. Unless of course you'd like to tell me the origin of your name?"

"I will retrieve the sound requested."

We go through this each time. And each time I refuse my name. I have a bit of a soft spot for the Bone Reader despite his eerie origins, perhaps because he's the only entity I've met as interested in the science of naming as much as me. I don't actually know his true name. I suspect it would cost more than I'd ever be willing to pay.

Deal complete, I lead the others back out into the snow.

Several steps later, Agatha pipes up.

"That's it? We're not even going to stay? Now what? And what does he mean about the rain? How is that a payment?"

I whirl on her, my patience at its edge.

"Little witchling, you are aware that your kind can essentially bottle different sensations, yes? Sights, sounds, and smells, saved in a way that can be preserved forever or used for magic?"

She nods wordlessly, chewing her bottom lip.

"But what does he use the sound for?" Her voice is soft as she asks, and I can tell through her tone even without my ability that she just can't help posing the question, even though she worries I'll be annoyed.

"I have no idea." I can read vague things about the Bone Reader, but nothing like what I can do with others. Besides, my ability gives me feelings, not visions. Which reminds me.

"By chance, do any of you remember what he looked like?"

Nadia laughs.

"Well, that's a ridiculous question. We all saw him ... he ... wait. Well, that's impossible. I just saw him!" she murmurs to herself as I turn to the others.

"Todd? Lynx? Aggie?"

Todd shakes his head.

"It's the darnedest thing, but I can't recall. Maybe his hair was ... well, no, that's not right." Todd abandons the thought as soon as he begins.

I nod to myself. As I expected. It's nice to know he pulls the same trick on everyone. Because that's the other thing about the Bone Reader. No one's ever seen him, even though anyone who's dealt with him has. Whatever we've observed while bartering with him has been wiped and obscured, a shifting shadow in our minds. I have no idea how he does it, whether it's an illusion in place while we're there or a spell that wipes our memory afterward. I just know I couldn't pick him out of a lineup to save my life. Annoying. And for that matter I have no idea *what* he is, although from all my interactions over the years he's the only thing like himself that I've ever witnessed. Truly one of a kind.

Chapter 16
Magikai Manipulation

The voice on the phone grates like gravel, deep and hoarse. I've never met the head representative of the Magikai. I've never actually even seen him. Normally this would send off alarm bells in my head, but as the leader of the group governing all magicals I can see how it benefits him to keep a certain level of anonymity.

I can only attribute being connected directly to the highest ranking member of the Magikai to the fact that I've left them in the dark on updates for a solid week. He wastes no time on pleasantries.

"What news of the girl?"

I fill him in on the bare bones of our mission thus far. Todd and Lynx's involvement, and a contract witch. I don't share extra information about Agatha, just as I withheld it from Representative Unkai. When I get to the part about the Jeweled Claw, there's a sharp intake of breath.

"Impossible!"

I anticipated that reaction. No one's seen hide nor hair of the group in over a century. They were the biggest threat to the Magikai, and by extension the way of life for all magicals, for some time. One of those magicals-should-be-out-in-the-open organizations. Now, everyone is allowed their point of view. The only problem was, they were fanatics.

The Claw set out to subjugate and use humans, for one. They also had an interesting idea about how to reorganize the power structure among magicals. Namely, demolish everyone's way of life and replace it with their own idea of what was better. No more packs, no more fated mates, and no more Magikai. Instead, there would be the Jeweled Claw. There was a king, or crown, as they referred to him. Underneath that were his 'jewels.' Very clever, right? The Claw set themselves up more like an organized religion than a government or any other magical species. The most devoted, no matter their kind, made their way into the inner circle. Everyone else would be forced to live under their authority. As one could imagine, this went over rather poorly with ... everyone, really. Still, they managed to gather a lot of magicals who were desperate for more power and had no other way to obtain it.

With or without Nadia, the group's continued existence presents a big problem. And the fact that they've kept themselves off the Magikai's radar is an even bigger one. I doubt they've been that subtle. More than likely there are some within the Magikai's ranks who are secretly working with the Claw.

"I know the information to be true. I verified with the Bone Reader," I inform the head representative.

While I view the Bone Reader as a neutral, if somewhat creepy, entity, I know he isn't perceived in the same way by the Magikai. Like most rulers, they don't care for things they can't control or explain, and as far as I know they've got as little information on him as I do.

"I do wish you'd thought to inform us before such a visit. Surely there were less unsavory means to garner the information you needed."

I shrug, even though the head representative won't see it.

"I had a spare bone on hand. Or rather, *from* a hand. In any case, his confirmation should suffice. We all know the Bone Reader's information is absolute. His abilities are even more foolproof than mine." I add the last part grudgingly. It galls me to say out loud, but I need to convince the head representative quickly. I'm not letting the Magikai debate and linger over whether the Jeweled Claw is back until they reveal themselves.

As I continue, I omit Damien's involvement. At least, I omit naming him or tying myself to him. He's mine to handle. I don't want a target on his back from the Magikai. I can take care of him.

"We'll need you to continue your protection of the other intuitive."

The head representative's words take me by surprise, but I can't sense any trickery. I had imagined having to fight to convince him of this idea.

"What are your plans for the Claw?" I ask, moving away from the topic before he can change his mind.

He sighs.

"We'll have to send quite a few enforcers out. To Romania, San Francisco, any location where they're said to be operating. We can't allow this to go any further than it already has. The Jeweled Claw almost ousted us in the past. If they had their way we'd be openly ruling humans, but it's not nearly as cut and dried as they like to make it. No factions agree on what to do with them. Do we kill them, rule them, breed with them, align with them? It creates all kinds of new tension and conflict between species. Which I believe is their ultimate goal. Infighting between us so they can further extend their agenda and control over us all."

I care about lives. Mine, and admittedly several others on a growing list. I care less about political intrigue. I'm more than happy to let him send others to San Francisco. I'd just as soon stay home. I think we've wrapped up the conversation when the head representative speaks again.

"Oh, and Never? Don't grow too attached to the Were. She'll need to report to our headquarters once this is all taken care of. She's clearly valuable, and an asset like that needs to be appropriately trained and utilized."

He's ended the call before I can protest. As if on cue, the Were in question strolls through the front door. Behind her, Aggie barrels into the house with a duffel. Todd comes in next, carrying two more suitcases, one propped on each shoulder. Lynx pokes his head out from behind the bear shifter.

"Mission move Aggie out was a success!" he announces.

I groan.

"I said to get what she needed for a few more weeks, not bring her entire apartment over here!"

"You should have seen the place, Never. Smells like mildew, leaky pipes, loud neighbors. And the heat's out to boot! You're not really going to send her back there, are you?" Lynx chides.

I find myself face to face with four pleading faces. I let out an exasperated huff. Or at least I hope it seems exasperated, because that's how I feel, and every so often it would be nice for people to read me.

"Fine! Fine! I'm being bullied by these inferior shifters and a witchling, of all things. How the mighty have fallen."

Todd just chuckles as he and Aggie move toward her room.

"Told you she'd take it well," he tells the witchling. Lynx trails after them, but I snag Nadia's arm before she can leave.

"I'd like to talk to you." I lead her down to the room I use as a gym. Extra padding for Were strength, which also means extra soundproofing, away from prying shifter ears.

"I think we need to start planning on your being here quite a bit longer as well. And given that fact, I'd like to start training you," I announce.

Believe me when I say many magicals and shifters would be thrilled by my offering them this service. Not the Wereling, though. She frowns, twisting her hands. I feel small ripples of resistance and hesitancy rolling off her.

"I appreciate all your help, but I'm just ready for all of this to be over. I want to see my family. I want to lean against the intricate base of a ceiba tree while eating fresh fruit. I want to watch honeycreepers flit through the canopy. I want to be back in my own colorful, crowded compound of a home without anyone trying to kidnap me!" A strong feeling of nostalgia gives way to a wave of frustration as her statement ends.

I nod, pretending to consider. It only hits me a few seconds after I begin this ruse that it's useless against her. I try instead for a vague truth.

"Some of the situation may be out of your hands."

"*Me gusta los cuentos claros y el chocolate espeso*!" Nadia yells, stamping a foot to punctuate the sudden anger emanating from her small form. "I can tell you're dancing around the truth, and you have intuition, too; you should know better. Give me the truth. I can take it," she demands.

Pesky little Were. She's been needling at me since we left the Bone Reader's. Fine, if she wants honesty, she'll get it. And maybe I'll get some peace.

"If the Claw gets you, they'll use you. If the Magikai get you, which is what they intend, I'm not sure what will happen. Best case, they'll try to educate you themselves. Bring you up in their academy system, try to make you an enforcer or official, who operates only for them. They're not going to risk another rebellious Were like myself. I'm constantly toeing a fine line between staying on their good side and going rogue. They tolerate me because to this point I've been useful, and they aren't ready to expend the force necessary to eliminate me. Also, I don't openly say or do anything obviously against them. That being said, I've come close."

It's true. The Magikai and I have a transactional relationship. One that both sides have exploited at times. I don't like being under anyone's thumb, but I do have a good sense of self-preservation. I am beginning to chafe under their rules, though.

"What's the other choice? You said best case. What's the worst case?"

"They view you as too much of an uncertain player and they eliminate you themselves," I confess. I don't add that they'll just as likely try to wipe us both off the map or force me into hiding if that happens. She wanted honesty, but that's not her problem. The Magikai are brutal in their decisions, something I can respect. I do have to say, though, it's never fun when you're the target. And I can't imagine them letting one intuitive go after they've killed the other. We need to make sure we're more valuable alive, while simultaneously ensuring we can remain free.

I brace myself for panic, or demands that we take on the Magikai, or any number of ridiculous and half-baked ideas like I would have come up with in her situation.

"The Magikai has an academy?" The witchling pushes the door open, walking over toward Nadia. I can feel her interest is piqued.

I sigh. In truth, if the Magikai finds out about her stripping, they're just as likely to acquire her as well. Why give up a two-for-one special?

"They have an ... institution of sorts. Consider it a very exclusive private education for the magical elite. Both the offspring of the Magikai and any magical beings they sniff out who demonstrate significant potential. Anyone who could be helpful or grievously harmful to them, they collect."

Aggie shivers.

"I don't like that word. *Collect*." She shoots a glance toward Nadia instead of me. "Maybe it's not that bad. The Magikai are powerful. Maybe they'd be able to train us, help us, protect us."

It's not a terrible line of thinking. They might do all those things. And yet I'm tempted to snap at her, fangs included, for the idea. Although, that could be because the idea of collecting is a familiar one to me. One I'd rather forget.

I nod, pretending to consider, but at least this time I intend for it to be sarcastic and not a true ruse.

"Yes, you could go running to the Magikai. They'd likely take you as well. A stripper is dangerous in the wrong hands, just as much as an intuitive. And if you walk through the doors of the Magikai compound, you might never walk back out, unless it's on their leash." I lean forward, eyes snapping black with the last words, to make my point.

Aggie still looks like she's considering it, but Nadia flinches. Leashes and Weres or wolves don't mix.

"You work for them, though," Agatha unhelpfully points out, "so they can't be all bad."

Pesky teens. Drawing attention to inconvenient contradictions and inaccuracies.

"True. I do work alongside them. But have you ever heard the term 'no good options'? They're not inherently evil, but nor would I describe our benevolent rulers as inherently good. They're just a way to balance everyone out. Not a terrible plan, but who have you ever seen with great power that didn't tip over the edges and land solidly in good or bad territory?" I demand. The Magikai are too powerful to understand when and why they should listen to others.

"You."

I blink at them both.

"Come again?"

"She's right," Aggie states, head nodding quickly. "You're prickly and sarcastic and lewd. You flirt and fight and curse. You pick and choose when you want to be helpful and when you want to be violent, and you've clearly got some stuff you need to work through from your past that you've avoided, for whatever reason." She tallies them off on her fingers.

I bat my eyelashes.

"You girls are making me blush. Those are all my best qualities." Truthfully, I'm surprised they've been paying such close attention.

Nadia picks up where the witchling left off.

"But ... you're also strong, and brave, and secretly compassionate. You helped both of us, and you didn't even know us. You care about

Todd and Lynx, whether or not you'll admit it. I'm willing to bet there's other people you care about, too. You could have wiped out that vampire coven, but you just took out Costas. And you've lived this long taking these contracts on your own terms, without selling yourself out to the Magikai or their enemies. I can even tell you feel a bit protective of the Bone Reader, no matter how odd he is. You forget, you can't hide your feelings from me. You're very powerful. Face it, you've got all the makings of a hero in denial." Nadia smiles, crossing her arms as she makes the pronouncement.

I nearly gag.

"You ladies have *got* to find a new role model. And stop attaching positive qualities to me that aren't there. I am tough, and *gorgeous*, which I note you missed, and very intelligent. All stellar attributes. But I am no one's hero but my own."

The girls just shake their heads.

"You're right. You're a horrible role model, but that doesn't change the accuracy of what I said," Nadia states, doubling down.

She might be less wrong than I want to admit. Hell, she might even be right. But I'm not ready to face that yet. So instead I shoo them out and shut myself into what would have been another guest bedroom if I hadn't set it up as a gym, and take my frustrations out on a punching bag.

There's an old saying in the magical world. Any time you find two incredibly discordant things, people will say, "Those go together about as well as Weres and water." Or at least they used to, it's fallen out of favor a bit as our numbers have dwindled and the younger generations of magicals come up with their own slang. It's not all about millennials and boomers, you know. We magic folk have our own terminology as well.

The thing is ... it's misleading. It's not that we dislike water, per se—I enjoy a nice bubble bath as much as the next gal. It has to do with death. Not all magical beings are immortal, but quite a few of us are pretty damned close, at least in comparison to our weaker human counterparts. Still, we can be taken out. A nice decapitation, or being burned to ash, for instance.

That aside, anything that eats away at someone over time can cause quite a bit of suffering while ensuring death. Being buried alive or dropped into the ocean inside a locked box, for instance. You don't just keep regenerating forever, at least not for most species. For a Were, you'd keep trying to heal yourself at an accelerated rate, bits and pieces of you wearing away with each time you're revived. A slow and excruciating way to go. There was a period of history where quite a few shifters and magicals were drawn to the pirate lifestyle. The most notorious of all the ships was run by Weres, of course, because we are awesome. That is, until it got destroyed by a conglomerate of other shifter ships and the entire crew was boxed right over the side and into the sea.

Yikes. And thus the saying was born. You may be thinking, what does any of this have to do with anything? Well, it does. Reality is a long and unending slog for magicals. Please note, the worst thing about the above, at least to me, is not the part where you die. It's the part where that reality is painful, repetitious, and torturous. So, going back to the saying, it's not the water ... it's the context.

Same thing here. I'm not naive. I can feel without intuition that I enjoy having actual company, actual friends, if that's what I want to call these beings I've been around recently. I know I thrive on my violence, but just in those moments when I'm taking down the true bad guys. I clearly have no problem admitting to my strengths, so I'm well aware that I could probably use them to make more of an impact. It's not even that I don't want to. It's just that I'm not sure I want to pay the price. The context of all those positives exists in the reality of other things. If I grow close to all these beings, it will hurt if they're taken away. Even worse if they betray me, or choose to walk away.

And if this were about a Were and water? I may already be in too deep.

Chapter 17
Training Montage Time

"Can't you get it up?" Aggie asks as Lynx lugs a sack of training dummies and targets up the hill toward us.

"No issues in that area, I assure you!" he shouts back. She just tilts her head, confused.

Poor witchling is all accidental inappropriate comments. Nadia gave in to my request that she train. Against my better judgment, *I've* given in to the girls' whining and pleas to do so outside my very spell-protected home gym. Or perhaps I've been won over by their declarations of admiration. Either, or. "We need *real* practice. You didn't get this good just by using a boxing bag. You're basically unstoppable—I mean, you run a whole coven of vamps now! We want to be like that," Aggie had argued.

We're in the woods not even an hour outside the city. After a rough trek past the popular areas where we'd be likely to run into hikers, I've set us up in a small clearing. We've got Todd and Lynx taking turns monitoring the perimeter and shouting encouragement alongside critique.

"You need to make more use of your fangs. Never forget your teeth; don't just rely on your claws all the time," Lynx advises the young Were on his turn while I demonstrate some moves for Nadia. She's small, but she could be mighty if she wanted to be. We've just got to work on her ferocity; find her something worth fighting for.

The training is helping me stay distracted as well. I hate waiting. And now I'm stewing about it until we hear from the Magikai again, or until I lose patience. Whichever comes first. I know which one I'm betting on.

"You ought to focus on some moves that start with them being in a position of vulnerability," Todd suggests when he returns from watch. "They are both small and seemingly easy to subdue. Let them use that to their advantage and lure attackers into a false sense of confidence."

"I'm doing the instructing so we'll be going with *my* plan, thank you very much!" I grouse. "Although ... that is an excellent idea. Todd, get over here and stand in as our unfortunate male who has bitten off more than he can chew." I wave the bear over, and he rolls his eyes as I simultaneously insult and accept his advice.

I can't help it. I'm not used to incorporating other people's ideas. In fairness, I don't even really have what I'd describe as a particular fighting style. I am largely self-taught, based on desperation and necessity. If I had to put a name to my form I'd say it's 'as needed.' I will flirt, fight, punch, kick, claw, and gouge my way out as the occasion demands. I do, overall, prefer a more aggressive approach. But, that's also because a more aggressive approach is often needed with magicals.

"All right, Aggie, you're going to turn away toward the trees there, and Todd's going to come up behind you." She turns, and he stalks after the little witch just as instructed.

"Now, when he reaches to grab you, you're going to duck down and kick your leg out as you spin. Try in slow motion." I demonstrate for her, and then they make an attempt at the move. It's semi-successful, so I add a step.

"Not bad. Okay, this next time, when you're sweeping out your leg, we'll put in an arm motion. As he loses balance and falls forward, jab up with a few fingers; aim for his eyes."

"Hey!" Todd protests. I sigh.

"All right, you big baby. I was going for accuracy. *Pretend* to aim for his eyes. Don't actually jab him in the eyeball, I guess."

Aggie turns, and Todd stalks up behind her. As he reaches over her shoulders to grab her, she ducks, spins, and jabs. And ends up poking him in the nose.

"Ugh, bear boogers!" She shakes her fingers off, her nose crinkling in disgust. "Can't I just strip him?"

"Hey!" Todd yells again, backing up. He's actually nervous. I don't blame him. She's nothing to laugh at.

"*No.*" I try to keep my voice patient. "You can't just strip him. Your powers are useful, but there may be a time when you don't want to give them away. Maybe there's a group behind him large enough that you can't take them all down. It'd be better to take a few out the old-fashioned way and save your power for the ones who come later, who will likely be the most powerful. The majority of villains send their disposable followers first. Or, maybe you're on the run and trying to hide your identity. Stripping's an easy way to get caught." I rattle off the excuses as they come to mind.

She lets out a burdened sigh.

"*Fine.*" She drops the word as only a teenager can. As if it's heavy with the weight of inconvenience. "But I'm not purposely sticking my finger in anyone else's eyes or noses unless it's a real threat!"

"Fair enough."

We practice with Nadia next. The Were requires a slightly different set of instructions. In theory she's got all the right equipment. The claws, the fangs, the muscle, the speed, the agility, and the near-indestructibility. And yet, there's no way around it—she's abysmal!

"No, no, no, no, no!" I repeat the word with each step as I make my way over to Nadia and Lynx. "You're trying to throw him across the grove." I gesture, pantomiming the motion.

"But, I don't want to actually hurt him!" she protests, looking positively ludicrous as she practically cringes away from the much smaller feline shifter. She may be short for a Were, but she's certainly taller than a four-legged feline. Her deep brown fur bends in the breeze, and I imagine it trembling with trepidation like its owner.

"He'll tuck and roll!" I insist, exasperated. I pick up Lynx and heave him several yards across the clearing. He yowls before landing on all four feet. His back arches as he hisses furiously at me.

"See? He's fine!" I turn toward the offended shifter. "You're fine!"

The feline curls his lips, prickly little fangs showing, but he does make his way back over.

Nadia's holding a hand over her face, in an expression of open-mouthed shock.

"You actually threw him!"

I run a hand down my furred forehead, squeezing just above my eyes.

"Look. I get it. Country witch and isolated Were. Two problematic situations. You"—I point to Agatha—"have never needed to fight, and you're relying on your very impressive power as your only option. And you"—I turn back to Nadia—"have been trained up and guarded because of your ability. While it is useful, it's not going to make you the winner of any physical fights. I know this may be difficult to believe, but I really don't relish being the one to burst this bubble for you. That said, this world, *our* world, is a violent place. You are going to have to get your hands a bit dirty. Because, the moon knows, your enemies will. I am trying to help, but sometimes the best protection you have is yourself. Terrible things happen to Weres who are unprepared. My family ... I ... for years ... never mind. The point being, you can learn now and live in discomfort, or be taught the lesson in a much bloodier way later. I can tell you which I wish I'd chosen, but it's your choice."

I pause my tirade, realizing I'm pacing and flicking my claws in and out in irritation. I flick them back in and leave them that way, turning toward her in what is hopefully a softer human form. She just gapes at me. I'm overcome with horror and a little bit of nausea as I read her emotions. *Pity.*

Oh no. Dammit. Will I ever get used to this Wereling's abilities? I didn't say anything, managed to keep from letting too much slip out, but it doesn't matter. She will have read it. The still-can't-breathe level of terror that encases me when I try to dip into certain memories.

"Never, what ha—"

"No more questions! Back to training!" My tone is clipped, and even I can hear the edge of unease that's crept into it. I shake my head, trying to banish the voices of my past that threaten to drive me mad. Lynx and Aggie are staring, and even Todd's watching from the edge of the clearing where he's come to swap back with Lynx.

Nadia tries again.

"What di—"

I round on her, teeth going pointed as I literally snap.

"Irrelevant! But as you're clearly so interested in reading my feelings, you should be able to tell that it was severe and unpleasant." I take a breath and snort, trying to bring down my attitude. It's not what I'm good at, but it's also not her fault. "Look, suffice it to say, I am *trying* to help you. For a reason. Hopefully you won't need some of this stuff. But if you ever find yourself in a bad situation, it's better to have the skills available than not. Can we leave it at that?"

Her eyes widen and she gives a quick nod. Then she turns back to Lynx and drops into a defensive stance.

"Run at me again. I'm ready."

I smile.

Hours later, we are all sweaty and smell like dirt and outdoors. I love it. Luckily some of the smaller towns around here are used to less-than-clean hikers, and no one bats an eye as we stop at a diner and polish off a plateful of cheeseburgers, two or three apiece. I lick my lips and order a round of milkshakes.

"Food always tastes better after a long day in the woods, am I right?" A dirt-covered group of hikers sits at another table on the patio, one of them leaning over toward us as he speaks.

"Oh, absolutely!" Aggie responds enthusiastically.

The group gets settled in and is digging into loaded french fries. One, the guy that spoke to us, walks inside to use the restroom. When he returns his body is tense.

"You guys." He starts towards his table. "You'll never believe it. We must have gotten so lucky getting out when we did. Another group I met inside said they spotted a mountain lion *and* a bear. Then they even heard them fighting. How wild is that?"

I can't help it. I snort into my milkshake. Lynx pouts later as we walk to the car.

"I mean, I understand that I'm much bigger than a real lynx, but a mountain lion? Honestly? My fur is *so* much more detailed than that. And luxurious."

Nadia rests a placating hand on his arm.

"Yes, it is. You are truly a natural wonder. They should have some appreciation and respect for detail."

"Yeah, they should!" he insists. The shifter is attentive to detail. His mate looks like a Bornean bay cat, with coppery tinted chestnut fur. Which reminds me, pretty soon I'll owe him a congratulatory baby gift. A negative of growing close to people? You're expected to celebrate things like baby showers. A positive? I love buying gifts, even if they're not for me.

Once back at my place, I shower off and leave the girls to do the same. Thank the moon for extra bathrooms. This is, I am convinced, the only way to host guests. Or at least it has been since indoor plumbing became popular in the last century. One of those human advances I find it hard to imagine I ever lived without.

I comb out my hair and trundle back to the living room in comfy pajamas. I am more magnanimous than words can describe, because I've agreed to share movie selection, and snack selection. Agatha insisted on some gummy candies not found in the US that she brought with her. Nadia volunteered to make empanadas for movie night, and I have supplied the popcorn and fancy hot sipping chocolates from a favorite local spot.

My movie selection for the evening is another old classic. Got to get these girls up to speed. Agatha picks a somewhat comical witch flick that's fairly entertaining, and Nadia has me rent a Colombian film she insists we'll all enjoy. I follow it more easily than I anticipated. My Spanish is rusty, although I was fluent at one time. The film is action-packed enough to hold my attention but a bit too dramatic for me to enjoy on a daily basis.

I'm cleaning up bowls, and by cleaning up I mean tossing in the sink as tomorrow's problem, after the last film ends.

"This is great! I wish we could stay here forever." I nearly drop the bowl at Aggie's suggestion. Partly because my initial reaction is not total and utter denial.

Nadia hesitates.

"I miss my home. I miss my pack. But I have to admit, I like it here a lot more than I would have expected. Not being worried I'll be kidnapped would be nice, but still, much better than I'd hoped." Ever the positive Wereling.

"Well *I'm* glad you're here. At most covens you'd have other girls around all the time, but ours was pretty small. And being a stripper isn't exactly endearing me to the other girls. Light magic is typically less aggressive. They're not sure what to make of me. It's like I get stuck to the side of everyone there." Her voice is sad. "Not because they're mean, you understand, they just don't know where I can fit in. Most of their keys are things like growing flowers for perfume, or other agriculture-based talents. Although we do have one girl who can communicate with birds."

It's quiet for a moment.

"Well, you fit in really nicely with Lynx, Never, and Todd. And I'm also happy you're here. I had a whole pack, but I've never had sisters before. Having two now is really nice."

"Yeah. You two are closer than the 'sisters' I had at the coven, for sure," Agatha agrees.

Nadia's voice fades as the girls walk up the stairs toward the guest rooms and continue to chatter.

I'm stuck, my feet rooted to the floor. Sisters. Two. Plural. If I were still holding the bowl I'd definitely drop it now. These girls think of me as family. And when I roll the word around in my mind, it fits. I should be horrified. After what happened to my real family, and with Damien, I never wanted that again. I've been alone for good reasons, and I ought to be running for the hills. Instead, I just feel protective. Like it or not, I do care about these girls.

Well, what's done is done. If the Magikai don't come through, I'll need to find a way to handle the Jeweled Claw. I'll take them down myself if I have to. I've lost everyone that mattered to me before, and then spent years captured and in misery. This time, nothing is going to rip my family away from me.

I hear a crack and realize I'm leaning over the counter, gripping it with my claws. Oops, looks like I'll need to call a contractor when this is all finished.

I leave the rest of the plates to soak and head to my room. Falling asleep is easy for once, but my dreams aren't. I keep seeing all the ways I could lose my second chance at a family, and I won't let it slip through my claws. For the first time in years, I wake to shredded sheets.

Chapter 18
Your Boyfriend's Back

I'm feeling an odd mix of nostalgia and worry that eats at me throughout the morning. I need some time by myself to think, without the chattering of two teens for whom I now feel responsible. Trusting that Chrys's spell is enough to keep them safe for now, and after calling Lynx to monitor the house as backup, I grab a leather jacket and head out.

Because I need it with the chill? No. Because I like the look. I make peace with getting soaked as I trudge down the street aimlessly. We are in full fall drizzle mode here. I'd drive if I weren't utterly convinced someone would hit the car. I've said it a thousand times and I'll say it a thousand more: Californians were not made for storms. So instead I take my time, kicking soggy leaves across the roads, simultaneously annoyed at their wet texture and enraptured by the gold and amber hues that I haven't grown tired of in all my centuries of life.

Thinking of my responsibilities reminds me: I have a debt to pay. Not to the Bone Reader; his price was purchased through a witch shop easily enough. I need to track down Chrys's potentially wayward vamp. On the heels of that thought comes another.

I still have no idea how to unsaddle myself from the vampire coven I've just acquired. I suppose I might be allowed to abdicate, but that has its own set of problems. Who takes over? A power-hungry vamp who's just doubled his territory? A Costas underling who will be dedicated to seeking revenge? Nope; for now I'll just sit on it.

It does occur to me, however, that I can take care of my first issue by *using* my newly acquired vampires.

"Hugh, my friend, I have a favor to ask," I announce as the vamp historian, or librarian, or whatever his exact title is, picks up my call.

"Yes, your ladyship. What is it you require?" As much as I've eschewed leadership, this kind of beck-and-call service grows on you pretty quick. So far, I'm liking Hugh. If I end up needing to eliminate most of the coven, he can stay.

"There's a certain young vamp in the Los Angeles coven. Goes by Travis. He's involved with a certain lady acquaintance of mine, and I'm afraid he may be entertaining himself with the available women of LA on the side. I need you to look into it and get me some confirmation one way or the other. When you find him, phone me." I'll still need to confirm everything with my own intuition, evidence or no. After all, a deal's a deal.

"Lady Vicious, to ensure I understand, you would like us to track down a vampire of a neighboring coven, to see if he's cheating on his girlfriend?"

"Correct," I confirm. He sighs, and I can just picture him running a hand down his face in agitation. I'm sure this is not what he thought he'd signed up for as a vampire. If he had an option.

Here is the thing with vamps. While you have variation, just like every species, some covens are less 'monogamy-minded' than others. The bedazzled and bejeweled ballroom at Costas's? Not just for special occasions. A nightly buffet of flesh. So, I'm fairly certain most of them are not going to agree with my sending a vampire off to get potentially poisoned just for sleeping around. Not my problem, however.

After the vampire confirms that he'll look into it, I shove the phone into my pocket as I continue my soggy stroll. Just having a few moments of silence to myself puts me in a much better mood. I'm near-chipper as I plop myself onto a barstool at Elios's. I shake my hair, droplets flying onto his floor and the empty chairs by the entrance.

"Dammit, Never! Were you raised in a barn? Stop messin' up my floor!" Elios curses from across the room, where he's dropping off a pitcher. I stare pointedly at the floor in question. It's cement, for anyone wondering. And questionably clean already.

I look back up at him. He's staring at me with a glare as I roll my eyes.

"Fallen Angel please, barkeep." I wink at him, flashing a toothy smile as he lumbers back to the bar. Another beverage I know he doesn't enjoy. Too tart, he's called it.

"You're a bit of a fallen angel, if you ask me. Perfect drink for you. A darned troublemaker is what you are. You're an unhinged thing who causes nearly as many problems as you solve, but beguiling enough to reel in your prey." He grumbles under his breath, but his feelings are in conflict with the harsh words. It's part of why I never take anything Elios says too seriously, and accept his barbs. I know he's joking, even though his sense of humor wouldn't come off nearly as well without intuition.

In return, he appreciates my sassy, flirty, harsh, and blunt, rollercoaster moods. Most of the time anyway.

I should be figuring out what to do about Nadia, but something the young Were said before has me posing a question to the cursed satyr instead.

"Elios."

"Hmm." The grunt is all the answer I get as he's making my drink, but I press on with my question as he hands it over.

"Have you ever given any thought to lifting your curse? Surely there's something in the contract that could be done to—"

"Nope! Don't go pokin' into my personal business, now. It's one of the things I like about you, rather than all the many things I merely tolerate." He pushes the glass toward me with a glare.

Then his face softens as he lets out a deep sigh. I can hear the resignation in it, and feel it as well.

"Look, Were. Your heart's in the right place, most of the time. I've seen you in here, downing drinks to drown out whatever's haunting you. And shockingly enough, I doubt it's all the cases you work on, all the good you do for magicals and humans alike while taking out the riffraff. That being said, if you've any notions of meddling in my affairs, get rid of 'em now. My business is mine to handle, or to let lie." Impassioned speech finished, he grabs his rag and goes to wipe down the table I spattered upon entrance.

He is fond of me. And honestly, I care about the gruff old satyr as well. I may have to add him to that list of people I want to protect. It's an unfortunate realization, given that I am on borrowed time. Which brings me back to Damien. I need to deal with him, sooner rather than later. Can't very well lecture Elios on looking for closure when I'm putting off my own.

As if on cue, the barkeep turns around, stopping at the till and then walking back over to me. He drops off a folded piece of paper.

"Almost forgot. You've got a message from some guy. Don't think it's an unsolicited phone number. He claimed to be an old friend. Now, I know that can be good or bad. I didn't read it, but have some caution before you just go doin' whatever it says, which I know you will, anyway." He goes back to wiping down the bar.

I open it and can't help letting out a curse.

"Hell's moon!"

Elios and a group of shifters across the bar look up, bewildered.

"Realized my drink's almost empty. Hate when that happens," I offer as an excuse before going back to the letter.

We need to talk.

I'll meet you outside the bar.

D

Not eloquent, not detailed, but effective. It's as if, by not including a threat, he's left it open to the imagination. I grind my teeth, canines lengthening as I envision him bursting into the bar if I refuse to come out. That won't do. I push up from the stool, ignoring the full drink Elios has set down beside my half-finished one as I head out into the rain.

He's not waiting right outside, and he doesn't try to jump me as I cross the parking lot. I know he'll find me, though. I scent the air as I go, and I catch his about a block away. I keep going. I've had plenty of practice at remaining calm in intense situations, but I can feel my heartbeat quickening as I lead him away from the bar. Maybe it's best if I do take care of him now, remove him as a player in this situation surrounding Nadia. It wasn't the original plan, but plans can change.

I veer to the left toward what I know is an abandoned building. An attempt at a local products store that couldn't quite find its audience. I smell it as I get close. No one else inside. Good. I wrench wooden boards off one of the windows and hop inside. I can smell as Damien follows me. The inside of the store, aside from being dusty, is in good shape. It hasn't been empty long enough to be taken over by mice. It's still got a for sale sign out front. The floors are a modernized faux-wood. The tempered glass of abandoned display cases is clouded with dust but intact.

I place one between us for distance as I turn to face the approaching Were.

"Well, you wanted us to talk. So talk." I waste no time with pleasantries. He surprised me before, but today I refuse to be thrown off guard.

He nods.

"All right. I wanted to warn you about what you're up against, but I couldn't find you. I assume you've got a second witch on the payroll somewhere who's hiding or protecting you?" He lets the probing question hang, but I don't answer. "A stripper and someone with those abilities? Either you've got very good friends or very deep pockets."

"Perhaps both. *Some* people find me quite likable," I respond, shifting into a more defensive stance and letting fur cover my features. For anyone who's been wondering, yes, speaking as a Were is much more difficult. It requires a very precise control over muscles and lots of practice, but I'm much more capable of warding him off in this form.

He doesn't change. He just gives me an up-and-down glance, head to toe, as my wolfish features lock into place.

"Stunning, as always," he offers. I just growl.

He holds up two pacifying palms.

"Right, right, straight to the point. I warn you, however, I'm not giving up. I know you're mad, and you have every right to be. But I'm going to win you over, Never."

That just makes me angrier, but I bite back a response. Literally, I'm pretty sure my tongue is bleeding. Still, I want to know what he has to say about Nadia.

"I know you work on a sort of as-needed basis for the Magikai."

I dip my head in confirmation.

"I know they've got all kinds of resources. Let them handle this. You don't know who or what you're up against, Never. If you're at all like you were years ago, you won't like hearing this, but, you could get hurt." I imagine for a moment that he's actually concerned. But that's what I assume it to be, imagination. I can never be sure.

"Hurt? By the Jeweled Claw, perhaps?"

His eyes go wide, and I feel empty air instead of the waves of shock I'd expect from someone else in his circumstances.

"You know?"

"Should have told all your Claw lackeys to hang onto their body parts better. It turns out a bird shifter's finger can garner all sorts of information." I can't help gloating, but I stop just short of mentioning the Bone Reader. He's one of my best sources. It wouldn't do to give him away to Damien, if the Were doesn't already know about him.

I wait for him to deny it. To try to lie to my face. Say he's not working for the Claw.

"I admit it." His voice is so quiet I'd miss it if not for my Were hearing. I feel the hair on the back of my neck rise as I prepare to fight.

"Consider what I've been doing for the Claw is a bit of freelance service, like what you do for the Magikai. Not for real, just to gain their trust. You and I are actually on the same side. I'm trying to help. Think of me as a sort of double agent. I volunteered for this mission so I could double-cross them and get the Were out of their hands. I planned to take her to the Magikai, where she'd be safe. It's why I was at the cabin. I'd won over a few of the others, but then a fight broke out between us. After that, you all showed up and the whole thing kind of went to hell." He runs a hand through his grey and brown hair, and I can't help watching the strands fall out of place, leaving behind a deliciously disheveled appearance.

"Did it ever occur to you that she doesn't *want* to become some puppy for the Magikai?" I snap at him. "If your story is even true, that is, not that I could tell, right? You found a way to mess up my abilities. Perhaps you really are with the Claw, or perhaps you have your own agenda after all. Maybe you've found a way to override *her* intuition as well," I accuse.

"You know that's not possible."

"Isn't it? I'm not even sure what we are. What we were."

His eyes flash and he growls, canines lengthening.

"You know damn well what we are! We're —"

"How long have you been doing this? And why wouldn't the Magikai inform us? Why risk having my group and you fighting each other when we could have been working together?" I throw the questions one after another, determined to bring the conversation back around. He lets me.

"A while. And I don't know. I'm in pretty deep at this point. Maybe they didn't want to risk blowing my cover? Maybe they figured I could handle myself, or that you could handle yourself, or both? Either way, now you know. Never, please believe me. I don't want to hurt you, and certainly not the girl. What happened between us, it's why I volunteered. I thought I'd at least save one intuitive Were, even if it couldn't be you. What happened to you was *my* fault. I made the wrong choice. I thought you'd be safe, for a long time I thought that you *were* safe, and I was wrong. I couldn't let that happen again if I could prevent it."

It's the closest thing to an apology I've ever heard him utter. I focus all my ability on him. But I can't get a read. It's maddening. I sense deceit. I don't think he's trustworthy. But is that actually intuition, or just my own worst fears coming to the surface? It's impossible to tell. And I'm not sure it matters.

"I don't care either way. We don't need you. I have this under control."

He shakes his head again before settling his grey gaze back on me.

"Wrong. You have no idea what you're truly up against."

"So tell me!"

"I can't. I can't risk someone in your group revealing details that could get back to the Claw. Things they shouldn't know. But the leader ... he's not your run-of-the-mill magical, Never. You need to be careful. And he wants the girl. Badly. He's planning an open rebellion against the Magikai, but he's cautious. He's bided his time, and he's not going to move until he's personally vetted everyone close to him. He's taking no chances. And that means getting ahold of the girl, or you."

I roll that information over. It could be true. It's likely true. At least part of it. We know they want Nadia, anyway.

"So why not just come for me in the first place?"

"The girl was more vulnerable. And also, easier to make an impression on. He thought he'd be able to train her and have more authority over her. He knew you existed, but we didn't realize you were here, either. I never expected to find both of you in the same place. That's a complication, but it could help us. Let me work with you."

"Never!" I spit before I can help myself. I'm aware of the irony, but this time I mean it as it sounds, not as a name.

"Look, we don't have to deal with things between us right now, but I can help you. You have something the Jeweled Claw wants. You've been hard to track down. Keep it that way. Find just a bit more leverage; extend him an invitation to meet in person. He doesn't normally do appearances himself, but I think you could convince him."

If he's as powerful as Damien says, I'm not sure meeting him on an open field is wise. Finding his identity, though, and passing that information to the Magikai, that could be something. And if I could find a way to take him out? They'd be willing to pay a hefty fee for eliminating the Jeweled Claw's leader, I'm sure of it.

"Get him to meet us. Then what? How do we get rid of him?" I ask.

"That's where you'll just have to trust me. I can take care of it. But you've got to get him away from his headquarters. You know, given whatever you're doing in your home to hide its location, that nearly all magicals put defenses around the places we reside. He's more vulnerable away from it. Try and get him to come to a trade or something. Ask for something you want and pretend to offer Nadia in exchange. I don't care. Just get him there. Then we find a way to get him isolated from the others, and I'll take care of it."

"You'll take care of it," I repeat dumbly.

"Yes. That's where you'll have to trust me."

It's a terrible idea. Trusting him. I don't want to, and I can't. The rest of his plan, though? It's more than my plan, which is nothing. And it solves my problem of wanting a backup for trusting the Magikai exclusively. I stick out a clawed hand.

"We have a deal."

Chapter 19

New Century, Old Mistakes

He smiles, like I knew he would. I expect him to thank me, or acknowledge my answer in some way, then leave. We've sorted everything out.

What I don't expect is for him to stride towards me with confident steps and wrap his arms around me. It briefly occurs to me that I'm missing almost all my guesses lately. Apparently the day is chock full of surprises, because I also don't anticipate practically melting back to human form as I lean into him.

I'm going to kill him. He's a betrayer. An obstacle. A snake.

None of the thoughts are sticking right now. After a long night of bad dreams and worse memories, I'm vulnerable to anything that reminds me of happier things.

Instead of attacking him, when he tips my chin up with one finger and lowers his mouth over mine, I let him. When his tongue demands entrance into my mouth, and his sharp teeth nip at my bottom lip, I sigh. Like a wanton Were with no self-control, I part my lips and let my tongue tangle with his. It's as if opening my heart up to all these new individuals has left me vulnerable for nostalgia to sneak in as well.

Somehow I've wrapped my legs around his middle, which I realize when he begins to carry me toward the only non-glass counter in the place. He sets me down, gentler than I would've anticipated, without ever breaking our kiss.

I hear myself gasp when he moves to bite my neck. I try to gather my thoughts, which keep slipping through my fingers. I force myself to try to read his emotions. Lust I can guess with certainty, but as a Were I'd be able to smell that anyway. No matter how hard I try, though, it's impossible to untangle what's real and what's my fear and what's leftover hope from our relationship before he wrecked it.

What's a Were to do? I owe him all kinds of vengeance, and instead I'm nipping at his neck while I rake claws down the front of his shirt and then pull the scraps apart. It turns out, under all the violence, all the bravado, and all the heart-crunching, soul-diminishing desire for revenge, there's still something there.

Not love. It's too twisted for that. But desire? Definitely. I tell myself he wouldn't be doing this if he were going to double-cross me. It doesn't work. I tell myself I'm going to regret this tomorrow and I should stop. That doesn't work, either. Then I tell myself it doesn't matter that it's Damien. It doesn't matter what our future holds, which is violence. It matters that I want this, and it's a form of closure. The sweet goodbye I never got to our relationship. And that does it.

I let myself be wrenched off the counter as he moves us to a wall, pinning me against it. He's got five o'clock shadow as a human, which scratches delightfully as he works his way down from my neck. My own clothes are ribbons, scraps on the floor, but it doesn't matter. I can change to Were and back again, and my problems will be solved. This may finally occur to Damien, who reaches down to rid himself of his jeans before my claws can savage them.

There's not a lick of furniture left in the boutique, so we make use of the floor. He's lying against the dusty faux-wood, but he's not complaining as I lower myself over him. His eyes dilate and I know my own are changing. He growls. I've braced my hands against his chest, and I can feel his voice rumble as he speaks.

"I love when your eyes go black like that. It's like you're about to hunt."

And I *will* be hunting him very soon. For one ridiculous moment I consider telling him the truth, all of it. Why, even if he's being honest now, and even if he had an excellent reason for abandoning me before, his days are still numbered. Or mine are.

Then he grabs onto my hips, rocking his own upward and accelerating our movements. I let my excuses and explanations fall as I lose myself in him. If it's a mistake—and who am I kidding, it's a big one—then we make it three times before I manage to get ahold of myself.

I step away from Damien as I'm putting on my fur.

"You know I love you in this form," he states, reaching for me again.

I just transition back, a new set of clothes on.

"Done already? I'm free the rest of the day. I wasn't sure how long I'd need to wait for you outside the bar." He's smug. Or just satisfied? I cannot put into words how frustrating it is to be completely incapable of reading the man's emotions.

My body is relaxed, wrung-out, and ready for a nap. My mind is going haywire. Magicals don't have nearly the same hang-ups around sex as our human neighbors. This is different, though. This is Damien. And there's a particular problem that may come up.

"Never, I *know* what you're going to say, and I know I have a lot to make up to you. But we're mates. Whatever apology from me you need, you can have. But we're meant to be together." And there it is. That dreaded word.

He just had to ruin it.

"We're *not* mates, actually. We're almost-but-not-quite mates that never officially happened because you abandoned me to years of torment and pain while you ran off who knows where, if I recall correctly."

This time his growl is one of frustration instead of desire. At least I think so.

"It counts. You know it does. I don't have to explain the ways of Weres to you, of all beings. What we said to each other in that forest is just as binding as the formal ceremony that would have followed. We chose each other." He makes the statements as if they're going to change my mind. As if I wasn't there. Why do I never learn? I'm telling you, there's something to names. Most names. It's like he can't help this need to subdue. And I'm not that same girl.

"Wrong. That ceremony is binding when the two individuals pledging matehood to one another are doing so with pure intention. It counts when they mean what they say. That whole bit about dying in defense of each other? Never abandoning your mate? Yeah, maybe you weren't paying attention to those paltry details, but I sure as shit was." I let my fury, and curse words, fly. They change with each new human era, and I've grown particularly fond of the ones humans use to decorate their sentences in this century.

He shocked me when he kissed me earlier, and he shocks me now.

"You're right. Never, I betrayed your trust and I am so, so sorry. I have my reasons, and when this intuitive situation is all over, I will take the time to explain. And if you can't forgive me, then I'll try and find a way to live with that."

That's different. I thought he'd push back against me. Against my independence.

"But I won't stop trying to win you. Not when I know we're meant to be together. We vowed to be mates to one another once, and I'll do whatever it takes for us to be mates again, officially. Hopefully helping you with the other Were will convince you."

And there it is. Old Damien. I don't want his help if he's doing it just so I'll take him back. I want his help because I want him to prove that he's not evil. Just for the sake of it. Because I need to know. Maybe I should tell him as much, but I'm not in the mood to argue with him.

I never claimed to be the most mature Were, or the best communicator. So instead of prolonging this discussion anymore, I grab his jeans and rip them right down the center. Then, I run. Good luck to him marching down the street without them.

"Dammit, Never!" he yells after me. I swear I hear those two words chained together so often I ought to add dammit as a surname. I'm not a total monster; I left his briefs. By the time he's found and donned those, though, I'll be long gone.

I don't stop running until I'm on the sidewalk outside my house, inside the boundary of Chrys's spell. I sprint past the girls in the living room and straight to my shower. If anyone's hoping for shame, you'll be sorely disappointed. It's just a place where I get some of my best thinking done. I let the water sluice the dust of the abandoned boutique off me as I roll Damien's words around in my head.

For so many years, I've been convinced he betrayed me. Convinced he did it on purpose, because he didn't love me. Because he must have hated me. I never understood his motivation. Maybe he sold me? But I have long assumed it was something evil.

Now that he's here, I'm stuck with a brand new dilemma. It's entirely possible he does have some excuse for abandoning me. Not that I'll accept it or let him off the hook easily. He may truly have thought I got out okay and that I just didn't want to see him. I know I was trying to fly under the radar for a long time after I did make my grand escape, and it's not like we had current technology back then. It's completely plausible he couldn't have found me for years, and then bided his time for the right moment.

He would have known if I were dead; that's one 'benefit' of our partial-mate bond that we've got. It's also why I haven't rushed my revenge. I knew he was still out there whenever I got around to it.

Now, though, there are other complications. Even if by some miracle he's not at fault. Even if by some second miracle I decided not to kill him and found a way around needing to, I'm still left with a scenario that in all these decades never once crossed my mind. In that reality I've forgiven him, and he's here, and I'm here, and we could be together. But even if all those other things came true, is that what I want?

Mate bonds—*real* mate bonds—are for life. In theory, if we were separated not because of Damien's betrayal but through some crazy coincidental and multifaceted tragic circumstance, I'm supposed to choose him. And after all this time, I should be over the moon at the prospect that, not only did he not betray me, but he loves me. I clearly am still attracted to him. I know him, or who I thought he was before. He's capable, strong, and fierce. And he cares for me.

Yet, sitting under the water of my shower, even after what just happened, I have to admit the truth, at least to myself.

Mate or not, I don't think I want to bind my life to Damien's. No matter what apologies he gives. And that, more than anything he or I have done, makes me question whether I really am a villain.

Chapter 20
Why Wait

I stew over Damien's words for another week. My mind's been a maze as I try to work through all potential outcomes. I'm really more of a 'loose outline and then barrel in and fill in the details as needed' type of gal. Although in this situation ...

I rotate between taking him up on his offer for help, waiting on the Magikai, or hunting him down now just to eliminate the complication. There's also option D: come up with my own plan. That's been impossible, though, unless I want to charge into San Francisco with my claws drawn and challenge the Jeweled Claw myself. Direct, but destined to fail. Despite Elios's statements, I'm a lot more sane than I come off. I'm not facing an unknown number and species of foes on their home territory while other choices are still on the table.

I sip coffee and glare at the crack that now runs through my countertop. I'll get it fixed once things settle down. As if to punctuate the direction my thoughts have been going, my phone rings.

"You will hand the girl over to the Jeweled Claw." The Head Representative doesn't waste any time on niceties, so neither do I.

"The hell I will!" I yell back, all my effort focused on not cracking what is a very fragile phone in Were hands, or claws.

"This is about more than just you and whatever loyalty you may feel for the girl as a fellow Were or intuitive. We need to stop the Jeweled Claw. I must admit our enquiries into their endgame and locations have produced less than satisfying results."

I mull this over. Was Damien lying when he said he was helping the Magikai, or is the Head Representative pulling one over on me? It's possible. If he's not feeling deceitful, I won't pick up on it, either.

Given his high level of authority it's plausible he doesn't find it necessary to include me in all the details of his various plans. Even so ...

"And your bright idea is to give her over to your enemies? Why in the moon's name would you—" I suck in a breath, all my teeth sharpening to points at once, when it hits me. "You have no intention of leaving her with them. You're going to use her as bait, track her somehow."

The silence and the confirmation I feel are all the answers I need.

"You bastards really are pieces of work, you know that? Using a teenager who trusted you to lure out the biggest and most violent group of magicals you've ever faced down. Very brave. You do realize that by putting her directly in the center of this, it's nearly impossible she won't get hurt. If your plan fails, she's in the Claw's clutches. If it's successful, it's likely they'll realize how you found them, and they'll kill her to prevent her being used by the Magikai."

"The sacrifice of one Were, even one with her abilities, is worth our way of life. Is it not?"

He's lucky he can't read *my* emotions. At this moment, they're not fit for the general public. If the Head Representative were here now, we might be looking for his replacement very soon. Listen, I get it. I really do. Every battle and every cause involves sacrifices. It's not real life to expect everything to be easy. That being said, I am *not,* have never, and will never, condone sacrificing innocents to achieve a goal. Particularly children, which I still truly consider this Were to be, at least emotionally.

"Never? Are you listening to a thing I'm saying? I do *not* like to repeat myself." The Head Representative has become annoyed. My first instinct is to push him over the edge, but that won't do.

I force a smile onto my face. I've been told people can hear it in your voice, and I'll take any help I can get. I don't want to sound murderous.

"Yes, sir. So what is the timing of all this?"

"We're coordinating and dispatching a team of our very best enforcers ..." *And I'm not included? Ouch.* "... to retrieve her and make the transfer. They'll go with her to San Francisco, where she'll be instructed to take herself to meet the Claw and hand herself over. With any luck, they'll take her back to their leader immediately." He's confident in his plan at least. Not that it's brightening my mood any.

"Then what?" I barely snap my mouth shut before a growl escapes at the end of the question.

"She'll say she escaped you. That you and the Magikai were trying to limit her and her abilities. We'll play into the Jeweled Claw's love for power. If she acts like that's her goal, it's something they can understand."

It stings a bit that he still thinks this plan will work. Her? Escape *me*. Yeah, right. I let him ramble on, but I roll my eyes.

"In three days, meet us back at the carnival at eight a.m. sharp. Not a moment later, Never. Do you hear me? You've been a useful, if occasionally troublesome, enforcer. Do not force us to end this relationship with you. Because we can just as easily remove you from this plan if you're going to cause trouble."

"You know me. I put myself first. If you're dead set on handing her over, far be it from me to stop you. I assume I'll be receiving the pay initially promised with this contract?"

I can practically feel him waving me off as he rushes through the end of the conversation.

"Yes, yes, of course. The Magikai never renege on our contracts. You know that."

After I hang up the phone, I also let loose the thread that my anger has been hanging by. I throw my head back, muzzle growing as I yell. The sound turns to a howl that draws the girls into the kitchen.

"Rough morning?" Aggie asks as they stumble into the room. She's still in pajamas, but Nadia's in yoga gear. She's been taking full advantage of my gym, and I have to admit her skills are much improved.

Oh, things are going to get rough. But not for me. Plans are hatching. If I were nicer, I would thank the Head Representative. He's settled my internal debate for me. I do *not* respond well to threats. However politely veiled his words were, I took them for what they are. I conform, or they eliminate me. And risk Nadia to boot. Not on my watch.

Yes indeed, the wheels are turning now. If you'd told me a week ago that I'd be setting aside my tenuous loyalty to the Magikai, or rather their money, for an ex I'd vowed to kill, I'd have laughed. Not today. This plan does set me firmly in align-with-Damien territory. But perhaps that's a good thing. Two birds, one stone. I'll know where he stands for sure after this.

"Ladies, we are going to call a meeting!"

Two hours later we've got Todd and Lynx, and are all seated around a table at Elios's. I fill them in on my call with the Magikai. I've been mulling over our options since I hung up the phone. I'd prefer the advantage of my own territory, but I don't want to risk Sacramento, either.

"I know what we're going to do," I state as the last piece of my mental puzzle falls into place.

"What's that? It all seems pretty hopeless to me," Nadia opines, her shoulders drooping.

"We're going to bring the fight to us. We'll lure the leader of the Jeweled Claw out."

"And just how do you suggest we do that?" Todd demands as Lynx snorts behind him. "The leader of the Claw hadn't been seen in years *before* the group itself seemingly disappeared. Clearly, he's content to run things behind the scenes. Why would he put himself at risk? Up until now he's trusted his lackeys to get the girl, even when they've failed. What's to keep him from putting forth more of the same type of strategy?"

"Emotion. That's what drives so many decisions," I announce, letting my features go furred as I pace in front of the group.

I wait for the inevitable question. Lynx poses it.

"What are we going to try and make him feel? And please don't tell me you're going to flirt. I don't think that'll work in this scenario."

I level a glare at the feline.

"Firstly, my seductive powers are nigh irresistible. But no, I'm not going to flirt."

"Then what?" Nadia asks.

"We're going to piss him off." I smile, as much as a muzzle allows for such things.

I really should thank the Head Representative for the plan. Or Damien. Or any of dozens of men I've had interactions with over the centuries, Todd and Lynx respectfully excluded. I'm talking about powerful, pushy, stubborn males who are used to being in charge and getting their way. I'd bet any amount of money or magic that the leader of the Jeweled Claw fits that category. I know Damien said it was a *he*.

The Head Representative was annoyed just by my hesitation to accept his total one-eighty of a plan with Nadia. Damien may have apologized, but he continued to press the issue. I don't think he even wants to consider that a betrayal that cost me years of freedom is worth more than a thirty-second 'I'm sorry' speech. These guys don't like to be challenged, or to have their plans disrupted. So that's exactly what we'll do, and with any luck it'll goad the Jeweled Claw's leader into action. Which will land him straight in my trap. I won't even have to rely on Damien to hold up his end of the bargain. Why it didn't hit me before, I don't know. Probably because I've been sheltering the girls.

I'm not going to lay them out on a platter, but they can still help. And we've got a stripper. If I can trust the others around me, and that's a big *if* for me to overcome, I think we can pull it off. I still have my reservations, but these individuals are the first in years that I'd be willing to take such a risk for.

Plus, if we do this, I think I can get us out from under the Magikai's thumb as well. Taking out the Jeweled Claw before they can rise again is going to be an unspeakably noteworthy accomplishment. The kind of job an enforcer doesn't have to take a contract for, because I'll be able to name my price afterwards. Just like the Bone Reader. And I know just what I'm going to ask for.

I fill the others in and then urge them to pack quickly. Because we're going back to Vegas, baby.

Chapter 21
Puzzle Pieces

I call Hugh as soon as I've got the others convinced.

"Have my orders to keep Costas's transition from power quiet been followed?"

"Yes, my lady."

"To the letter? I need to know if any of my new subjects have gone gossiping outside that little vamp manor. Has anyone leaked this information?" I hold my breath as I wait for the answer. If they have, then the whole plan falls to shit before we've even started.

"Of course not, Lady Vicious. As soon as you left, I drew up a spelled contract to such an extent and had them all sign it. Anyone who let such information loose would be obvious to spot, as they'd be missing their tongue. I saw to it myself, and if I may brag, paperwork is something I'm quite adept at." Hugh is proving to be much more than meets the eye. A dangerous foe, and a very helpful ally.

"You're gunning for a promotion here, Hugh. Very impressive. Now, I need you to go ahead and leak the power change."

I can feel his shock before he speaks, and indignation. I'm assuming over his wasted paperwork.

"What?" he sputters. Poor Hugh—all that work down the drain at the whims of a Were who must seem like quite a mad mistress.

"Yep. I need you to let it slip that Costas has been dethroned. But not by me. I need the identity of the new coven leader to remain very anonymous, shrouded in mystery. Perhaps give out some contrasting details from various sources. The new leader is a jealous vampire from the coven, they're a mysterious magical who did business with Costas, they're a vamp lord from a neighboring area trying to increase their power. Let all those rumors fly."

He sighs, and his voice sounds tense over the cell.

"And after I have worked through the mess that is amending this contract and done all those things, who are we leaking this to? And what is the intended purpose?"

"That, my fanged friend, is where it gets really interesting. I want it leaked to any and every magical you can find, discreetly of course. Have your vamps hit the party scene in Vegas, tonight. Have each one let slip to a friend or two, as if they've said too much, what we've just discussed. I have confidence it'll get to the right people. I'm willing to bet the Claw will be reaching out to find out what will happen to their funding from you, now that someone new is in charge." That's the hope, anyway. It's a key part of the plan. I doubt it'll take long, either. Rich or not, the vast majority of magicals are very defensive of their wealth and possessions.

"And once we hear from them? They're not going to be happy. They'll assume their deal with us is in jeopardy."

"Exactly. That's what I'm planning on. When they contact you, you will tell them that the new leader is no longer interested in funding the Claw. That we've decided to take the intuitive, and her mentor, and use them ourselves. Keep one of us and sell off the other to the highest bidder, as it were. That we've had the Weres under surveillance and captured them. That they've been taken to the dungeons and we're not letting them out until we're given the right price."

Hugh rolls rapidly through annoyance, more surprise, and fear. He's going to need a stiff drink after this conversation, I can tell.

"Lady Vicious, Miss Never, whatever titles you go by. They're going to be furious. Costas had official deals with them; we can't just cut them off. If we say what you suggest, then they're liable to come down here, and *not* to negotiate. They'll attempt to take what's technically owed by force." His speech speeds up as the message goes on, panic evident. My poor, precious Hugh, happy to relieve someone of a tongue via paperwork, but not one for bloodshed in person, I'd wager.

"Exactly. And we'll beat them to it. Once we've said everything else and gotten them good and riled up, we'll demand a meeting. Beat them at their own game. State that the new leader of the coven needs to know who exactly they're doing business with. That they may be willing to reconsider the deal, and let the coven have one Were and the Claw have the other, if they can meet the Claw's leader in person."

"What makes you think they'll agree to that request?" He's still hesitant, but I sense the smallest amount of anticipation.

"Because. This magical is the biggest, baddest villain on the stage. At least he thinks so. That's his whole goal, right? Control, and a need for it so strong that an intuitive is their highest priority. An absolute drive to know exactly who is with them and against them. He'll be furious, but he'll agree. Either he shows up as intended, confident that he's impressive enough to convince you to hand over the Were."

"Or?"

"Or, he does show up with a massive group intent on decimating you and taking both intuitives for himself, just to prove a point. Either way, he will make an appearance. If he doesn't when he's called out directly like this, he risks losing face, and therefore the control he so clearly craves," I explain.

Another sigh on the other end of the phone.

"I have to admit, it does sound plausible. We will, of course, do what you've instructed. I just hope you're right." He hangs up the phone.

I hope I am, too.

I've given both Todd and Lynx assignments. I have faith they'll deliver. In the meantime, the girls and I are in for a final round of training. But not before some refreshments.

"Hot chocolates and pastries!" I yell, not bothering to name our destination. There's a particular spot within walking distance they've grown rather fond of. Still, I grab my keys. Once we finish dessert, we're headed for the woods.

"Heaven," Aggie declares, both small hands wrapped around a hot chocolate cup in the back of the car.

"And if you spill that on my seats I'll send you straight there," I mutter. She just giggles, and Nadia snorts. I'm seriously losing my touch.

"What exactly is it that we need to practice? It doesn't seem like we're going to learn much more in only one more night of training," Nadia observes.

"This is going to be less a typical training session, and more of a rehearsal." I refuse to elaborate more until we're there.

Hours later, we return to my house. I can't recall a time I've ever been more grateful to see it. Preparation with the girls was rigorous, but soon enough we'll know if it was worth it. I drag myself to my shower and twist the water on. My arms ache, and I lean forward against the tile while water, so chilled it raises goosebumps, slides down my skin. I don't even move; I just wait for it to warm up. I stay until there's no hot water left.

The good thing about being magical is ... okay, there are a lot of great things. One of the bad things is that nearly everything seems to have a magical solution. Want to take a two-hour shower with water that remains one temperature? There's probably a spell or something for that. The thing is, those all cost something. Not always money. And, you can become overly reliant on magic. Just like humans have with their technology. I mentally argue with myself against finding a witch who can bespell my water heater as I walk down the hall.

As I enter the living room I see duffels dropped unceremoniously on my couch and floor. Everyone will be staying together until we head to Vegas. This means the boys are here as well. They've both been in their fur tonight. I can smell bear and feline in my kitchen. I round the corner to see Todd leaning into one of my cupboards waist-deep, pulling out what I'm fairly certain is every snack I own. Lynx is at the stove, where he's managed to use all the burners, and has something sticky dripping out of at least half the pots he's using. I note that both are wearing borrowed jeans from my front closet, despite the luggage they brought along.

"You two are going to owe me a cleaning service and a grocery run," I inform them.

Todd pulls out of the cupboard, arms full and a cookie hanging out of his mouth.

"Hey, bears like to eat a lot when it gets cold. And I've been one all afternoon. Don't blame the grizzly-sized stomach," he states after horking down the cookie.

"Did it work, then? Did you both get them to agree?" The half a second it takes for me to feel their triumph stretches forever. Lynx grins.

"Did we pull it off? Please, who do you think you're dealing with here? Of course we did."

My plan involves some backup from Todd's bear relatives, as well as several enforcer contacts Lynx knows. I also tasked the cat with talking Elios into providing a few bar-related individuals for our cause. As much as I hate to farm out work, I'd rather trust their friends and family than leave everything to vamps who have already double-crossed me once.

Todd feels a bit more reserved.

"The bears will come, but they expect to be compensated. Heavily."

I wave him off.

"Not a problem. If we can manage this we'll be able to name our price to the Magikai." The wheels in my head are turning again. "Or possibly plunder whatever treasure the Jeweled Claw is sitting on."

They may have been getting funding and help from Costas, but I'm willing to bet they've got plenty of their own cash stashed away.

Todd just shakes his head.

"They don't want money, spells, or bewitched objects. They want you."

"*Moi?*" I gesture toward myself, trying to make light of the situation. But I'm utterly confused. I've become a hot commodity lately. Not that I haven't always been hot, but this is ridiculous. First the Claw wants an intuitive, then Chrys requests my services, now the bears?

He just nods.

"Yes. And not a one-time service. I don't even know that they have anything in particular they expect you to do. They want you available on retainer. It's a status thing. If this goes well, you're not going to be able to hide among the enforcer ranks anymore, known and feared only by targets and your peers. Your name is going to be huge in the magical world. My brother wants in. Having someone like that essentially on his payroll elevates him within our kind."

Strong connections make him look like an even stronger player. I get that. Still, Todd's just brought up a point that, for all my scheming, I hadn't considered. I'm not ready for the spotlight. I like to be the center of attention in certain situations, but I don't relish the idea of being known and notorious everywhere I go. I'll never catch a moment's peace.

My thoughts are interrupted by whatever Lynx has on the stove catching fire.

Chapter 22
Unexpected Visitors

The girls are in a guest room, sound asleep, as I clean up the kitchen later. With two magical teens, and a bear to boot, I'm lucky I had enough food. I yawn as I set a plate in the dishwasher and pick up a knife to run under the water. Maybe it's my age, but I seem to sleep less and less as the years go by. A bit of a cruel joke, when I feel I deserve the rest. Still, this means I'm already wide awake when my sensors catch movement on the sidewalk. Given Chrys's spell, I don't even bother holding out hope that it's nothing more than a late-night dog walker. I see reflective, animalistic eyes on the cameras.

Aw, hell.

Without a word I set the knife down in the sink as I feel fur along my back and limbs. I flex my hands and feel the weight of claws as they grow. Through a long snout of fangs I form a silent snarl.

I'm already making a mess of my vow with Damien, but I am deadly serious when I promise myself that no one will make it past me to the girls. As quietly as I can manage, I open the front door and slip out into the darkness of the porch awning. My eyes blink a few times but adjust quickly.

Standing on my lawn is a single figure. Even with my improved sight I can't quite make out what he is, as though the air around him is more shadowed than the rest of my lawn. I sniff but smell no one else. After a few moments of silent stare-down, I walk across the lawn toward him, tail swishing through the grass.

As I get closer the shadow seems to fade toward the individual, and then directly inward, eventually revealing a man. Or something similar, anyway. Whatever he is, I've never seen one before. Which is saying something. He's slightly taller than I would be without my fur, with hair so dark it's as if all the shadow that was around him was absorbed into the strands. His eyes are a striking blue, but that's not the most fascinating feature about him. His anatomy is clearly that of a muscular man, but the way his skin turned colors and faded until it was fair says something different. He's magical. He has high, sharp cheekbones that give a look of sophistication, but regardless of his species, something about his stance tells me he's more dangerous than all that. He's too still, like a predator waiting to pounce.

"Who are you?" I barely stop myself from asking *what*. I can indulge that curiosity later if the opportunity presents itself. If the male proves an enemy, perhaps I'll save a piece of him for the Bone Reader and get my answer that way.

"The Bone Reader sent me," he states. Speak of the devil. Or whatever that mythical being is.

He certainly feels truthful, but even for my abilities it's almost too fantastical to be believed.

"What purpose would the Bone Reader have to send someone after me? And what proof do you have that he's the one who sent you?" I've never known him to initiate contact with any magical.

"You're skeptical. Even as an intuitive. That's good. When you last visited, you brought him a bird shifter's bones. He traded you information for a sound from a Scottish loch. Convincing enough for you?" One brow rises slightly.

"Maybe. The information is correct, but how did you come by it? You could have gotten those details by torturing the Bone Reader, for all I know." A growl slips into my voice as I finish the statement. I'm almost surprised to realize how defensive I feel of the mysterious cave-dwelling creature I wouldn't exactly consider a friend. But he's been a dependable, albeit infrequent presence in my life for years.

"I could have. But I didn't." He lets the short response hang while I chew on it, feeling out the words for lies. There are none. "The Bone Reader is in excellent health, and I can assure you that it would be unheard of for any magical to best such a creature," he adds.

"Do you know what he is?" I can't help the question. I want to know that much more than I want to know about the identity of the magical in front of me.

"I do."

"And I don't suppose you're willing to tell me?"

"I'm not."

This time the growl rumbles as it makes its way up my throat. Curiosity evaporating, I begin to grow irritated with my visitor.

"If you have a real message to impart, get on with it. If not, and you're here to cause harm, then get on with that as well." I stamp a leg into my lawn, the claws in my feet ripping up turf.

"My, my. You *are* testy. No matter. I find Weres fascinating. I volunteered to come, Never. I wanted a closer look at this magical the Bone Reader is so interested in. To observe you in your natural environment, if you will."

Wrong choice of words. I am *not* a zoo animal or museum exhibit on display for people to gawk at. The statement hits all the wrong chords. My hackles rise, and I let loose an open-mouthed snarl, saliva dripping off a front fang and onto my tongue.

He shivers but smiles, as if the whole thing is a joke to him. Humor exudes from his frame.

"Oh, very nice display. Ferocious. I bet you'd be fun to see in action." He holds out two palms as I inch forward. "Not that I'm planning to initiate a fight. It's not why I'm here."

"So why are you?"

Quicker than I can react to his movements, he's slipped a hand into his pocket and pulled out a small vial. The contents swirl on their own, shimmering and bluer than the clearest sea. I find myself mesmerized.

"I came to give you this." He holds the vial out before going still again. I glance back and forth between the contents and his face.

Either I'm imagining things or his skin is going blue as well; then again, it could be a reflection off the vial. I don't move to grab it.

"The Bone Reader gives nothing for free, and I have no desire to accept a mysterious gift with an equally mysterious cost. What does he want?"

The man shakes his head.

"Nothing. This isn't a product to be bartered. This is a present."

"Like hell." His eyes go wide and I can feel I've finally surprised him. If he was hoping for someone as formal as he appears to be, he's sorely mistaken. And I'm done playing around.

"This is no joke, Were." He glares, offended at my outburst. "You are correct. The Bone Reader does not make a habit of giving out things for free. Nor does he readily associate with many other magicals in anything but a transactional sense. That being said, there is something about you. Not just your species. Not just your abilities. He sees something in you, and in your future. And you will need this. It will help you defeat the Jeweled Claw. Do not put all your trust in the other Were."

That gives me pause. Is he speaking against Damien, or Nadia? I eye the vial suspiciously before swiping it. I hear a sharp intake of breath from my visitor as my claws scrape the edge of the glass, but I'm careful as I cradle it in a paw.

He watches me intently, and I catch a faint hint of ... desperation? It's incredibly important to him that I keep it. Relief washes over his face when I wrap a paw around it, then drop my arm to my side.

"How do I use it?" I demand, eyes locked once more on my mysterious guest.

When you need it, you will know."

"And what does it do?" I press.

"It will help you accomplish what you seek. But do remember, everything comes at a price."

"I thought you said it was a gift."

He waggles a finger.

"Providing the vial was the gift. What is in there would be impossible for anyone but the likes of the Bone Reader to acquire. Using it, though, he has no control over *that* cost." My visitor holds up a hand, perhaps sensing my question as much as I sense his emotions. "It will not kill you. And it is the answer you seek, even if you don't know it yet."

I want to ask something else, but my tongue freezes as the man starts to change. Shadow, or darkness, leeches outward and across his skin. His hands go black. Not the shade of any skin I've ever seen, but glossy and dark like a crow's feathers. His face is an iridescent blue, yet another feature that reminds me of birds I've seen in flight. I almost expect to see feathers or a shift, but it doesn't happen. Instead, the figure merely disappears, slowly, as the shadows overtake him.

"He will see you after." The voice of the magical sounds in the air, but I can't see him clearly. A thought hits me and I sprint back in the house for a few items. By the time I return he's hardly more than a shapeless blur against the night. I lunge for him, then he disappears entirely.

For a few moments afterwards, the air where he stood seems heavy. Thick, like a fog, even though it's the same color as the space around it. I'm equally curious and frightened to touch it. By the time I make up my mind and reach out my empty hand, the feeling is gone.

I don't wake the others when I go back inside. The following morning at breakfast I'm distracted by the thought of the vial, even though I ought to be preparing. The stopper for it is small and metallic, a loop at its edge. As soon as I'd come back inside from meeting with my mysterious visitor I headed for my room. I managed to find a necklace in my possession with links slender enough to fit through it. I slide the charm that used to hang on the necklace off, and put the vial on instead. I can feel the glass, cool where it rests against my sternum.

"How long are we going to just sit here?" Lynx demands, jittery and jumpy. He's stood and sat and stood and sat at least ten times in a row.

"You're going to make me tense!" Todd growls, in a tone that suggests he's already well on his way.

"We stay put until it's time," I remind him.

"And just when will that be?" The feline is at the end of his patience. Todd and Lynx are shifters of action. It's part of what makes them effective enforcers. But while they're far from unintelligent, they're certainly not masters of strategy. They don't typically go for plans that involve preparation more than a step or two ahead.

The girls are still packing up in their rooms. Somehow the teens have managed to make a couple suitcases' worth of items cover two full bedrooms in the span of their stay here. Once they finish and bring down the bags, I call Chrys and have her remove the protective spell around my house. It won't do if our escorts can't find the place.

"Todd, any idea when your brother and pack plan on arriving?" I enquire.

"When they arrive." He's getting terse. I know he and his brother have a complicated relationship, but not why or the extent of it.

"Lynx, what about your enforcer buddies and Elios's guys?"

He snorts.

"You know, I wouldn't call them buddies; more like acquaintances on the payroll. Which we'd better be able to back up, by the way. If this doesn't result in our taking down the Claw, I'm not sure how you expect to be able to pay them all off," he reminds me.

If we don't accomplish taking down the Jeweled Claw, the reason will be that we've been killed. I don't say that, though. Not in front of the girls.

"Oh, there they are!" He jumps up and runs outside, where, one and two at a time, a bevy of magicals are walking to the door. Another feline or two, a warlock, and a handful of wolves.

Todd helps the girls grab their duffels and I put on my fur to meet the guests. Outside. I do not host this many magicals. Bad for the breakables in one's home.

"The infamous Never." One of the wolf enforcers, currently human and sporting a mischievous grin, holds out a hand for me to shake. I don't think he means anything by it. In my work circles I *do* like to maintain a reputation. Keeps me from having to fight for the best contracts. As I drop his hand the shifter goes still, then drops to the ground as he starts to shift.

"Vamps!" yells the feline next to him before doing the same thing.

Todd's tossing bags into his car; the girls are cluttered together next to him as they wait to load into the backseat. They cling to him as vamps come swarming onto the lawn.

None of the neighbors are coming out to gawk, and the vamps aren't so much as blistering in the cold sun, so there's a witch or two somewhere who's made quite a hefty fee off this whole endeavor.

"Stay behind me," Todd growls at the girls before he drops. The magical is a master of the shift, and he's back up several seconds later, pawing away an over-eager vampire that goes sprinting toward Nadia. Agatha raises her hands to handle it, but I see Todd turn and snarl at her, warning her off of revealing her key.

A group of males and females comes lumbering down the sidewalk toward us, all swagger and thick muscle. That and the scent gives them away as the bears Todd has been waiting for. I see his brother, Rex, already a bear as he meanders up to greet us. Some of his guard, also already shifted, surrounds him. Lynx and the other enforcers are battling our errant vamps while I run over to the brothers.

"Thank goodness you're here. The vamps are out of control. They're going to try and take the girl."

Rex lifts his whole, heavy head as he looks at me head to toe, then glances at a bear shifter in human form still next to him. Unlike some shifters who *cannot* speak in their animal form, Rex chooses not to. Makes him feel more in tune with the animal, or something along those lines. At least according to Todd.

The female steps forward.

"King Rex regrets to inform you both that our deal is moot. His brother failed to tell him the girl was an intuitive, or that you're also harboring what we hear may be a very powerful witch. And *you*, Never, would also fetch quite a price."

"We had a deal, bear!" I yell at him, flecks of spit flying. He flinches as one lands on his face and wipes it away, slowly, before the female responds on his behalf.

"Deals are renegotiated all the time. Clearly your vampires have decided to seek profit instead of whatever previous agreement you had with them. Our idea is similar. We take you, *and* the girls. Cut out the middle man."

"Why, you—" I cut off my own statement as my words sink into a low growl just before I launch myself at him. One of the other king's guards blocks my path, and I bowl into a female bear shifter with auburn fur, rolling her across my lawn.

Whatever witches someone paid must be well worth the cost, because my lawn and the surrounding street are now a chaotic scene full of fighting bears, vamps, a couple of Weres and a few other assorted shifters. In spite of all this, no one else has exited their homes.

I abandon the stunned bear as I look across the melee to see the girls back to back, with vamps coming from one side and bears from the other. Nadia's actually got her fur on and is getting in some good hits, but I can tell she's nervous. Her movements are shaky. Aggie's glancing back and forth between several vamps as they slowly tighten the circle around the girls, seemingly undecided on whether or not to reveal herself. I sprint toward them, tucking and rolling under one of the bears as he launches himself over me and lands in the dirt. My lawn service is going to *hate* me.

I manage to take down five of the vamps and a rogue bear before I hear a yell behind me.

"Never, help!"

I turn to see Nadia struggling against one of the bear shifters. Next to her is Rex, his paw on his brother's head. Todd is unconscious, his tongue lolling, but I can see him breathing. I have no idea what's happened to Lynx.

"Take off your fur and come with us, or we'll execute the bear," Rex's guard, still in human form, commands.

"Go. To. Hell." I growl. Rex presses his claw down and I see Todd grimace, but he doesn't open his eyes.

"Seems we've got a bit of a problem here. You've got the intuitive, and we've got the witch. Along with the feline shifter. How about that?" The voice behind me is sniveling and cold. It belongs to one of Costas's vamps. I turn, and his words are confirmed. I see Agatha held by one of the other vamps, his hand clamped over her mouth as she struggles.

"Blood-sucking leech!" one of the bears accuses.

"Taxidermy project!" the vamp shouts back.

Growling and taunting ensues on both sides. And I feel it pertinent to add that each group seriously outnumbers the rest of us.

"Enough. We could sit here and insult one another or come to a much more lucrative deal." This voice is more calm than the others. More formal. I growl so hard my head vibrates from the tip of my snout down through my collarbone as Hugh steps forward on the vamp side.

"You traitorous little corpse-drinker," I seethe.

He grins, unbothered as the breeze lifts his hair. He's enjoying himself. Immensely.

"If you don't mind, please keep your mouth shut. Your betters are speaking." I feel my fur bristle, but I keep my muzzle snapped closed as I wait to see how this will unfold.

"I propose a deal." Hugh raises his voice across the crowd. "We have a bargain already in place for the Weres. One will remain with us. The other will be sold. We'll sign a magically binding agreement that the profit will be split with you."

"We're listening," Rex states, back in human form. While I apparently do not warrant speech, the vampire does. One of his guards has already handed him a robe that he has wrapped around himself.

"One Were for us." Hugh tallies it off on his pale, color-leeched fingers. "One for our buyer, with the profits split between us. Once all is done, you may take the witch and your brother to do with as you'd like. In exchange, we end this fight now, and get out of here to conduct our business before those enforcers bring back more of their kind to interfere."

Some of Todd's bears are nervous; I can feel it. The bear king doesn't hesitate.

"Deal."

Hugh's smile grows, reaching his eyes. It would actually be a handsome expression if he wasn't in the middle of selling us down the river.

"Excellent. And to show our good will, please feel free to make use of this on the troublesome Were." Hugh pulls the collar Costas used on me before from behind his back. He tosses it over to one of the bear shifters, who sprints forward to snap it around my neck.

"Hugh. Many who double-cross me are sorry. The rest don't live long enough to realize they should be," I warn.

He gulps, real fear wafting off him. I let it wash over me and relish it.

"Get them in the vehicles," he orders through a clenched jaw. We're corralled by a mix of bears and vamps to the panel vans he points out. I glare directly at my captors, not breaking eye contact even as the door slams shut.

Chapter 23
What's Her Name

"Not bad, everyone. But do you think the Claw will buy what we're selling?" I ask the others in the back of the panel van as a vampire drives us down the highway toward Vegas.

Todd rubs his jaw from across the van.

"Well the hits were certainly real. This smarts!"

"Now, now. Let's not be overly sensitive. I'm sure your brother was just letting out a bit of frustration."

"He didn't have to send his best guards!" Todd whines from his seat. But I see him smile. His sibling has done us all a solid. He knows it. Rex's performance was excellent. I'm certain that's in no small part because he got to rough up his minutes-younger but larger twin brother just a bit.

What can I say? When I commit, I commit. If I wanted this plan to be foolproof and draw in the Claw, it wouldn't have been enough to just *say* the vampires had gotten the Weres. They've got to actually have us. So, we staged a kidnapping. Now, I may be selling myself pretty highly here, but I felt it would take more than some vamps to believably take us out. Or maybe that's just because I already did that single-handedly.

Either way, I had instructed Hugh to send the coven's best. I admit I was a bit nervous to cast him in the lead role, but he did quite well. Aside from his fear of me, which no one else will have noticed except perhaps Nadia.

I'd asked Todd to reach out to his brother and relay our plan to the bears. I'm just relieved they went for it, even if it does involve me being 'on retainer' for them. Elios did Lynx a solid by recommending some muscled-up bouncers he uses for the rare occasions on which his bar holds a crowded event. They helped bulk up the ranks of the few real enforcers we had at my house. The hodgepodge group looks very mercenary-esque. Which is great for us. Even the collar was an impressive touch. It's utterly useless now, of course, but I still hate the thing. I wrenched it off the moment we got in the van.

Now Nadia and I are in the back of one vehicle with Todd, while Lynx and Agatha are in a separate one speeding toward the coven's mansion, where we will be staying in the best rooms, not the dungeon. If this were a real kidnapping, it's unlikely they'd risk both pieces of valuable cargo going in the same van. Particularly with two opposing factions negotiating over us.

Presumably, we're being followed by the Claw. Some of the enforcers should be tailing the magicals who are tailing us. That is, if Hugh's instructions to leak the new vampire leader worked. It all hinges on that. If nothing else, I believe in Damien. Not his word, but that he's been keeping tabs on me. There's no way he didn't have someone watching for me. Either he'll come after us because he's genuinely worried and wants to help, or he'll follow us just to get Nadia for his boss.

I pace the grand entrance of the vampire mansion—I suppose it's my mansion now—as soon as we arrive. Hugh follows me back and forth, peppering me with questions about the running of the coven, trying to get me to engage. I ignore each and every one. I'm too antsy for bloodsucker politics, even if I will eventually need them. One thing at a time.

"Lady Vicious, please if you could just —"

I hold out an arm to signal for silence as Lynx strides in, alongside a slew of Elios's bouncers and a couple of trusted enforcers.

"Well, are they taking the bait? Was anyone following us?" I tense as I await his response.

He smiles.

"Oh yeah, and they're not even being subtle about it. They've got glistening claws emblazoned on bands over their arms to mark themselves. It seems you've goaded them into their end game."

Well that's good, or bad. Or both. If they're showing themselves, it's more likely someone with actual power will arrive. For the thousandth time since this plan has gone into motion, I question my potential stupidity. This time, it's not just my own life I'm placing on the line. And that bothers me.

Less than an hour after our arrival, one of the vampire butlers scurries into the office where I've been lounging. He bows to Hugh and me.

"There are guests at the property gates. A representative for the Jeweled Claw, demanding an in-person meeting with our new ruler."

"What did this representative look like?" I demand.

The vamp gives me a once-over.

"Like you, Lady Vicious. At least his species. The visitor is a male Were, large and steely grey. He did not give the impression that denying him entrance to our grounds would be well received."

I laugh.

"I imagine not. Very well. This is working out even more quickly than I'd hoped. Trot on back down to the gate and inform this Were that the new vampire leader is prepared to meet with the leader of the Jeweled Claw. And *only* with the leader. They're welcome to bring a small entourage, but if the leader is not present, then the negotiations are off. And they know we're not bluffing, because we've got intuitives. We'll be able to tell."

He nods several times quickly before running out of the room and back toward the gates. I suppose that means it's time for me to get ready.

Upstairs, in the center of a bedroom that is so luxurious as to be laughable, I stand in front of a large mirror. I'm decked out in what one of the vampires described to me as a 'combat' bustier, fitted pants, and heeled boots that zip up to my knees. No one's kidding anyone here. This would be a horrible choice for fighting and flexibility. I do, however, look stunning in it. I've taken the time to curl my hair into ringlets, more to distract myself while I wait than anything else. I turn a circle in front of the mirror, appreciating the exacting, tailored fit of the black ensemble. If I have to fight, it'll just get shredded regardless. Perhaps that's truly the biggest expense for magicals. Clothes. As a final touch I cover up the mark on my arm that singles me out as a Were. Human make-up has come so far. Although it is another large expense.

I'm busy considering this and tabulating different species' potential spending when I hear a soft knock on the doorframe. I turn to see the girls.

"We heard the Jeweled Claw is coming," Nadia starts.

"Holy moly, Never, you look like a battle queen!" Agatha gushes. "Like you could just take our enemies and wham, kick, slam!" She mimes some of the movements I taught them.

I smile at her before looking toward Nadia.

"You're nervous," I observe. She nods.

"*Sí.* I can feel that you aren't. You're mostly just confident and on edge, but not exactly worried. How do you do that?"

"Timing. I've lived many years. I'm just waiting for the action. Once that starts, either way, we'll have our answer. And then you'll be headed back home and I'll go back to my regular life, or ..."

"We'll both be dead or captured," she observes, still not convinced.

"Yes. Or that. And if I'm still alive, I'll concoct a new plan to get us out."

I don't add that I've added a small failsafe. One I hesitate to use but am near-certain would work to get Nadia and Agatha out of almost anyone's clutches.

"I won't lie and say that I can guarantee a happy outcome. You'd know it wasn't honest, and I have no desire to try and deceive you both anyway. But I *will* promise you both that Todd, Lynx, and I will do everything in our power to prevent anything from happening to you all."

"We know that. And that's part of why we're worried. We don't want you three hurt, either." Agatha protests.

"You two just focus on sticking to the plan. Stay out of sight, and if that falls through, then remember what we worked on in the woods. And when I give the signal, don't hold back. Either of you."

They nod in unison.

"Now, go get ready." I move to shoo them out of my room. Aggie gives Nadia a knowing look before slipping out.

"Um," the small Were starts, looking at her shoes.

"You have something else to say?" I am careful to keep my tone and my emotions in check.

She takes a deep breath and sighs. I feel her determination, combined with reluctance. Whatever this is, it's not an easy topic for her.

"I want to know about the other Were. Damien. I smelled him on you that one night. You remember? You came in and ran straight to the shower." She blushes, and I can tell she knows exactly what we were up to. I've been trying to account for her intuitive abilities, and I've overlooked her nose. Weres have an excellent sense of smell.

"He's ... a complication. It's possible he'll be helpful to us, or he could be an enemy. I can't quite figure him out."

"*You,* an intuitive, can't figure him out?" Her tone is skeptical.

"We have a history. And for reasons I won't get into now, I can't read him like I can everyone else. There was ... a relationship, and it ended. Badly."

"You know, *donde hubo fuego quedan cenizas.*" She lets the phrase slip quietly, but I hear and feel the chiding tone.

I tsk, this time able to figure out the gist of the meaning. Where there was fire, ashes remain.

"That's *exactly* what is left between us. Ashes. But this time, I won't be the one who gets burned," I promise.

"I don't believe you, Never. I don't even think you do, deep down, beneath the anger I can feel. Where something as big as true love has been, there is always the possibility of a spark. Get your closure if that's what you need, but be careful you don't burn the rest of us down."

Look who's getting wise. The worst thing is, it won't matter if she's right. I set myself on this path too long ago to deviate now.

"I've been thinking. You say names are powerful, and dangerous at times, right?" Nadia asks. It takes me a moment to pick up on the change of topic.

"Exactly," I confirm.

"Then I think I need to change mine."

"Explain," I demand, intrigued.

"My family wanted me to hide, and for good reason. I understand now the danger of being what I am, but I think there's a better way. I want to help the other magicals. At the same time, I can't give up my home. I don't want to endanger the people I care about. You said if we're successful here, everyone will know who we are, yes?"

"That's right." I pause, giving her space to put her thoughts together.

"Then I don't want them knowing me as Nadia the Colombian Were. I need my pack kept safe. After tonight, I think it'd be best if I take on a new persona. Don't misunderstand, I'm proud of my heritage. I love where I came from, but that's exactly why I don't think I should keep my name. If I do, they can use my real information to track my family down. I don't want them to have to run and hide for the rest of their lives. I need to see them after this is all over, but I don't plan on staying hidden on the compound again."

"So you need a new name. I get it. And just what have you decided on?" I'm proud of her ingenuity. I did just what she's thinking of doing, though I came to her conclusion in my own way.

"I've decided on *Ever*."

I freeze. I roll the information around in my head. Then, I laugh.

"It's perfect. On the surface level, just like me. Never and Ever. And yet, I don't think that's why you chose it, did you? I listened to you and Aggie listing off the qualities you've observed about me. You two respect me, but neither one of you wants to *be* me. And your name's more about that, isn't it? People will hear it and connect the two intuitive Weres, but you'll know that it's actually a statement of our differences."

"Are you mad?" she asks, tentative.

"No." I shake my head, my answer honest. "Far be it from me to determine another individual's growth. The truth is, you're not like me. And while I'd still love to see you embrace the ferocity you're capable of, there's plenty about you that doesn't need to change. Plenty that I hope doesn't have to."

"Thanks, Never." She slips out the door just as Hugh arrives.

Chapter 24
The Jeweled Crown

Showtime, I think as Hugh informs me that our guests have officially arrived. Even with the thick curtains down the aisle of the throne room, I can tell it's well and truly dark outside as well. I debated back and forth between letting myself and Nadia be led in like the prisoners we supposedly are. Perhaps it's my past warring with my good judgment, but I decided against it.

Instead, I've seated myself directly on the throne, where I belong. Hugh clears his throat from where he stands next to me.

"Lady Vicious, shall I have them shown in?"

I wave a hand, signaling for some of my vamps to open the double doors. I hear two sets of heavy steps making their way toward the throne. Hear, but don't see. I've added a swivel to this throne, and chosen to face away. I want my first impression to be emotions only. They roll over me like a monsoon. The intimidation of the vamps. Not sure if that's because the leader of the Claw is actually here, or they're just easily cowed, now that they've seen one leader bested. I have Todd and Lynx hidden within the crowd of vamps, and I'm not happy when an edge of worry creeps into the wave from Lynx's direction.

From my new guests I feel confidence, and—this is interesting—also worry. Are they on edge, then? Good. I scent two males. One is *very* familiar.

"Gentlemen." I allow my voice to rise, echoing across the hall while I pause for effect. Then I kick off, sending the chair swiveling around as I hook my legs over the edge in a 'look at these boots' pose. I sweep my arms out in welcome.

There's a small contingent of Jeweled Claw members waiting back by the doors, but only the two males directly in front of my throne. I feel my brows scrunch as they turn downwards into a glare, my mouth clamping shut before I quickly give my face a shake and let my features fall back into something neutral.

Damien is standing in front of me. Damned Were said he was a double agent, but not that he was this far up in the organization. I take a deep breath, attempting to calm myself. Shockingly enough, it fails, but I settle for lying my ass off and pretending to be fine. It's not like they can read my emotions, and this is certainly a situation that calls for a confident Never.

"I'm so glad you were able to meet for a renegotiation of terms," given the unfortunate demise of my predecessor." *I burned that two-timing bloodsucker to ash* just doesn't sound as professional.

"I must admit," the taller male next to Damien speaks. He's got to be the Jeweled Claw's leader. "I was disappointed to hear you had no intention of honoring our previous terms." His voice rolls and rumbles like thunder in a stormy sky.

He's broad-shouldered, and he's wearing a tightly tailored suit. The cuffs glint, and I see gaudily large sapphires as the links. The buttons down his jacket are also varying kinds of precious gems. It's rather on the nose, given the name of his organization. Instead of a traditional crown he's wearing something that has ridiculous horn-like antlers coming off the sides of his face. As he finishes speaking his hands start ... steaming?

Oh no. Oh wait, oh crap. None of that is armor or costume. I scent the air, and catch wind of his species. *Dammit, Never,* I chide myself. I was too focused on Damien's scent and the emotions of the others to notice.

He's a dragon.

Of all the supernatural bad luck. Remember when I said they're similar to us in many ways? Well, they're also similarly hard to kill.

"I don't need my promised intuitive to see your surprise, and if I am not mistaken, recognition? You didn't anticipate the leader of the Jeweled Claw to be a dragon, then?" he asks.

Nope. Not in the slightest. Dragons in general are as few and far between as Weres, each variety having their own specific attributes. And they're notorious loners. They've all got some version of a hoard or a home that they guard with their lives, as far as I know. They've also got the pesky habit of passing down different magical genetic traits. There are no dragon intuitives—that anomaly is just in Weres—but they have their own gifts and banes that bolster and afflict small numbers of their kind. It's an additional detail I'll have to watch for.

"I'm surprised a dragon would agree to an in-person meeting," I say, leaving it at that.

"I thought it best to handle this quickly, and personally." His deep voice reverberates against the stone walls. "I don't suppose the threat of my dragon form is enough to entice you into providing my intuitive to me?" He's running one hand along the sapphire scales coating the other, and I see blackened claws lengthening from his fingertips. He glances up at me without lifting his face. Completely unconcerned. He thinks he'll win.

I'm not so sure he won't. Screw what I said to the others. I'd told them my plan was to negotiate from the throne, to try and establish an uneven balance of authority. I'd pictured that provoking him into action. I can already tell that won't work. I need a closer look at this new foe. With only a second's thought, I decide my strategy will be femme fatale after all. Slowly, with exaggerated movements, I extend each leg before planting my boots on the floor. I rise from my throne, drawing myself up to my full human height. I don't answer the dragon at first, but put an extra swing in my step as I walk down the stone stairs from my throne, down the carpeted aisle toward my visitors.

Damien goes slack-jawed. The leader of the Jeweled Claw finally lifts his head, quirking one eyebrow up. Amused, more than anything. But he's not suspicious or angry, yet. Thank the moon I decided to greet them as a human, and doused in the same species-hiding perfume I normally hate. You never know what different magicals will find attractive, and the human form is more universally appealing.

The dragon allows me to plant myself directly in front of him, close enough that if he took one small step forward our chests would touch. I quirk my chin up at him, a small smile playing on my lips before I answer.

"I do *love* the personal touch. My newly acquired coven here has dubbed me Lady Vicious." I don't bother clarifying how I got that title. "Would it be too much to ask the names of the two of you before we proceed with the details of this negotiation?"

I have to assume Damien hasn't told him about me, because there's no feeling of recognition coming off the dragon. I do catch him sniffing, but he comes away with nothing but confusion as he hits the perfume.

"My dear lady." The dragon sweeps into a bow and grabs one hand, planting a kiss on it. "That is the minimum level of politeness we could provide. Allow me to formally introduce myself. I am Ekaitz, one of the last of the ancient dragons. My companion is Damien, second in command of the Jeweled Claw, and a most capable Were warrior."

Second in command? I put all my mental effort into focusing on Ekaitz. He's the real target today. My desire to claw out my lying ex's eyes can wait. He has some explaining to do.

I turn further toward Ekaitz, while presenting my back to Damien. I want it clear who has my attention, and who the real threat is. Ancient? His words rang with truth. That makes him even more deadly. Some magicals maintain fairly solid powers with age, some increase, some decrease. It really depends. Dragon powers are city-decimating events in some cases, and most only become more volatile as they grow older. I reach a hand out, tracing a finger over one of Ekaitz's sapphire cufflinks, pretending to admire it. Then I let my fingers graze the dragon's scaled hand before I meet his eyes again, once I'm under control.

"Forgive me, Ekaitz, but I haven't heard such a name in quite a while. Does it have a meaning?"

He waves a claw as if it is of no real importance.

"I am a storm dragon. It is a common name for us. Or it was, a few millennia ago."

He truly *is* one, then. To be an *actual* ancient, as the title implies, you must have been born prior to the common era. This dude is BCE-confirmed. In other words, well and truly old. Older than sliced bread, and while not older than dirt, certainly around long enough that he preceded most inventions we currently enjoy.

"How fascinating," I croon, as I lean toward him. "I would *love* to discuss your experiences in a more intimate setting once we conclude the necessary talks."

I've piqued his interest, but he's suspicious. I expect nothing less from someone hell-bent on obtaining an intuitive.

"We shall see. But first, my Were. She is necessary for my plans. I'm afraid that this is not something I am willing to bend on, even for someone as intriguing as yourself." He leans down and puts a finger under my chin, lifting my face as he locks his gaze on mine. "This can go one of two ways. You can either agree to our original terms and provide me with my intuitive, or we will be forced to resort to more violent methods, Lady *Vicious*." If I were a lesser being, I'd shiver. From fear or excitement? Take your pick. This male is massively powerful and handsome, but I have more noble aims than bedding a dragon right now.

"What about option three?" I hold my breath as I await his response.

"I'm afraid there is no option three, my dear. You've won over this coven, so you're clearly intelligent or physically powerful. Perhaps both. But make no mistake, I am a trickier entity to tangle with than Costas. Compared to me, that vampire was no more harmful than a troublesome insect." I believe him.

"Perhaps it would help if I revealed my true nature to you, Ekaitz." I step back, and his gaze follows me. I reach up, pulling down the edge of the zipper holding my ridiculously tight outfit in place. It's all for show, all for a purpose. I'll rip right through it anyway. His eyes drop with the zipper and I feel it. Lust. I put on my fur, letting the clothes shred and fall. I've played card number one. His gaze is hungry as he takes in the fur. He's surprised, but impressed rather than upset. Still staring, and still attracted to me. Time for card number two.

"*I* am an intuitive as well. So perhaps a third option could be negotiated after all?"

More shock on the part of the dragon, but also delight. I think I've got him snared.

Damien's looking back and forth between his master and me. He growls and then turns the snarl toward me.

"Enough of this! What makes you think you can so easily sway the Jeweled Crown, leader of all the Claw? Foolish female. Why would he deal with you, now that you've so readily exposed yourself? Now we can take the girl *and* you." The emotions behind his statement are as muddled to me as ever, but I'm furious that he's clearly attempting to sow mistrust between Ekaitz and myself.

I put on my haughtiest stare and tone. I don't have to fake my annoyance.

"I am negotiating with the Crown, not *you.*"

"Silence." Ekaits sweeps a sapphire-scaled hand out and stops his lieutenant from stepping any closer to me. Damien glowers but stays behind his master's scaled hand.

"My second in command does have a point. You are currently the leader of a vampire coven, however that came to be. However, I am not in need of someone with their own interests. I am in need of your abilities. More so than the enjoyments your body might bring, I am afraid. Take her." He points at me, and the Claw members behind him converge.

Ekaitz steps back and then stands still as five Claw, not including Damien, circle around me. The dragon is waiting; he feels expectant. I'm betting this is a test. He wants to see what I can do, and what I *will* do.

Three of the surrounding individuals drop to the ground to shift. A fourth launches himself forward. He's a vamp, but not one of mine. He's overconfident but not skilled, and I'm easily able to grab his head and yank. It gives a satisfying crunch as the neck bones break, just before I wrench it off. I toss the head towards the three shifters now crouched in front of me.

"Who's next?"

There are two wolves and a leopard. The wolves run to my front, and the leopard circles around. I manage to scoop one wolf up like a rag doll, while the other goes for my leg. I toss the first aside. It's not a pretty throw, but it does the trick. He slams into a column and slumps. The second wolf I kick away as he sinks his teeth into my leg. That tears it. I bend down and sink my claws into his back, drawing blood. I wrench him off and toss him toward his comrade. The first wolf is just standing and shaking his head dazedly when his buddy slams into him. They both go down in a topple of fur.

I have just enough time to turn as I hear a snarl. The leopard ran all the way around me. She's sailing through the air with serious momentum. I duck, but she lands easily and turns back toward me, beginning a second run. As she charges, I note the smallest movement coming from the fifth individual. He's reaching a hand into a long, sweeping purple robe for something. Warlock, if I had my guess.

I make my choice, turning my back on the leopard as I run toward the warlock. She yowls, and I feel her offense that I've indicated she's not even a worthy threat. I hear her pursuit. The warlock has his palm back out, powder in it. His lips round as he begins to blow. I slide, my furred and clawed foot slamming into his very human-like shin. He yells and I hear it snap as he hits the ground. Whatever the powder is hits the leopard square in the face. She yowls some more and starts to shift back to human, tears running from her eyes.

I'm breathing heavily as I stand to survey the damage. The wolves are mobile but limping. They take a few half-hearted steps, and I lean down and roar at them with all the volume I can muster. They cower, tails tucked under.

"Anyone else?" I turn and face Damien and Ekaitz.

Ekaitz slowly claps.

"Not bad. I can see how you managed to procure a vampire coven for yourself. That aside, you've proven my point. I have no need for a combative intuitive." Oh no, I've failed. I can still feel his interest in me, but it's not the type I need right now. "We will require an intuitive that is more malleable. Thank you so much, though, for the demonstration." Ekaitz turns his gaze to Damien and snaps a clawed hand.

"Get the girl!" Damien yells the instruction at some of the other Claw members, his furred arm ending in sharp points of his own as he gestures towards the stairwell. It's clear he intends to search the mansion.

"Don't do this!" I know I sound like I'm begging. Damien doesn't even look at me. He turns towards the other Claw members instead, and gestures in my direction.

"Kill anyone who tries to stop you." He tells them.

He may as well have slapped me. The filthy liar. The Claw members spill out the double doors and head for the entrance stairs. He turns to run after them, and panic consumes me.

Chapter 25

Two Can Play At That Game

"No!" I throw myself at Damien, determined to tear open his face. He will *not* find Nadia. A sapphire-scaled arm hits me across the chest, stopping all forward progress.

I double over, wheezing. Dragons pack a punch. When I can catch my breath I stand and run at Ekaitz, but he holds me at bay easily enough. He grunts only once, when I first make an impact, but other than that he's not even breathing heavily. And he's mostly human now. If he chooses to fully transform he could wreck the ballroom, if not the whole mansion. Dragon sizes vary wildly, but 'big' is an apt enough descriptor. And yet, I don't care about the mansion or myself. I care about my friends getting out safely. Nadia and Agatha, especially. It's taking a backseat to even the pain I feel at Damien's second betrayal.

Which gives me an idea.

I go still in the dragon's arms, my limbs limp. I let my eyes go unfocused as he stares at me, confused. When I speak, I keep my tone monotonous and haunted. He wants an intuitive so badly? He's that insecure in his followers and his rule? Fine. I'll use it.

"He will betray you, sapphire one. The Were seeks your destruction, and he plans to deliver it tonight." I lift an arm, pointing one solitary claw in the direction Damien ran. It's not lost on me that, for all my ex knows, he's abandoned me to death by dragon. Well, two can play at that game.

Ekaitz squeezes my biceps where he holds me, hands steaming without burning me. His breath smokes as he glares at me.

"How do you know? Is this a trick?" He shakes me, and I let him.

I move my head left to right, slowly, trying my utmost to seem as if I'm in a trance.

"No tricks. Only truths. Intuition does not lie. Your second in command has planned your downfall. He harbors resentment, and envy." One great thing about the rarity of intuitives is that no one knows how we work. This whole display is insultingly dramatic, but I feel him growing nervous and eager.

Ekaitz's eyes go wide as he drops his hold. *Now* his breath quickens.

"I should have known. He's been a trusty enough lieutenant, but he demanded this mission personally. He never planned to return the girl to me, did he? He was going to take her for himself. Tell me, has he turned my army against me?" He reaches down and wraps a claw around my wrist again.

"Some," I say, answers remaining vague.

"Traitors! They will pay. They will all pay!" Wow. This guy's even easier to sway than I thought. With great power comes great paranoia, apparently.

He turns his face upward, his features going reptilian and snout-like as mist pours from his mouth. The two of us are enclosed in a perimeter of sorts, and the liquid spreads in a circle away from us. As it touches the skin of several gathered vampires and Claw members alike, I hear screams. Then I see its effect. It's acid rain. If I'm not careful, he'll burn us all to the bone.

I say a silent, mental apology to the gathered vamps. I don't feel any loyalty to them. They were more than willing to follow Costas, and some are likely getting what they deserve. Still, I'm not down for killing innocents. I turn my face back toward the remorseless dragon, determined to win him back over.

"Jeweled Crown, forget the girl. She is young and untested; she cannot help you. Let me take your lieutenant's place, and I will vet every magical in your army to determine their loyalty."

"Let the girl go? And be used by my enemies? Absolutely not." His denial comes quickly, but I anticipated it.

"Then allow me to train her for you. In this mansion." I feel his hesitation, the distaste. "Or a castle of your choosing. Surely you have several. I will relocate my coven." Appealing to an ancient's vanity and wealth seems a safe bet.

He nods, considering.

"Yes, that would be acceptable. But why offer yourself? You didn't want to be taken."

I shake my head.

"I didn't want to be a captive. I wanted to be appreciated for my talents, not used for them. I also don't want to get hurt. You saw what I've done with the coven. They came after me, so I responded in kind, but I know I'm nothing compared to a dragon." Sort of true. They're unquestionably stronger, but I can still outsmart him. "I don't want to keep fighting for my safety. I want to be protected, but I need someone strong enough to provide that. I see by your demonstration that you're more than capable. I will happily barter my services to you in exchange for safety. I can see you value my abilities."

It's a deal I'd never really make. Being on the run, living in fear of what's after you, is still better than being captive to a crazed king.

He pretends to ponder for a minute, clawed hand under his chin. I can feel his answer before he gives it. He isn't seeing the downsides. He's seeing a very valuable item to add to his hoard.

"Very well. You shall have my protection. And a castle of your choosing, near where I reside. The girl will stay there for training with you. I need you at all times available to me, so I may vet my army as we mount our attack against the Magikai. You will only grow more valuable as we enact our plans. Soon, the world will know of us, and I will have many new recruits." I suppress a shudder.

"And what will you do with the magicals and humans who resist this new order?" I hold my breath as I wait for an answer. It's a short wait.

He shrugs.

"Eliminate them. I have no time or patience for doubt and betrayal. We will build a better community from the ashes of this one, if need be."

Not surprised he's planning to go scorched-earth, but it's nice to have it confirmed, since I have every plan to betray him myself.

"We have a deal." I offer him a hand to shake, but he just stares at it.

"We will settle this through a magically binding contract, once my business today is concluded. For a whole army, and a whole world, an intuitive is necessary. For *my* intuitive, I would rather have insurance. I am no fool."

We shall see. I'll just have to beat him before he ever gets around to that step. Which means Hugh had better keep himself scarce, the darned contract-wielding vampire.

"Come, my new lieutenant, let us destroy your predecessor and claim the girl." Ekaitz offers an arm to escort me. I gently push it away.

"She's not where Damien thinks she is. I will retrieve her for us. You deal with the lieutenant, and we'll meet you on the lawn." I can feel his hesitation. "My Crown, If we go together, he could try to steal me back from you. Do this for me, as a gesture that you mean what you say about protecting me," I urge.

"Yes. This is acceptable. Fetch her and meet me on the lawn. I will bring you his head." He kisses my hand with full lips, but I see his face going scaled again as he turns to exit the ballroom. Unless I am very much mistaken, I'm going to end up with a fully transformed dragon on my lawn very soon.

At this point, I wouldn't complain if he did kill Damien, although I'd prefer it be me. I'm a do-it-yourself kind of gal. As soon as the dragon is gone I sprint back toward the throne. I pull a sconce on the wall, opening a passageway Hugh showed me earlier. It seems the vampire lord who had this mansion built, Costas's predecessor, was a true fan of all things medieval, including a few hidden passageways. I run down a set of curving stone steps.

Nadia and Agatha aren't in their plush rooms upstairs, or in the dungeons. I had them hide in a passage adjacent to the cells. There's a panic room of sorts at the end, loaded with supplies. I fling open the door, expecting to find the girls.

Instead, I'm staring at the exit on the other end of the room, the door wrenched off its hinges, hanging at an awkward angle. The grounds of the mansion stretch before me, flashes and bangs sounding as Claw and vampires battle each other on the lawn. I sincerely hope someone thought to bring witches or some magical object for sound control. The Magikai are going to be furious if we put on a battle royale for all the humans in town to enjoy. Then again, it is Vegas. Maybe we could write it off as a stunt for a casino opening. That's for future Never to handle. Right now, I need to find the girls.

We're still in the deep of night, much to the use of my vamps. I'm surprised as I run through the gardens that there's a wide array of night-blooming flowers. Who would have thought they'd put effort into gardening? Or maybe they have their food do it? I know some covens illegally keep a few humans on hand for such things, although I haven't seen any here yet.

I'm halfway across the garden, catching and losing the girls' scents in increments. I find them in the air, follow the smell a few feet, and lose them again under the confusion of all the other magicals battling it out. The progress is maddeningly slow until I hear a shout.

"Never! The canyons!" It's Todd's brother, Rex. He looks comically terrifying with his face halfway back to human as he yells, his body still a hulking bear.

I give him a salute to let him know I've heard him and go sprinting after the girls.

I cut down every shifter in my path as I follow their trail. I'm deep into the canyons and can scent that I've almost caught up to them when I hear screams.

"Get away from us, you creep!" That one's Aggie.

"*Para, déjame en paz!*" That'll be Nadia. Her tone is nicer, but I feel the desperation as she beseeches their pursuers to leave them alone.

I only hear growls and response.

"*Ya basta!*" Nadia again, and her voice shakes as she makes her words more firm.

I push myself to move faster, rounding a boulder to find a half-dozen shifters closing in on the girls, whose backs are against steep walls of rock.

Aggie's eyes go wide as she sees me behind them. Despite all her fear, she's stayed true to her word not to reveal her abilities until asked. Behind the back of one of her attackers, I give a slight nod.

I needn't have worried she'd be too timid or scared to do what needs to be done. The moment I give the signal, Aggie's concerns falls away. She's grown confident in herself. She smiles at an advancing feline as she holds out a hand. The cat doesn't even have time to leap at her before she strips him, and he's left staring down at a naked chest, wondering what happened. She does the same to a scarred bear, not one of Rex's. The ursine shifter twists in discomfort as he transitions back into a man and she strips his abilities away.

Nadia is sinking her teeth quite effectively into the leg of another wolf. She flings her head around and the shifter's body is hauled along. As she releases her jaws, he goes flying, and I hear ribs crack as he slams into the rock.

I'm so proud I could cry. And I don't weep easily.

I see attackers number four and five are vampires. If they were Costas's they must have abandoned him before I arrived. They're wearing Claw armbands. I know I saw one of them in the ballroom earlier this evening.

I creep up behind that one and snap his neck before wrenching the head clean off. It really is the most efficient way to handle them. The second is a woman, and I see Nadia hesitate for only a moment before she sinks her fangs into the vamp's throat, ripping down to the bone.

Behind her, Aggie has our last assailant, another wolf, on his knees as his fur fades away.

I stride over and shake my head in disappointment as I stare down at him.

"And to think I tell everyone you wolves are my favorites," I chide before I kick him in the nose. He topples over.

"We'll want to burn them," I instruct Aggie. A small spark out here will go a long way. We don't need her to use a lot of power. The biggest challenge will be containing it. "Then we should get back to the mansion. I don't know how this group of idiots found you, but—"

"Never!" Aggie lifts a shaking finger as she points behind me. "They didn't find us, he did."

Damien, in full fur and frustratingly handsome as ever under the moon, strides out from behind the rocks.

"Hello darling," he croons.

Chapter 26
Fight Night

"*Malparido!*" Nadia yells from behind my shoulder. No love lost between these two. *Yeah girl, I think he's a bastard as well.*

"Want me to strip him?" Agatha offers. I angle myself so that I shield them both. I shake my head.

"No thank you. This feud needs to be settled, and it's long overdue." I try to convince myself I'm ready. After two hundred years, with less than one more year to go, I'll finally be rid of it. My vow to destroy him. And the deadly consequences if I fail.

"Never ..." Damien lets my name hang in the air, his voice almost pleading. As he holds out a furred arm, I still have to wrestle with the small but vocal part of me that insists he cares for me. It's a thought I can't afford to linger on for more than a second, and it turns out even that's too long.

I'm so caught off guard that I register his intent with hardly enough time to duck as he swipes claws over the space where my head was moments before.

I punch upward, intending to hit him in his lying gut, but he jumps back.

"Are you insane?" I seethe at him. Even now I'm in disbelief that he could have lied to me so thoroughly.

"Never, you don't understand! I'm trying to help you here." Damien wraps his hands around my arms, trying to pull me in closer. I'm so mad I can feel myself shaking under his grip. I manage to spin around and face him, but he keeps his hold.

"No, *you* don't understand. You seem to be under the deluded belief that you can pit me against you on opposite sides of this fight and still somehow be on my team." I snap at him, spittle flying off my muzzle. We're so close we could kiss, and some of it hits him in the face. Sometimes fury isn't pretty.

"Girls. Run," I instruct. They do just what they promised me and follow the direction without question, sprinting back toward the mansion's grounds. I twist in Damien's arms again to keep him distracted, biting at his shoulders.

He ducks out of the way and then lunges close, grabbing hold of my wrist.

"We're not on opposing sides, you stubborn, ridiculous female. Did it ever occur to you, even once, that I was telling you the truth about this whole double-agent bit? If it had, maybe you would have seen fit to warn me about your little kidnapping scheme and the fact that you're a vampiress. Or vampire lady. Or whatever you are. I could have told you how to play Ekaitz."

It is possible, and if our relationship was built on a foundation of trust, I might believe it. The tiniest part of me wants to. That part is probably the one responsible for missing the gigantic red flags that have always been present with Damien.

I go still, not fighting him anymore. Not because I agree, but because I want him focused on what I have to say. I want him to hear these words.

"Maybe you are on the Magikai's side. Maybe you're not. It may matter to them, but it doesn't matter to me. Because you and I have bloody and unfinished business, Damien Onasis. You left me in that forest years ago, at the mercy of our enemies. Dead, for all you knew, and for many moons the fate I would have preferred. That would have been kinder than what was done to me."

He flinches, his gaze falling to the ground. But he doesn't let go.

"Never, I'm sorry. If I could ex—"

"Save it." Flecks of spit fly off my fangs, but this time he doesn't back away. "Today, you left me sitting in the throne room with a deranged dragon king who controls acid rain. Once again, you abandoned me to potential death. I could be a bleached pile of bones now, for all your help."

"I —"

I bowl right over him, holding up a paw to cut him off.

"I am telling you this so that you understand why I will never forgive you or forget what you did. Today, my focus is keeping Nadia away from your boss. I will protect those girls no matter what it takes, even walk away from my vengeance against you. We don't have time right now to fight this out, with a field of enemies behind me. But once this is settled, you had better watch your back. Because, Damien darling, I am going to sink my fangs into it."

He does drop me then, releasing me so fast it's as if I've burned him with my words. If only. I take advantage of the opportunity, and as he stumbles back I spin myself around, leg out. I roundhouse him right in the jaw. There's a satisfying crunch as a canine pops loose.

"Dammit, Never!" He cups his bleeding lip. As the fang falls, I catch it and pocket it before he can see. He glares at me over his hand, red seeping through.

I blow him a kiss before sending another kick straight to his groin. Some males never learn. He grunts as he drops, and I lean down so he can stare me in the eyes.

"Well, while I *have* been on better dates, this is certainly the most fun I've had with *you* in ages. Toodle-oo, lover!" I give a wave as I poke fun at his last name. If he'd been a true lover, or mate, if that's the term shifters need, I'd be settled in happy Were suburban bliss and not fist-fighting him in the Nevada wilderness.

I sprint away before he recovers his breath. I don't hear him follow me as I make my way through the melee on the lawn, cutting through my opposition in my pursuit of Nadia and my crew.

I spot the girls, tucked behind Todd and Lynx in the fray. Nadia is swiping at anyone else who gets close. Aggie is dropping shifters one at a time. She's grinning from ear to ear, and I can tell she's in her element. I pause for just a moment to watch the ferocity of my four friends at work. They're outlined by the moon, and they look fearsome.

As I begin to move toward them again, darkness descends as something large blocks the moonlight. I glance up and see the belly of a dragon. It seems Ekaitz has decided to join the fray. He's just as enormous as I feared he might be. Not as big as a house, but certainly large enough to crush a charter bus.

The massive blue beast falls on the lawn. The ground quakes beneath us, rolling under my feet. I stumble, barely catching myself as several of the others fall. As the dust settles, fighting stops all over the lawn. Ekaitz blinks, two sets of eyelids moving over vertical pupils. His sapphire scales glint in the moonlight.

On instinct, my paw grabs at the Bone Reader's vial. It's swinging from a chain around my neck. I purposely put it there to prevent losing it when I transformed. Now, I like to think of myself as hard to scare, but I admit to some nervousness as I take in the beast before me. The Bone Reader's messenger said I would need the vial at the end. I have no idea what it does, but I'm really hoping smashing it against a dragon will do the trick.

Ekaitz's gaze lands on me, and I feel, larger than life, the fury. He lifts his head to the skies and roars, the ground shaking again. Against all my instincts, I begin to sprint toward him. I'm well aware I'll probably get only one shot at this.

As Ekaitz lowers his massive head and opens his maw, mist swirls in his throat. *Please let me be able to dodge this.* I keep running, even as my thoughts turn toward the likelihood of being burned, my skin melted by magical acid rain.

Just before he lets the swell of acid loose, he lets slip one word around the mists forming above his tongue.

"Traitor."

Behind me, I hear steps pounding the ground. I turn and see Damien. He's right on my heels and gaining. There's no way to know which of us Ekaitz means, and I'm done placing my bets on Damien's fickle choices. I suck in a breath and push myself well past my usual limits, determined to beat him to the dragon.

As Ekaitz begins spraying acid, I leap forward, rolling under his neck. I miss the worst of it, but droplets still spatter on my arms and I clench my jaw against the pain, willing myself not to look. As I stand, my arm reaches towards the dragon's belly. I'm stretching toward his heart, wrenching the vial from the necklace and preparing to smash it, when a furred arm reaches over mine.

No.

With one arm, Damien slaps my hand away. With the other, he reaches out with some small, glowing silver blade I didn't see on him before. He slams it into the spot I was aiming for, in the process falling on me as he loses his balance.

Above us, Ekaitz's roar causes more small quakes. The dragon's legs waver around us and I scramble, pushing and pulling against Damien to get out from underneath him. We're a scrabble of limbs as we struggle to get away.

I fall on the grass, the bottom of my muzzle slamming painfully into the dirt, Damien twisted up somewhere over my leg. I feel the ground move again once more, this vibration larger. And then, stillness. I extricate my limbs from Damien's.

I wipe dirt out of my eyes, staring at Damien as he stands.

"What did you do?"

I'm not even expecting an answer. I just don't know what else to say. Behind him is Ekaitz's body, still in dragon form. Possibly a side effect of how he died? I know he'll transform back eventually if he's really dead, but I keep an eye on him just in case. There's no movement. No breath from his snout, no air ruffling Damien's fur. No up and down below his ribs.

I turn my eyes away from the very likely dead dragon and toward the crowd. Everyone is mixed together. I wouldn't be able to tell friend from foe if not for the Claw's jeweled arm bands. Some are stone-still and silent, others chattering to each other. A few moans and groans come from the wounded. And we're surrounded. Whether intentionally or not, the crowd has formed a circle around us.

The eyes of the Jeweled Claw members turn to Damien. This is it. Surely they'll tear him apart. I still can hardly wrap my mind around the fact that Damien did what he told me he would. I don't know what it means for us.

I may even have to apologize. The ridiculous thought flits through my head as Damien turns to me. For a moment I think he'll say something, but he snaps his muzzle shut and turns back toward the crowd instead.

"We have been betrayed by our hosts!" Damien's voice booms as he yells across the field. "The intuitive has used her abilities to slay our king. This insult cannot go unanswered! Brethren, I will guide you in revenge! "

The group, bloodthirsty, begins to yell. A sickening feeling settles into my chest. Not just rage, which I'm more than comfortable with. It's the feeling of something breaking. The last bit of my affection and trust for the lying, slimy Were by my side.

"Long live the Claw!" Damien yells, raising both arms into the air. The others shout and cheer. Those with fists pump them in the air, and the ones with paws stamp the ground.

The crowd of shifters and vampires creates a din I can't hear over. I have no idea if my friends and allies are yelling for me, or if they can even get to me. As Damien lowers his arm, the crowd becomes silent. His eyes meet mine.

"The Claw will have its intuitive. *This* intuitive. She has proved herself more useful than the girl, but she must still pay. I will challenge her, and retrieve her for the Claw." He shifts into a fighting stance. "Face me, traitor!" he yells, before he sprints toward me, fangs bared.

Chapter 27
Aftermath

It's instinct alone that carries me through the motions of combat as I swipe, duck, kick, and roll. I know there are all sorts of emotions coming at me from the crowd that surrounds us, but I can't feel any of them. They're blocked out by the turmoil inside my own mind.

Numb disbelief on the surface barely contains what's beneath. Rage. The type that can only come from love. Twisted and betrayed love that has to be repurposed into something new. I've felt it before and shoved it deep down, to be unleashed on other enemies.

Not to brag, but to brag ... I'm a pretty decent fighter. I hold Damien at bay while coming to all these realizations. Years ago, I felt this same anger toward him. By the time I escaped and went after him, though, it had transformed into something more centered. More purposeful. Once I actually came into contact with him in these last several weeks, I had allowed it to fade. To become useless. I'd grown complacent.

I tell myself that this more recent, indisputable betrayal is a good thing. Now there's no hope. No lingering 'what if.' Nothing to hold me back from my vow.

Still, curiously enough, I feel a tear slide down my fur when I do manage to break through his defense and slice into his face. He yowls and I kick him in the chest, right over his deceitful heart. He flies across the grass, slamming into Ekaitz's now harmless jaws.

Damien looks up at me, starting to push himself back up. I stand over him, staring down with what I hope is easy-to-read anger. In my periphery I can see jeweled bands as his followers close in. This is it, then. I only hope the girls are able to get away from here with Lynx and Todd, and that I can finish Damien before they reach me. I have no plans to be anyone's intuitive captive again. I won't be making it out of this alive.

I open my jaw, preparing to sink my fangs into Damien's neck before he can hurt me in any other way.

A yell sounds behind me.

"Never! Duck!" Agatha's voice. She's one of the few individuals in this world I trust, and I throw my body to the ground, rolling away from Damien.

Aggie screams as she unleashes on Damien and the followers closest to him. I feel her power like a strong wind as it buffets the air. Damien drops back down, and the line of advancing Claw falls behind him. I squeeze my eyes shut as the gusts her power is giving off become too much. When the air stills and I open them, I see dozens of naked, human Claw members and burnt and gaunt vampires. She must somehow be pulling their ability to absorb nutrients from blood, or tolerate even the moonlight. Lynx goes sailing over my head, tearing into the weakened magicals. Todd is right behind him, swiping left and right as his paws send bodies flying.

Nadia is perhaps more noble, going after the still shifted members in the ranks, while enforcers and Elios's bouncers back her up like personal bodyguards. I look around for Aggie and see Rex, back to human, holding her gently in his arms. She's passed out, and her lips have a bluish tint at the edges. She's pushed herself too far.

"Aggie!" I yell, or at least try to. I'm stunned to realize my voice comes out as a pathetic squeak. I'm even more surprised when I try to stand and my wobbling legs fail me. I look down as I sink back into the grass to see very human limbs. I must not have gotten clear of her powers. No matter.

I manage to pull myself up against Ekaitz. I lean against his scales, too tired and weak to care that I'm propped up against a dead reptile. It's about this time I realize I can feel those cold scales all down my back and ... oh hell. Aggie's abilities ripped right through the magic that allows me clothes when I shift back. I'm well beyond caring. After several attempts, my legs shaky as a baby deer, I manage a few steps towards the others. One of Rex's shifters, a female back in human form, steps forward to wrap a wool blanket around me. My mind feels fuzzy.

There's something I needed to do. Something the other way, but I keep moving toward Aggie. Her eyes flutter open and she groans as I get close. She looks me over.

"Sorry, Never. Didn't mean —"

"Don't worry about it. Gives all these shifters a chance to see me in all my naked glory." I wink at her. She gives a tremulous smile before her eyes roll shut again.

"She'll be okay," the female who handed me the blanket informs me. I take a good sniff, and make a guess.

"You're the pack healer?"

She nods. At least Rex brought the right individuals. I keep my eyes trained on them as they move away. I smell vamp, and turn to see Hugh beside me.

"Lady Vicious, I —"

"Hugh. There's something I need to do. Something." *Damien!* My mind clears with a sharp pain. Aggie's all right, and he still needs to be taken care of. I turn back toward him. Too fast, apparently, because I stumble and fall. How embarrassing.

I struggle to keep my eyes open as blackness plays at the edge of my vision. Aggie really must have turned on her abilities full-force. I have hardly any strength left, but I'm determined. Hugh places a hand on my shoulder, pulling me back.

"No!" I shrug him off. Then more hands descend, lifting me up. I'm being carried away from my target. "No!" I kick and struggle, the darkness growing. I have to still myself or risk falling unconscious. I settle for verbal threats.

"Put me down. I will unleash violent vengeance on you if you do not drop me immediately!" I feel the terror of a few of the vamps carrying me, and a couple begin to lower me until Hugh waves at them to keep going. He turns to me as he walks alongside us.

"My apologies, Lady Vicious, but in this we must disobey. This coven has lost one leader recently. We cannot afford more infighting at this point. We *need* a decisive leader. One with a goal. One with at least, well, *some* morals." He clearly doesn't think mine are ideal, but apparently they're good enough.

"We need you," he finishes.

Vampires not only bowing to a Were, but fighting to protect and keep one weak enough to overthrow. Now I may have seen everything.

"Hugh, you are dangerously close to insubordination," I warn him.

"I know."

"There could be serious consequences to this," I try again.

"I know that, too."

"You have more spine than I gave you credit for," I acknowledge. He smiles, pleased as he recognizes the words for the compliment they are. I allow myself to be transported back to the mansion but have one last request.

"Hugh?"

"Yes, my lady."

"Bring me that traitorous Were. Bring me Damien."

He nods and then is gone. Speedy little things, vampires. At least in the night.

Aggie's powers really could be sold as an amazing sleep-aid, if it weren't for the troublesome side effect of temporarily losing all your magic. That would probably kill sales pretty effectively. Once I'm back in my room and the vamps have receded, I sleep until the sun is high in the sky outside my window.

When I do manage to drag myself out of bed, I don't even bother with sifting through the duffel I brought along, still unpacked and sitting in the corner of my barely used rooms. Instead, I grab a silken lavender robe hanging over a bathroom door and wrap it around myself. It lifts in the back as I move, the slight breeze created by my steps enough to set it in motion. I walk down the hall toward the girls' rooms. Nadia is sitting up in hers, Lynx and Todd with her. They're chatting over coffee, if my nose is correct, served in china so fine you'd think we truly were in a castle.

"Aggie's all right," Todd informs me as I enter. "The healer saw to her. She's resting now, but her color's back to normal. She'll be fine."

"She'd better be! I still have to rough her up for stripping me ... both magically and otherwise. I'll feel rotten doing that if she's not at full strength." The threat sounds weak even to me, but no one calls me on it.

I hadn't planned on Aggie using so much power at once, but I knew she'd likely need her key. Before we came to the mansion, I had her practice on me in the woods. I hadn't felt nearly as sick then, but she'd also been holding back. Even that had affected me more than the other shifters she's stripped. My working theory is that when she strips the shifters she's mostly working on the animal soul, and they still have a fairly strong half left. The human half. Even stripping a vampire, she's leaving a body that used to be human. Stripping a Were? We may *look* like the others, but we only have one self. So if I get stripped, I feel the full force of her abilities.

Once I stop by Aggie's room and confirm her health for myself, I head downstairs. I walk past the throne room and make my way to the dungeons.

Hugh is waiting at the entrance. He shakes his head before I can even ask the question out loud.

"He's not here. I am sorry, Lady Vicious —"

"Never," I correct him. As fun as the nickname is, there's no use in hiding behind it now. News is going to be all over the place through the Claw, the enforcers, and Todd's crew that I'm the new vampire lady.

"Lady Never. But I'm not sure if you heard. We were unable to obtain the male Were for you. His supporters took him. He's beyond our reach now." He cringes back a bit, his anxiety growing with each word.

"And the dragon?"

"The. Dragon?" He blinks at me, taking a few moments to follow my change of topic. "Still on the lawn, my lady. We can take care of it, if you wish?"

I nod. Gruesome as it is, dragon's teeth and scales are profitable items.

We sit in silence for several minutes before Hugh dares to speak again.

"If that is all?"

I don't respond; I just wave toward the stairs. Hugh moves up them gracefully and quickly, and then he's gone.

I push open the wooden door to the old-fashioned hall of cells. The one I busted out of still has a pile of rubble, but several of the others sit intact. I don't even know why I'm here, since they're all empty. I lean my forehead against the door I've just pushed open, then slowly sink to the floor. It's dusty and dank, just like you would picture a proper dungeon.

I don't rage. I don't yell. I don't pound the dust or cry. I just sit there on my knees. Tired. Exhausted. My sleep wasn't so restful after all, it seems.

After what may be a minute or an hour, I smell bear. I don't bother turning to look until I feel Todd's reassuring hand on my shoulder, deep brown fingers squeezing just enough to shake me out of my thoughts.

"He got away," I state. It's not as if I've bothered explaining the whole situation, or even most of the situation, to the others. Todd's unbothered by such things. One thing I'll say for the bear, he takes situations as they come.

"I know," is all he says.

"I couldn't do it. Todd ... I have to kill him. I could have killed him. I failed. In truth, I've been failing for years." And after all this time, the truth spills out.

I tell Todd everything, while he sits silently and takes it all in. How Damien and I promised ourselves to each other. How he abandoned me to enemies who took me captive for years. I skim over some of that time, but I do tell him about my magnificent escape and the deadly consequences. Then I tell him about the vow.

"I was so angry, Todd, and so directionless. I needed something to focus on. And I was afraid. Afraid that if it took me too long to find Damien, I'd lose my rage. I'd let it simmer and fade into nothing. I thought, maybe I'd find him and I wouldn't be capable of actually killing him, or I'd let him deceive me again. Which is exactly what I did."

"Because you loved him," Todd supplies. It's the first time he says anything.

I start to nod, then shake my head.

"Yes, and no. I *did* love him. Whatever is left now ... it's not that. But it's the memory of that. It's enough that it kept me from hating him even when I should have. Kept me from bothering to pursue him. I'm sure I could have found him before now if I'd put real effort into it. But instead I let myself fall into the role of enforcer. I told myself I'd wait on clues for his whereabouts; that I had time. And then time began to run out. That vow is magically binding. I wrote a contract to myself, to ensure I'd have to see it through. Either I kill him, or I die."

He doesn't tell me the terms are stupid, which he should. That I behaved like a lovesick fool and could have handled it better, which I could have. Instead he asks a question.

"How much longer do you have?"

I sigh.

"Halloween next year. If he's not gone from this world by that time, I will be."

I wait for him to chastise me.

"You know, Never, I've been familiar with you for years. Not close to you, like now, but familiar. You wouldn't have allowed our friendship before this point. Even though Lynx and I kept trying to offer it by sharing our missions with you. Those girls, though, they've softened you, and that's not a bad thing. Do you know why Lynx and I sought you out? Why we'd want to work with you?"

"Because I am very adept at kicking ass and taking names?" I give a half-hearted giggle at my own joke.

He laughs.

"You may be, but that's not why. You're prickly on the outside, Never, but that's not all there is to you. You're strong. And you're a *good* magical, for all the complications you have. Lynx and I observed you. Which contracts you took, which you did off the books. We were fascinated by your species and ability at first, but then there was more. You don't go after those who don't deserve it. You do a lot more pro bono work for magicals and humans alike than you'd ever admit. You're a protector, a defender, more than you've ever been a killer for hire."

"And so?" I press, instead of telling him what his words mean to me.

"What I'm trying to say is, there are different kinds of strength. You've decided it's all about fighting and hunting. Vengeance and violence. And that does have a role to play, especially in our world. But the way you care for the girls, the way you watch out for innocents, even the way you tease Lynx and me. The way you didn't decimate this coven, when many would have and no one would have questioned your motives —"

"They had a bad leader. Vamps aren't my favorite, but they're not evil," I insist.

"Even so. It's what many would have done. Or they'd have used them. And not to ward off the Claw, but for their own convoluted purposes. Face it, Never, you're one of the good guys. And all those things. All those soft qualities like caring and compassion. *Those* are the signs of strength that made me determined to get close to you. I wasn't sure Aggie would work, but I'm glad she did."

Realization dawns.

"You brought that witch along to meet me on purpose! You knew I'd want that contract and you picked —"

"A girl who really needed help and guidance. And I hoped you'd provide it. I must admit, the results are beyond what I expected. You care about her, and us. And we care about you. Now, from what you told me, taking out Damien may be something you need to do yourself. But we can help you get there. And while you may feel like you have to kill him, don't discount the other things that make you strong."

I don't know how much longer he stays while I sit silently, but I feel his absence when he leaves.

Chapter 28
Uninvited Guests

I park just in front of my house. Aggie and Nadia are back with Todd's pack for the night. The bears are quite taken with the spunky teens. While I love this new sense of family, I was happy when the enforcer volunteered his home. I need a night to myself. No vamps, no Weres, no exes or dragons or jobs. Just me, working through my thoughts.

Which reminds me. I need to settle one more thing before I can have the evening to myself. Preparing for teenage drama, I dial Chrys's number.

"So he's going to propose to me, *and* keep a bevy of vamps on the side?" Chrys demands through the phone after I fill her in on what my vamps found out.

"Side vamps, and a siren. Yes," I confirm.

"The hell he will. That sneaky little boy has another thing coming. Thinking he could lock me down like that!" Okay, not exactly the point I would have homed in on, but whatever works. Chrys continues her rant. "The dishonesty! Honestly! His proclivities are his business, but when he tries to drag me into a marriage? With deception? That I cannot abide."

"Are you going to have him poisoned, then?" I question, unable to help myself.

"No. No, I'll come up with something else. I don't want him dead. I just want him to know that if he's going to fuck around with me, he's going to find out." Teen lingo. I tell you, I both love and loathe the changes that each new decade brings. So many fun new curses, but so hard to constantly change one's vocabulary.

I offer something I almost never extend: a free service. Given what she actually should have charged for protecting my house, I'm still getting off way too cheap.

"I'd be happy to pay him a personal visit if you'd like. Or, if you prefer, I can easily have him relocated to the Vegas coven and charter you a flight?"

I can feel her desire for revenge and the glee that comes with it.

"Now *that* would be lovely. I could use a vacation. If you don't mind recommending a good spot to stay and gamble while I'm there, we have a deal."

I promise her one of the best rooms at the coven. I have no idea which one that is, but I'm sure Hugh can get some of the others to take care of it. Come to think of it, I should strike another bargain with Chrys while she's there. Having the vamp grounds protected by a spell like hers would be invaluable.

After I hang up, I sigh. All I have to do is walk up the sidewalk, but it feels like an impossible task. It's been three days since our battle on the mansion lawn. I really haven't had to do much. The bear healer saw to Aggie. Lynx informed the Magikai what happened with the Claw. We'll still get paid out for our work with Nadia, but they're being argumentative about Ekaitz. They're claiming they don't owe us since none of us actually killed the dragon, even though I'm the one getting blamed for it. My name truly is becoming infamous.

I reach into my jeans pocket and place my fingers on the vial from the Bone Reader. I didn't use it. I've never known him to be wrong before. Either his ability is imperfect just like mine, or there's more to come.

I called the Magikai myself yesterday; left a message with the snarky secretary they keep up there. I want them to leave Nadia alone. I'm not sure what bargain I can make for her, but I'm hoping they'll be willing to listen. If not, I'll help her myself.

I know I need to look for Damien. I just feel so tired. Not myself at all. I need something to fire me up. I appreciate Todd's words about real strength, but I don't know how to motivate myself without righteous fury. And I can't feel that. Haven't managed to feel much at all the last few days.

I realize something is wrong as soon as I place my hand on the door. It's not locked. And I know for a fact that Chrys put her spell back in place. I press it open and smell something new. Someone who doesn't belong. I actually offered the house to the girls on a more permanent basis, and they're thinking about it. This scent, though ... it's male. And there's more than one.

Fur rips over my skin and I move into a defensive stance, letting out a low growl that rumbles from my throat through my toes. This is *my* home, and I tolerate no trespassers.

"What are you doing here?"

The male on my couch stays relaxed, leaned back against my plush decorative pillows. He's got one leg thrown over the other, lightly bouncing his foot to and fro. The lights are off, small slits of sunshine illuminating the room through the blinds. It doesn't matter, though; I can see him easily. Deeply tanned skin, olive undertones, aquiline nose, full lips. He'd be handsome if he weren't breaking and entering. And if he weren't sending shockwaves of dangerous signals straight to my brain. Whatever he is, he's powerful. Extremely so.

"Never. Good to meet you in person at last. I do hope you'll forgive the intrusion, and my arriving unannounced. I did consider extending you an invitation, but after all the trips you've taken recently, I thought it only polite to meet you in your own city." His voice is hoarse and rough, a deep rumble when he speaks. At odds with the polite words and the feeling I'm getting from him.

I'm in no mood for games.

"Explain yourself, or get off my couch," I demand, not breaking from my defensive stance. I feel the smallest hint of fury, and I relish it. Finally, an emotion. *This* is something I'm comfortable with. I lift my claws in warning.

He just holds up a conciliatory hand.

"There's no need to be rude or make threats, I can assure you. I am Amun, and I am here on behalf of the Magikai." This is shocking. The Magikai are the elite of the elite. I run his name through my head. Egyptian god of mystery, and a king. I'd bet any amount of money that he picked it, and his real name is something ridiculous.

"You're Head Representative of the Magikai," I guess. I feel his confirmation.

"Yes, and I have a deal for you. We've been contacted by the other Were, Nadia."

"Ever," I correct automatically.

"Whichever. She's a powerful entity, or at least she will be, with the right training. She has unfortunately declined our generous offer of a spot in the Magikai's academy." Smart girl. Also, a small-town girl. She wanted more time with her family.

"She did, however, express an interest in a mentorship program. Once she's wrapped up her studies in Colombia, she'd like to apprentice herself to one of our top enforcers and train to join the Magikai ranks."

It reads as the truth, but it can't be. She said she didn't want my job. But she also said ... aw, hell. She wants to make a difference, and I'm betting she came to the realization that might be easier if she understood more about who she's up against.

"She wants to work for you. At whatever hidden headquarters you all keep," I guess.

He gives the smallest nod, chin barely dipping.

"Precisely. And given you're the only other known intuitive, we'd like *you* to train her. Formally, not this come-and-go business you've done for us in the past," he adds.

She's stuck us both in it now. If I refuse, I could risk our safety. The Magikai don't like to be refused, and I recognize this for what it is. A last chance. She already got out of their academy. If she turns this down, they'll know for certain she can't be brought under their control. Looks like I'll be going undercover.

"I have a few conditions."

He waves a hand. "Name them."

"Firstly, I go where she goes. So if you're sharing the location with her, you're sharing it with me."

"Done. Next?"

"Time. I have a few things on my to-do list, and I know the girl does as well. Did she specify how long she needed to finish her studies?"

"Six months." He informs me.

I shake my head.

"No good. I need eleven. Then I'll work with her."

He purses his lips, then sighs, as if I'm being wildly unreasonable. A year is a mere blip in magical time, but I'm sure he's happy to make a big show of magnanimously agreeing to something so small by making it into a much bigger deal.

"Fine. But not a day longer. When the time gets close, we'll send you the needed information to report to our headquarters. Any other demands before we write up this contract?"

It will be magically binding then. I'll have to go, or risk some very painful repercussions.

"How long will I have to be there? Am I going to have to get a housesitter?" I stall, and as we speak two males appear from the shadows of my hallway. They're wearing suits, as if they're some kind of undercover government agents. Could the Magikai be any more cliché? One has deep brown skin, coiled hair on the top of his head, faded on the sides. Smells of shifter.

The second one is pale, slender, shorter, and smells wholly human.

"A non-magical?"

"We find they can be quite useful in certain capacities." Amun doesn't elaborate further. "Now then, it's difficult to say how long your tenure would be. It's impossible to predict how long it will take for the girl to gain a level of independence with her skill, and for us all to determine the best professional position for her. I'd wager a year, though, or at least that's what the length of your contract would be. After that, it would be up to you."

I nod. The shorter man has opened a briefcase and is pulling out an old-fashioned quill and parchment. The shifter grabs the quill and begins scribbling furiously in glowing ink. At the bottom of the page are blank spaces for Amun and me to sign.

I reach for the offered quill, hesitating at the last moment.

"Just one more thing, before I sign."

"What?" Amun growls, calm facade breaking a bit. It's enough for me to scent out what he is, and I nearly drop the quill. A shifter, but a very old one. Barbary lion. Felines are a dime a dozen, but he may be the last of his kingly kind. Older than me by far. I'd guess several hundred years older.

"I'd like to know your real name."

Epilogue

My visit from Amun, or Vizier, if I used his real name, really kicked me into gear. My life on the line is one thing, but Nadia's future is another. I have to get this done, and sooner rather than later.

I shed the faux-fur coat that I've worn since stepping off the plane and into the icy environment. I chose to make this journey as the ice princess instead of the Were, given the hunting parties I saw forming near the airport, but there's no need to hide now. No one encroaches on *his* home.

I let out a sigh of relief and comfort as my Were features roll over me, more content in this form than the human one. Perhaps there's something to be said for living in the wilderness after all. I'd get to be this way all the time.

I make my way through the icy entrance, the shadowed ceiling cavernous above me. Not for the first time, I wonder how and why a magical being found itself living within the icy walls here.

The echoing and contrasting tones of the Bone Reader sound around me as I shake my fur, small icicles flying.

"Beautiful," he croons, his tone welcoming and suggestive.

He doesn't fool me, though. The others guessed the Bone Reader is interested in me romantically. That's not quite the right word for it.

The Bone Reader doesn't feel lust for me. That's a suffocating emotion that's easy to pick up on. No, he doesn't love ... he possesses. My novelty, as the first intuitive he's met, is driving the need to add me to his collection of magical oddities. I don't even know what he looks like, and so it's tough to determine what he'd find attractive in anyone.

"You sent me a visitor," I accuse.

"I did." At least five voices answer back from the one being in front of me.

I reach into a pocket and pull out the vial, moving to return it to him.

"I didn't need this. Thank you, though." The Bone Reader is one of the few magicals for whom I will make an effort to be polite.

He shakes his head but pulls a paper from his own pocket. I recognize my writing. It's a note I slipped into the pocket of his messenger when he was leaving my lawn.

"So he found my note. Did you open it?"

"No. I do not accept payment without providing a service." He scowls, but just as I place the shape of his lips, it slips from my mind.

On the outside of the folded paper are the words, *If I fail, save the girls. Payment inside—my real name.* The one piece of information I knew he'd do something so costly for. He's been as curious about it as I have been about his.

"Would it have been enough?" I can't help asking.

"Oh, most certainly. But you needn't fear; I haven't opened it." He leans toward me again, proffering the paper.

I wave a hand.

"Keep it. Who knows, depending on how this next year goes, I may need you to do what it asks."

He pockets it, in clothes I couldn't describe. I'm left standing awkwardly with the vial as he continues to ignore my attempts to hand it to him.

"It was a gift. I do not take back my gifts. And know this, Were: they are rarely given. I can think of less than a handful of occasions in all my time where I have offered something without taking a price in return."

I am quite certain asking for that history *would* cost me something.

"You bring me a new challenge, I presume?" His eyes, whose color I know I'm seeing but not registering, sparkle in the light reflected off the icy walls as he changes the subject, full of curiosity.

I pull Damien's tooth out of my pocket, and he curls a lip.

"Pulp. Enamel. Dentin ... useless. I have no need for these materials, and I cannot use them to help you." He waves a hand dismissively. I hold up a finger and wave it back and forth as his eyes lock on the movement.

"Uh, uh, uh. Not just a tooth. Look closer."

He does, and while they could be black, blue, or hazel and I'd have no clue, I do swear his eyes light up as he catches the small piece of jawbone.

"Delightful! Delicious! Drop it in the goblet."

I hesitate for a second; I'd been reaching out to hand it to him. The Bone Reader always puts his own samples in. Until now, I've assumed it's part of the process.

He quirks a brow.

"This individual means something to you, yes? I may not all have your gifts, Never ... but even I can see that much without your bones. It's obvious. In cases of high emotional ties it can actually work better for the individual who desires the information to provide the bones for the goblet. Go ahead."

Any secret about how a magical's abilities work is valuable. I'm sure this one's going to cost me.

When I first bargained with the Bone Reader I assumed he'd want my skills at hunting people down as payment. Once he expressed an interest in my intuition, I thought perhaps he'd make use of that. Instead, he always demands magic, or items he can use for magic. He doesn't even ask for bones, which he either reads or pays for. I'd be willing to bet anything the Bone Reader can be violent, but he's not cruel.

Still, I don't think I like the eagerness coming from him. He knows how badly I want this information, and that's bound to up the price.

I hold my breath and march forward a few steps before dropping the bone in. The liquid in the goblet is a deep purple, and it fizzles as the tooth dissolves. As the Bone Reader moves to lean over it, I step away.

He lifts a tiny shred of bone from the liquid, tooth eroded away. He stares at it intensely for a few moments.

"Hmm, interesting. Not just close to him, a mate. Or an almost-mate. How intriguing. And he betrayed you. Not without reason, but then again, who am I to judge motives." A few weeks ago, I'd be dying to ask what those motives were. Was there any chance they were pure? Now, I don't bother. I don't care. There's nothing Damien could say to stop me from coming after him.

"You can't read him, can you?" the Bone Reader asks me.

He looks away from the bone, his intense gaze falling on me instead as I shake my head.

"How fascinating. That must be so bothersome to you. I can only imagine. I have never failed to read a bone."

For a moment that lasts less than a second, I get the briefest feeling of sorrow coming from him, but then it's gone as he settles back to the task at hand.

"He has traveled quite extensively. From Greece, originally. Then met you elsewhere in Europe on your own travels. He's younger than you. What, fifty years or so? Then more Europe, after he left you. Romania with the Claw, then San Francisco. But you already knew that. You need to know where he's going."

I wait. The Bone Reader likes his buildup, and I'm not going to be the one to deny him.

"He planned to betray his leader from day one. It would always have ended that way. The weapon cost him something very dear, but he believed it to be worth it. We shall see, I suppose. Now that he's head of the Claw."

That part isn't surprising. It was clearly a power move. Again, I wonder at the origins of the weapon. But that would be another cost, and I'm already in deep.

"Where would he hole up, though, after this victory? Where to shore up his defenses and build up the loyalty of his fellow Claw members? Where would he feel safe? Not his master's strongholds. No, no. Getting all the Claw that's in the US back to the forests of Europe, where he'd feel most comfortable, would likely prove difficult. They've spent a significant amount of effort garnering support over here." I growl at the location. Damien had better not steal the sanctity of a former home from me. The Bone Reader holds up a hand.

"However, I think you'll find him much closer than you expect. Deschutes National Forest in Oregon, to be exact." I breathe a sigh of relief. It could be so much worse.

"And the vial?"

"You haven't realized by now? It was never for the dragon. It's for Damien."

I take a step back, eyes still locked on the Bone Reader. I nearly smashed that vial onto Ekaitz and wasted it. The Bone Reader doesn't say anything else for several minutes, and I determine his portion of our transaction is concluded.

I turn back toward the entrance of the cave, staring at the icy wind and bracing myself for a long walk back to the airport.

"You really are exquisite, you know," the Bone Reader remarks behind me.

"What do I owe?" I question, not bothering to ask whether he means my appearance or my abilities. I'm not sure I want to know what would pass as a compliment to him, or an explanation.

"I want you to make me a new Were."

I drop the coat. My first instinct is to tell him absolutely fucking not. But that's not how the Bone Reader works. I took the product,

I owe the price. I just never thought he'd ask for something like this. And that's the problem: I didn't think. I wanted Damien, and I didn't consider that there might be a price too high to pay, or too impossible.

"I don't even know if I'm capable of that!" I protest, and that part is true. Shifters are born. Weres are born ... and made. It's sheer fiction that a shifter can bite you and turn you. It doesn't work that way. And if they've discovered some other magic to make humans like them, it's certainly been kept secret enough that I don't know it.

A Were, though, we can make more of our own kind. You might think I'd have been dying for the chance, given how near extinction we seem to be, but there's a catch. When you create magic, or magical beings, you are responsible for them. Otherwise, we'd have rampant new vampires and all sorts of things out there blowing our cover and ruining the good time for the rest of us. Truthfully, I've never had the motivation to make another one of me. It's not like I can bring back my family. I'd have to pick from the human choices available and start from scratch, and that's never interested me. I'm no one's babysitter. Which is probably why I'll be facing another significant obstacle ... I truly don't know how. Creating a new Were is not nearly as simple as biting someone. And it's a ritual that was kept traditionally by Were historians, of which there are, to my knowledge, zilch, zip, nada, zero left. So there's me screwed.

The Bone Reader shrugs as I look at him.

"I guess you'll need to find a way. No Were ... No Damien."

I growl, the sound reverberating off the walls. Not that I'd actually attack. That would be monumentally stupid.

Here's the thing about the Bone Reader. He won't let me use his services again until I've paid, but more importantly, I can't find Damien until the balance has been settled. I've never shorted him, but stupider magicals have tried. That's part of why he offers the product before the payment. He somehow can block your goal. If I leave the cave now, without an intent to pay, and without doing it, then my tracking of Damien will all come to a dead end. No idea how he does it, but that's how he works. My goals will spiral out of control as I meet with failure after failure, until he gets his bloody Were. Dammit.

"Just what are you intending to do with this new Were once I create them?" I dread the answer. He can't collect them. If that's what he wants, I'll be stuck with no other option than to abandon my hunt for Damien, which I cannot do. But I won't sell a person.

He raises a hand at me, palm out, his tone soothing as several octaves of it echo around me.

"Nothing unsavory. I don't keep living beings as objects in my collection." Creepy, but a good start.

"Call this a curiosity. I merely want to see it done. Live as long as I have, and with my abilities, and you begin to grow weary of certain things. I've mastered many magics. Creating a Were, though ... there's no shortcut for that. Your kind is dwindling, and whether their motivations are altruistic or not, no one but a Were can save your kind. So, I want to see it done. I have confidence in your abilities. If anyone can do it, it's you. I only ask that you bring them to meet me once. Do that, and I'll consider your debt paid. And I'm generous. You're welcome to continue pursuing this Damien in the meantime, as long as you're also actively searching out how to make the Were. My magic will know if you're not. Then, once you've turned the Were you can settle things with Damien."

"Oh yeah, damned generous of you," I can't help grumbling under my breath. Now I'll be gallivanting around Oregon seeking revenge on my ex while also looking for a human to turn. So many issues with that. Still, less horrible than it could be.

"It's a deal," I say, louder.

"I know." All of his tones are in sync on this one, smug, just like the feeling that jabs at me from where he stands.

As long as I'm deep in debt ...

"I don't suppose you'd be magnanimous enough to point me in the right direction? If I'm going to create you a new Were, I need at least the texts on how to do it, if not a Were historian. I don't suppose you've got any of those lying around, in spite of your 'no living things collected' declaration? Because if you do, it'd be damned helpful."

He just laughs. Deep and booming, high and shrill, short and staccato all at once.

"You know I'm not known for giving anything away for free. However, just because of the amusement your impertinence brings me, I'll provide you a starting point. If you're looking for information on turning one of your kind, you don't need a Were. You need a lover of history and information. If you want to locate that individual, you'll need to go back to the place you most fear to go."

His statement echoes in the cave, and in my mind. I don't have to ask where he means; my own terror at the prospect is answer enough.

This is Damien's fault. If it weren't for him, I wouldn't have to face this. I let that anger replace my fear a little at a time.

Then, I exit the cave.

Note From The Author

Thank you so much for reading Never! I hope you enjoyed this first in series, and will join Never on her future adventures. And numerous misadventures, if we're being honest.

If you enjoyed reading this book, I would truly appreciate you taking a moment to leave a review on Amazon, Goodreads, or wherever you prefer to look for new reads! I would love for more people to be able to find and enjoy this book.

Book 2 in the Shifter Vengeance series, "Never Again", releases July 2023 and is available for preorder now on Amazon.

For updates on new releases and events, sign up for my newsletter at nightlochpublishers.com or join me on Instagram @reameswrites

Thank you,

S. Reames

Acknowledgement

I've seen it written on many acknowledgement pages that completing a book is not a one person job. That's so true. I am thankful beyond words to have amazing, supportive people around me. Lizzy and Ally, thank you for trying to read these manuscripts as fast as I was putting them together and giving such helpful feedback. Alyssa, thank you for always having the best book recommendations, and thank you for hyping me up every step of the way. Anna, I cannot thank you enough for all your help with this. From your patient explanations of Colombian idioms to your encouraging phone calls. There wouldn't have been any Nadia in this book without you. Thanks to my supportive family and husband for listening to my constant writing updates and encouraging me. Doreen, you are the best editor and I appreciate all your feedback. I am thrilled to be working with you on future projects.

About The Author

Silas Reames

Silas Reames has long been a lover of all things reading. Each time she's set loose in a bookstore she comes out with several purchases because "this particular book spoke to me."

She is often found reading or writing while drinking what might well be considered too much caffeine. She loves swimming and spending time with her husband and two dogs. Both of whom feature heavily in her newsletter, the dogs, not the husband.